THE NECESSARY CAT

A Car'l Hobbes Mystery

Stephen Stillwell

The Vision Tree, Ltd.

This novel is a work of fiction. The author either created names, characters, locations, and events from his imagination, or used existing names, characters, locations, and events fictitiously.

Cover Art by Annette Wisniewski

Published by The Vision Tree, Ltd.
216 Waterbury Circle, Lake Villa, Il 60046
Jo@TheVisionTree.com
847.356.7550

Printed in the United States of America
ISBN: 978-1-933334-37-0

Stephen Stillwell

Dedication

I dedicate this book to my wonderful family:

To Zenovia, my wife of more than 50 years –
You are the love of my life.

To my children, Annette, Michele, and Richard –
I have had so much pleasure watching you grow
up and have your own wonderful families.

To my grandchildren with love and laughter,
Alex, Ethan, Sean, Niki, Desaray, and LeeAnn –
You bring me such joy!

To my grandpups – Lucy, Archie, and Boomer –
Thanks for all of the giggles and
embarrassing surprise kisses.

Acknowledgments

Many people volunteered the help and input I needed to keep my story believable. Or almost believable. There are too many to list, so I won't even try.

I'll just say thanks to all of you.

A special thank you to my daughter, Annette, for volunteering to edit this book and see it through the publishing process.

"As there is no firm reason to be render'd....
While he, a harmless necessary cat,
Must yield to such inevitable shame
As to offend, himself being offended..."

                                    Merchant of Venice

Chapter 1

One of the mildest Decembers I could remember was coming to a close. It was a month of frequent rains and October temperatures. Christmas had come and gone without snow, and today — New Year's Eve — had begun like a day in March, wild and unruly, with storm clouds gathering.

That changed abruptly when an uneasy rain heralded the start of a major storm. Lightning tore the black sky into scores of brilliant flashes. Thunder erupted in a cacophony of roars and drum rolls. Wind-driven rain gusted against the patio chairs and the screen door, knocking the chairs over and forcing a deluge of water through the screen. The storm lasted for only moments, during which I was forced to jump back, as one of the creatures of the night slammed its body into the screen, puncturing it in several places as it tried to find its way to a dry place.

"Harmless the Cat," I murmured to the biggest mouser in the world. "Come on in." I pushed the door partway open, but the wind was strong. The best I could do was a five-inch opening. That was enough. He forced his way through, leaving bits of cat fur on the doorframe and a four-inch scratch on my right arm.

I followed him to the kitchen and cleaned my scratch with hydrogen peroxide. The only creature in the enclosed patio when I returned was the cat known as Harmless. Harmless? My mad Aunt Molly was harmless; this guy was a natural born master of the house. He took possession of a cushioned wicker chair and calmly watched me walk by. He had everything under control.

As for me, I had a job to do.

A battle had come to Car'l Hobbes' office. It was a conflict where each combatant pretended the other wasn't there. Grandma Agnes Kelch, who drives a pickup truck, and Katya Ransom, who calls herself a practicing witch, would never yield in their battle of wits, or one-up-ness. They needed a third person to be the referee — that was me. I am Abel Houston and I work for detective Car'l Hobbes. I am his all-around handyman and surrogate legs, and I get paid to put up with things like this.

Personally, in this battle of wits, I thought both of the combatants were unarmed.

Katya finally broke the silence.

"Does her god make it rain like this at the end of every December?" she asked.

"My boy," Agnes said. "Tell her He makes the rain fall on the just and the unjust alike, regardless of the month."

Katya's reply was to me, but clearly meant for Agnes. "She's an idiot, Houston, so you probably understand her. Tell me what relevance rain on the just and the unjust has to do with rain on New Year's Eve."

"Hmmph," said Agnes. "Sarcasm is her specialty. It's too bad she thinks I care."

And so on.

They were a little less vocal this morning because of the violent early storm; the thunder interfered with their witty remarks. It kept them quiet while they were in Car'l Hobbes' house.

After a while, they ignored me as well, and sat in stubborn silence. At least fifteen minutes passed, and they still refused to acknowledge each other's presence.

I said a quiet thank you to whomever had made the storm. While it raged on, the room was peaceful, if not quiet.

In the meantime, I was finding out that women, especially these two, could easily become two women too many.

I tried talking to them. "Would you like some coffee?"

No answer.

"Tea? I could make some instant tea."

They ignored me.

"How about water? Ice water?"

I gave up. Katya could have won any number of beauty contests when she had been in high school, but that was at least forty years ago. She still had the looks, but, in her case, the beauty was quickly eclipsed by the sarcasm and bitterness of an unrestrained tongue. I suppose I could consider her silence a blessing of sorts, except that it wouldn't last.

Agnes Kelch, *Grandma* Agnes Kelch, was four inches taller than Katya and about a hundred pounds heavier. At seventy-seven, she was charming, witty, and as homely as a pan of fried bacon and eggs, sunny side up. (That was her description, not mine.) She looked comfortable enough, wearing a flannel shirt and blue jeans that did not flatter her figure, but didn't look out of place on her either.

Suddenly, Harmless padded through the hallway by the office door. He stopped long enough to lock eyes with me, hiss, spit, and then slip away. He was no doubt Katya's familiar; supposedly every witch has one. Katya fidgeted her way through three minutes, but when the cat appeared, she gave up her silence. She threw the ancient *National Geographic* in the direction of the coffee table. It landed awkwardly near the edge, spun around, and began to slide off. She darted forward, grabbed it, and slammed it down ferociously. Then, she glared at me, daring me to say something. I knew better and kept my mouth shut. Not that I was afraid of her, but until two or three months ago, she had called herself a practicing witch. She gave that up only when her coven had excommunicated her, which I thought was a brave thing for them to do. Personally, I still thought of her as a bona-fide witch.

She had stored up plenty to say though, and finally started saying it. "I know what you're thinking, Houston, and you'll make a fool of yourself if you start broadcasting it." She snorted. "But then, you're quite the young idiot anyway, aren't you? What's your IQ, thirty? Thirty-seven? Same as your age, I imagine, whatever that is." She glanced at my boss's desk. "Are you going to tell that crippled slant-eyed meddler to come in here or do I have to sit here all day?"

I really didn't have a respectful answer to her question. It would have been mostly about getting rid of her anyway. She waited an hour for Hobbes to make an appearance, but the only person to come in had been Agnes. Katya had given her one scathing glance, then sat in deliberate silence and gazed out the glass patio doors.

She watched with me as gray clouds the size of football fields floated sullenly out of the west like some giant's dark balloon creatures on parade. They had been on a straight course toward the city of Mercater since I'd first seen them half an hour earlier, and now it became clear that they would pass directly over the old house on River Street — this house, the one that belonged to Car'l Hobbes, and which also happened to be the place where I lived and worked.

The clouds swarmed overhead in a sinister grayness. It was easy enough to imagine that an intelligence leading them, something that could control a convoy of clouds two or three miles long and stop it directly above Hobbes' house, and then wait impatiently for the rest of the convoy to catch up. Controlled or not, in minutes, a master cloud developed, half a mile in diameter, that transformed daylight into twilight and then twilight into nightfall. Even that darkness came and went as brilliant flashes of lightning pierced the sky and sent thunder rumbling in that shook the old windows.

One cloud roared downward — a violent shape-shifter turning itself inside out. In less than a minute, it slammed against the ground and made the backyard an ebony fright-house of invisibility and thunder. Trees shook in terror and the river climbed its banks. In the distance, warning sirens went off.

Then, as quickly as it had begun, the storm quieted itself and let the cloud hang silently as if undecided whether to destroy the old house or depart in peace. I felt rather than saw something slipping through the darkness and gliding across the patio. It paused and stared at me for a long second, its eyes — cat's eyes — Harmless' eyes maybe, reflecting and distorting the faint light from the house. At least, I thought it was cat's eyes; the shape of whatever the creature was seemed too big even to be *him*. It made some guttural noise that could have been human or animal and then faded away, leaving only the faint sound of padded feet on flagstones that echoed vaguely here and there and down toward the river.

The backs of my hands suddenly began itching — a clear warning of danger. Before I could analyze it, the cloud began to lift, and the itching stopped.

I was brought back to the problem of the two ladies. The return of daylight didn't make it easier. I took a deep breath and turned away from the glass door. "Mrs. Ransom," I said at last. "You can sit on that sofa until next year if you want to. He's too busy to see you." I tried to sound reasonable, but it was hard.

"Liar. Idiot. Fool. Jackass. Toady!" Katya Ransom didn't look sixty years old, nor did she talk like it. She bristled with energy, and was as slender and wiry as one of the stray tomcats I'd seen her bring home. The difference was the tomcats had a better disposition.

"It's my job to relay his messages." I shrugged and walked to the door. I held it open for her. "You can talk to him at the party tonight, if you care to come."

"Me? At his party? Don't be an ass." She stood up. "Very well, give him this message: Tell him to leave my cats alone. They're not hurting him."

"Cats?"

"Yes, cats. My Harmless, especially." She glared at me. "If he throws dirt clods at one of them again, I'll call the cops and have him slammed in jail, wheelchair and all!"

A cat. She rescued cats from the street, cleaned them up, fed them, and then took them to the animal shelter where they were probably put to sleep. The room had become light enough to read her expression, but it didn't tell me she was here about a cat, not even one she called Harmless. The people in the kitchen, if they were listening on the intercom, must be having a good laugh. It was impossible to picture Hobbes throwing dirt clods, or anything else, at a cat.

"It wasn't him, Mrs. Ransom."

She pointed a finger at me. "Just tell him." She walked past me into the hallway and stopped. "You're thinking those clouds are driven by some sort of malignant intelligence. You think they have purpose in coming here. Bah! Idiot!" She couldn't help but send a last split-second flash of loathing at Agnes, and then she slammed the door behind her. As near as I could tell, she wasn't bothered by the darkness. Anyway, minutes later, the cloud left the ground, drifted back into formation, and resumed its journey.

She was wrong. I didn't believe in malignant intelligence of any sort, except for the kind that some humans had.

It might have seemed there was something supernatural about the way the clouds had moved, but I worked for Car'l Hobbes, investigator of the paranormal, and her opinion could not have been further from the truth. His purpose in life was to debunk frauds and hoaxes and prove there was more *natural* than *super* in *supernatural*. He believed that everything could be explained with logic or science, and I agreed with him, for the most part. It was my job to be a skeptic, to doubt that there could be anything like an intelligence driving those clouds. This was nothing more than one of Ma Nature's most unusual weather displays.

Well, maybe so. Maybe not. Something was out there, running across the yard and stopping to look at me even though Katya apparently hadn't seen it. It wasn't necessarily my imagination.

Grandma Kelch was still waiting, and I nodded to her. I started to go after Hobbes, but she stopped me with one quick sentence.

"It was there," she said. "Something was there."

She picked up the *National Geographic* that Katya had thrown down, and started paging through it.

So I said thanks and went to find the boss. Grandma Agnes Kelch put her head back against a cushion as I went out the door. During the five minutes it took me to find Hobbes and bring him back, she had stretched out on the sofa and passed out. She would have embarrassed a power saw — I had never before heard that kind of snoring from a human being.

"She must live alone," Hobbes said as soon as he pushed his wheelchair into the room. "Has to live alone. No man with hearing could tolerate that. Wake her, Abel, before the ceiling collapses."

The snoring stopped abruptly, and Grandma Kelch said, "Ain't nobody's business if I live alone." She sat up and added, "Unless you're putting in for the job.

"I doubt if I qualify," Hobbes said wryly.

"That wheelchair wouldn't be a problem." Her homely face broke out into a wide smile, "Long as you can play checkers. That's what I do since my last husband died."

The corners of the boss' mouth went up an eighth of an inch. "I play chess on occasion, but not well, and I treasure my hearing. I must decline the offer."

"Weren't no offer," she said. "I've come to hire you, but not for that."

Hobbes studied the old lady for a minute or two and then looked my way as if he wanted my opinion. I shrugged. He turned back to Grandma Kelch. "I only investigate things related to the supernatural, and my fee is seldom small."

Her smile disappeared. "I'm seventy-seven years old, Mr. Hobbes; old enough to call you Car'l, if you'll allow it?" She made it a question, and Hobbes nodded without hesitation. Now, it would take two hands to count the number of people who called him by his first name. It was a select group.

"And I have some money — enough, I think, to pay you and still handle my needs for the next year or two. After that, I doubt if I'll care."

Hobbes shook his head. "You seem to enjoy robust health, Mrs. Kelch."

"And you can call me Grandma, or just Agnes, if you feel like it — so can your partner."

Partner? I had to clear that up pretty darn fast, before the boss had time to think about it. I liked the kind of responsibilities I had now, and I didn't want to branch out. I said, "I'm just a worker here, Agnes."

"Hah!" she said to me. "You are what you are, and it ain't no worker." To Hobbes she said, "Suppose I tell you what I want, and we go on from there."

Hobbes leaned back and said, "Please do so."

Chapter 2

She nodded and inhaled a gallon or two of atmosphere. Then in a rush of exhaled air, she said, "Okay. Forgive my bluntness, but I don't know any other way to say this. Seventeen years ago, my daughter, Mattie, committed suicide. This was right after she stabbed her husband to death. She killed him because he was molesting her daughter Susan, who was, of course, my granddaughter.

"Susan was fourteen years old when the court made me her legal guardian. Poor thing, no one else wanted her. There were plenty of aunts and uncles that could have taken her, but she was tainted. She said she never let him get *that far*, but no one believed her. For a while, there was even a rumor that she had seduced him, and that he really wasn't to blame. I don't believe there was any truth to that, but no aunt or uncle wanted her growing up with their kids. She was the rotten apple that could spoil the good ones. I was the only one who would take her."

Grandma Kelch stopped to give Hobbes a chance to react, but all he did was nod his head.

She took another deep breath and went on.

"Susan was an outcast. A loner. She had one friend, a boy her age name of Lucas Ransom, come from the good side of town. He called her 'Little Sister,' and for two years, they closed the world out. I think they were happy together, but at the end of that second year, everything changed. They went swimming down near the dam, and she got caught in an undertow and drowned. They got her out, but the rescue took too much time. She weren't breathin'. They did CPR and got her lungs working again, but it was too late for her brain. She was in a coma. After eleven days in the hospital, they sent her home, still unconscious. Her body was healthy, but there was nothin' in her head. The boy spent every day with her, talkin', tellin' stories even though she never heard, and helpin' her get some exercise. He blamed himself for what happened, but she just laid there.

"Then about six weeks after she was brought home, she woke up."

"Mrs. Kelch," Hobbes tried to interrupt her, but she held up her hand.

"This will make sense in a minute, Car'l. There ain't a lot more to say."

Hobbes glanced at me. I shrugged. We had heard worse in this house.

She continued. "But, first, I gotta back up a little, before the drowning, and tell you another sad story, and then you'll see how the two come together.

"The boy had a sister name of Linda, eight years older than him. Rumor said she was a spiritualist. She talked with the dead many times according to her ma and pa. She started when she was thirteen years old, going into a trance and speaking in different voices. That made her sorta famous and her ma didn't mind; as a matter of fact, she enjoyed it. Some of her ma's friends even seemed to envy her. Then, Linda spoiled it all. When she was sixteen, she had a baby by some boy in town, but she never told who the boy was.

"Bein' a spiritualist weren't embarrassing or humiliating to her family, but being pregnant and unmarried was. So they sent her away. The baby was born someplace in Galena and she came home without the baby. When she was nineteen years old, she started having fits, and they brought her to Mercater State Hospital, right across your river." She nodded in that direction. "She shared a cottage with another woman for about four years while she learned how to hold meetin's where she talked to dead people — abominations called up from hellfire. One night, the cottage burned to the ground. She burned to death with it.

"This is where the two stories come together. A week after the fire was when Susan near drowned and went into that coma. When she woke up, or rather, when the body that had been hers woke up, it was not Susan that was inside. The boy's sister, this other girl, the Linda I been talkin' about, had returned from the dead and taken over."

Grandma Agnes Kelch stopped and waited for our reactions.

Hobbes said, "You saw her come out of the coma?"

She shook her head. "The boy didn't call me into her room until maybe fifteen minutes after she woke up, and then she didn't know me. My granddaughter didn't know me. And I didn't know her. When I looked into her eyes, all I saw was a stranger."

13

"And the boy? Did she know him?"

"Yes, obviously. It was funny, but he said to me, 'Grandma, I'd like you to meet my sister, Linda Ransom,' and she said, 'Pleased to meet you,' and held out her hand. It was like they'd known each other all their lives, and I was someone she'd never seen."

Grandma Kelch held both her hands out, palms up. "I could do nothin' but call her doctors and take her to the hospital. The doctors were surprised by her recovery. They could find nothin' wrong with her body and she didn't say nothin' about her new identity. I didn't say nothin' either. They kept her overnight, and then sent her home."

She put her hands down. "I didn't know much about Linda, or the hellfire that killed her. I just kinda sat back, relieved, and let Lucas take her to his parents.

"Within hours, she convinced them she was their daughter returned. Within a month they asked to adopt her. By then, I was convinced that she was... who she said. I signed the papers, and she was gone. For a while after that, I still believed in her, and then..." she let her voice drop off.

"For a while?" Hobbes repeated. "Why did you believe for only a while? What changed your mind?"

"I was a sucker," she said wryly. "I wanted to believe her. She been in a coma, practically dead, and she come back to life. At least, she still looked like my Susan. I wanted the best for her. We were poor folk from the poorest part of town — I was a widow, sixty years old and we were just getting by. I had a small

14

widow's pension and I made a little money cleaning house for some of the rich folks up on the hill. Once in a while, Susan helped. She saw how the upper class lived and it bothered her. She said someday she was going to live like them. I think that was what Lucas and her were practicin' for those two years.

"Later, I got to thinking about their story and figured I had been fooled. They must have planned this for a long time and had simply fooled everyone. She wanted out of my house, and he taught her everything she needed to know to be his sister."

Hobbes stroked his moustache and said, "This happened seventeen years ago?"

She nodded and swallowed hard. "Seventeen. Yes."

"And what is it you want me to do now?"

"Prove that she's a fake. That she is really my granddaughter, Susan, and not that Linda come back from the dead."

"It is always difficult to prove a negative, Mrs. Kelch, and this is made more difficult by the passing of nearly two decades. Why have you waited so long to begin an investigation?"

"I waited because I didn't know what else to do. Once the adoption was legal, she completely shut me out of her life. I only had a hunch and no proof. I tried twice to talk to her adopted mother, but that woman refused to discuss anything about her Linda's return. The second time I tried, she flew into a rage and chased me out of her house. She said the next time she'd use a gun. I guess she refused to even think about losing her daughter a second time. So I let it drop. Everyone was happy but me. That was good enough."

Hobbes considered her story, briefly, and then said, "How long after Susan's near drowning did the supposed spirit–possession take place?"

"Best I can remember, it was a little less than two months."

Hobbes crossed his arms and said slowly, "That would support their claim, wouldn't it? Susan would not have had time to learn enough about Linda to pretend to be her, so Linda's takeover was real. If Susan had seen the opportunity to move out of your house and in with Linda's family, even as soon as the day Linda had died, then she had only two or three weeks to prepare herself. She would have to learn all the small details and quirks that would make her believable to people who had known Linda well, like her parents."

Grandma Kelch moved her bottom jaw side to side as if she was grinding something with her teeth. "Unless they'd been planning on it for a long time. They'd had almost two years."

"Then," said Hobbes, "They would have to have known when Linda was going to die."

Grandma Kelch began slowly, "If that was so, then the fire that killed her...."

"Was set by them," Hobbes finished. "And that would be murder. But there are other scenarios. One is that Susan longed to escape the life you described, so she played at being Linda, with Lucas to guide her, with no reason other than escaping an unpleasant reality. In two years, she could have been nearly perfect at the impersonation — if she had the talent for it. Linda's death would have been the perfect opportunity for Susan to become the Linda she had pretended to be."

"Yes," she said. "That's it. A perfect impersonation, learned by play-acting. She is still my grandchild. Linda died in that fire, and she remains dead."

Hobbes was silent for several minutes. He turned his wheelchair sideways and gazed at the painting on the wall — Canadian Geese flying over a marshland with a grace and sense of freedom that man, crippled or not, could never match.

He closed his eyes and began tapping out the rhythm of a song on the arm of the chair. I recognized "The Stars and Stripes Forever!" Finally, the tapping stopped, and he opened his eyes.

He turned away from the picture and shook his head. "Seventeen years is too long a time, Mrs. Kelch. The chance of proving anything against Susan, who has been Linda for all those years, is extremely slim. You would be wasting your money."

"There is more," Agnes began, "Susan..."

Hobbes raised his hand, "Please. I find calling her Susan some of the time, and Linda the rest of the time, confusing. She is Linda, both practically and legally. Let us call her that."

"That's what I been doing all those years, except for this morning. Long as it's clear who we're talkin' about." She looked at me for the first time in many minutes. "Make sense to you, Sonny?"

I nodded.

"Okay," she said. "Linda it is. But whatever we call her, we got to do something about her now. Car'l, I'm going to give you the bare facts of why we got to stop her, and if they don't get you goin', well, I guess I'll get goin' myself. Okay?"

Hobbes nodded. I grinned; the old woman had charmed him.

"She's been married three times," Agnes began. "Her first husband died of a heart attack after seven years marriage. Her second died two years later, or two years ago, depending on how you look at it, also of a heart attack. And last night, I met her latest husband, Clyde Butler. Clyde doesn't look at all well." She left it hanging there.

"You are saying that Clyde's life is in danger? Middle-aged men are notoriously at risk for heart attacks, and Clyde has already had one. The simple truth is that, even though her two previous marriages ended that way, it doesn't necessarily mean anything. Especially if she is a woman of intense physical appeal, such as Linda Butler."

"Well, I'm positive about it."

Hobbes glanced at me, and I shook my head a bit. "I don't want to sound negative, Mrs. Kelch, but it all sounds like a..." I got hung up trying to find the right words. "Like a confused old woman's fantasy?" She gave me a pleasant, homey smile and then laughed. "Sonny, I know what it sounds like, but that don't mean it ain't true."

Hobbes took over again. "And if I find the proof you're looking for, what will you do with it?"

"I will show it to Linda, and she will stop whatever she's doin'. I would give it to Lucas' mother, whose been duped all these years. I think she would be happy to get it. I think, too, that she might get the police to start lookin' into the deaths of Linda's first two husbands."

"I see," said Hobbes. "And Lucas' mother is...?"

"Katya Ransom."

"Of course."

The corners of his mouth went up a fraction. "And you think she'll listen to you, or to anybody else for that matter?"

She parted her lips in a thin smile. "I think she's known the truth from the very beginning and hates herself for believing a lie. That's why she's so bitter and mean, Car'l."

"And you would see Linda go to prison, even though she is your granddaughter?"

Grandma Agnes Kelch looked down at the floor while the big hand of the grandfather clock moved a sixtieth of the way around the dial. When she looked up, she had a grayness to her skin that hadn't been there before. "Murder is a despicable act, no matter who does it. It should never go unpunished."

"Very well." Hobbes leaned back in his wheelchair, and then turned to me. "Abel, will you prepare a standard contract? The fee will be one dollar, or more, at Mrs. Kelch's discretion, subject to her satisfaction, at the end of the case. Expenses will be extra."

With the standard form already in the computer, it took only five minutes to print out three copies. They were all signed by Mrs. Kelch and Hobbes, and witnessed and notarized by me.

"Mrs. Kelch, you have hired a detective," Hobbes said.

"Hope he's worth his fee, else I'll have to ask for my money back," Grandma Kelch said with a straight face.

"I would have it no other way."

"Startin' today?"

"This is New Year's Eve. We can do little either today or tomorrow because of the holidays, so we'll begin the day after New Year's. Is that all right?"

She nodded, "I'm visitin' with my friend, Kelly Decker. She lives next door in one of the small apartments in the upstairs of the big old Butler house. I believe I can stay there a few days more."

Hobbes' raised an eyebrow and said, "You are staying in the house owned by the Clyde Butler who is married to your granddaughter, who, you say, may be going to kill him? That stretches the laws of coincidence. You must have been keeping a close watch on her."

"Hell, yes! And then Kelly called me besides. Why else do you think I'd come to this godforsaken part of town?"

Hobbes gave her one of his rare smiles where he actually showed his teeth. "Why, indeed. And Kelly is an old friend?"

"She was a schoolteacher for ten years, before the school had to do something about its budget and let her go. She found a job here and moved into that apartment. While she had been a teacher, though, she roomed and boarded with me. That's how I saved the money to come hire you."

Before she left, Hobbes invited her to come back that night to the party.

She said, "No, thanks. If I wake up in the morning, it'll be party enough for me.

Chapter 3

Morning of New Year's Eve crept slowly past on its way to noon. Rainwater ran off the patio almost as quickly as it had fallen onto it. Smaller clouds moved out as if they were being herded by the monster cloud that followed them. Another storm was over.

I grabbed my jacket and headed out for a morning's jog. When we weren't busy, my schedule was almost like clockwork. Today, I was a couple of hours late, and that nearly got me mauled by the same tomcat I'd seen earlier. I was on Hobbes sidewalk, just heading out when the cat leaped from behind a Spreading Yew, hissed, spat, bounced off my hip, crossed the driveway and disappeared under the Butler's porch. He had almost knocked me down.

I wondered if Katya Ransom's 'Harmless,' was what I'd seen in the back yard just a few hours earlier. Whatever it had been had looked even bigger, but I supposed that could have been the lighting, or the lack of it.

Forty-five minutes later I was back home and in the shower. I reflected that it had been an interesting morning so far.

As I said before, I'm Abel Houston, Hobbes' number one (and only) leg man — one of the three people who work for him and share his house. The other two are Fireman Fred, a seventy-year old ex-fireman who has developed a morbid fear of fire, but nevertheless is the cook — one who categorically refuses to cook on the four-thousand-dollar Viking professional gas range; and Sally Wilson, a.k.a. Cemetery Sally, a twenty-something-year old girl who has no memory of her past, but is Hobbes' research assistant, and a damned good one. Sally believes she will find clues to her past in some graveyard somewhere, and spends her free time searching through them. So far she has built a computer database that cross-references several hundred mostly ancient graveyards and maybe fifty thousand graves. Her latest find was a tiny family gravesite near a rusted windmill, about ten miles south of Mercater. Three hand chiseled stone markers in a row said Born 1920, 1921, 1922, and Died 1920, 1921, 1922.

A fifth member of Hobbes' household, but not of the house, is Charon. He is the ancient boat-keeper who lives in the boathouse, although the only sea-worthy craft Hobbes owns is a rowboat.

Hobbes himself had been paralyzed from the waist down in an accident about twenty years ago. Now, he does his thinking and detective work from a wheelchair, limiting his detecting to cases that involve the paranormal or the supernatural. He doesn't believe in either. I went looking for them. For any one of them. I wanted someone else's opinions about the clouds and whether they thought it had anything to do with the cat. I found all four of them at the kitchen table. Before I had a chance to say anything, Hobbes told me to sit down and eat. Sparks were flying at the table anyway. I could wait.

We were going to have a New Year's Eve party. After more than twenty years of peacefully ignoring New Year's Eve, Hobbes had decided that this year, it was going to be different. This year, we were going to rock out the old one and roll in the new one, whatever that meant. There were arguments about what we were going to do, and who was going to do it. Hobbes, who was normally inscrutable within the limits of his wheelchair, had become abnormally scrutable. It was obvious that Sally and Charon weren't going to give him much help, although they would probably do better than Fred.

"Cornbread and Great Northern soup beans is good enough for this old body." Charon said and winked at me. "Ain't much for New Year's Eve parties, no how."

"And I'm not your cook, Car'l," Sally said sweetly. "I wouldn't dream of interfering."

We shared a moment of silence when I could have spoken up about the storm clouds, or the cat, but I thought maybe Katya was right. Maybe I was being an idiot, and talking about clouds as if they were intelligent would prove it. I let the moment pass and the opportunity with it.

Hobbes, whom I call Boss, Chief, or Sir, depending on my level of cynicism at the moment -- growled across the kitchen table, "Fred, will nothing persuade you to make baked beans according to this recipe?" He tapped a yellowed piece of paper. "It was my grandmother's, a family favorite."

"No, sir," Fireman Fred Lynch glared back, "I'm seventy–one years old, and I want to see seventy–two. I'd have to use the oven and that stove's a death trap."

Hobbes choked on something –– the words he was going to say, probably. The stove was almost new. He took a deep breath and slowly ran his fingers down both sides of his moustache. He was losing the argument and he knew it.

He glanced briefly at the food Fred had placed on the table, then for the third time since lunch was announced, or at least for the third time since I'd joined then, Car'l Hobbes and Fred Jones glared at each other.

In that brief silence, Hobbes allowed the old Rex Stout novel he had been rereading, *The Mother Hunt,* to fall to the floor by his wheelchair. We all knew what he was thinking: Nero Wolfe, the eccentric genius who solved all the crimes in the Rex Stout series, did not have to tolerate cold mashed potatoes and gravy, canned green beans, and tapioca. He would have been eating pheasant under glass or something. Hobbes had my sympathy, and not just because he was my boss. I had to eat at that table too.

The problem was that Fred, Fireman Fred, was afraid of fire –– and he was paid to be the cook.

Hobbes pushed his plate away, untouched. "Is there any chance of ever receiving digestible food at this table?"

"Ain't my fault, Boss," the retired firefighter ground out the words. "We need a new stove, an electric one. That old one just ain't safe — it could blow

25

up in a minute." He shoved four sheets of paper in Hobbes' face. "Look at this! I got it right off the Internet; a hundred gas explosions!"

Hobbes glanced at the papers. "These go back to 1944."

"Dates don't mean nothin'."

Hobbes drummed his fingers on the arms of his wheelchair. "That gas range is less than two years old, Fred. It's the one you wanted."

"It ain't no good, Boss," Fred insisted. "Last night I dreamed it blew up and took the house with it!"

And some night before, he had dreamed that carbon monoxide had killed everyone in their sleep.

We'd had the stove inspected by the manufacturer, the local service department, and the fire department that Fred had retired from. They all said that nothing was wrong with it. Fireman Fred wasn't convinced.

Hobbes turned his glare to that expensive Viking range. It was what Fred had insisted on at the time, although he might have thought Hobbes wouldn't buy it because of the price tag. If so, he would have a good excuse not to cook. "Maybe you should try the front burners before you throw it out."

The sarcasm was wasted. I doubt if Fred even noticed it. He merely shook his head. "Too risky for kids. They might grab a handle and pull hot grease over on 'em." The fringe of white hair that barely covered his ears and resembled a marshmallow and coconut sundae looked better than what I was eating.

His bald head shone like a scoop of peach ice cream –
– that didn't help either.

"Kids?" Hobbes sighed. As far as he knew, no
child had ever been in that kitchen. "Well, if it will help
for cooking safety, I suppose I have to look into
replacing it."

I almost choked on the tapioca. I could imagine
just how much difference a new stove would make.
Fred was Fred.

"What will you want done with the old one?" he
asked. I couldn't tell if he was gloating or not. "Call the
Salvation Army store?"

"If we get a new stove instead of a new cook, I will
offer the Viking to Clyde Butler, if he will accept it. We
are still in his son's debt."

The Butlers lived next door. Not too long ago,
Clyde's seventeen-year old son Rich had helped solve a
mystery Hobbes was working on, and saved my life in
the process.

"I dunno," Fred replied. "That new wife's pretty
smart. She might be too smart to cook with gas."

"You can ask them tonight, Chief," I said.

"What time is it now?" Hobbes seldom wore a
watch. I was not only his surrogate legs; I was his
surrogate timepiece.

"Half past noon."

"Plenty of time to order pizza for lunch?"

"Plenty of time." I reached for the phone. "With bread sticks and Diet Coke, right?"

Fred glowered at us, but began clearing the table. Mashed potatoes, green beans, and tapioca were scraped into the disposal as I dialed Johnny's Pizza.

Cemetery Sally, who had been fairly quiet up until then, said, "Don't throw away that tapioca, Fred. Please."

"You like it?" Hobbes asked as if it was the strangest thing he'd ever heard.

Fred looked suspiciously at her. "You want more?"

"Greg and I can use it to patch headstones. When it dries, it's as hard as cement."

The corners of Hobbes' went up a sixteenth of an inch — for him a broad smile.

"Funny," Fred said. Then he changed the subject. "That boy Greg sure got it bad for you, Sally. Ain't never seen no one get hooked so fast."

"I don't think there be a net strong enough to hold him," Charon said, speaking for the first time. "He bears watching."

"We're just friends," the twenty-something year-old said. She was completely unruffled.

"Does he know that?" Fred asked.

"We have related interests; he buries people and I study headstones. What could be less romantic than that? Besides, we haven't known each other long enough to get serious."

"Mebby not, but he's been seeing you pretty damned often for the last eight or nine months. Ever since him and his uncles buried Jane Butler, and that seems to be long enough to me."

"Oh, Fred," Sally's eyes sparkled, "I don't even know what he sees in me. Look at us; I'm just a poor country girl while he comes from a wealthy respected family."

"Well," Fred said. "Regardless, he ain't good enough for you."

She reached over and rubbed his bald head. "Thank you, Fred, but like I said, we're just friends. Besides, he's got that great Viper!"

"He's got a snake?" Charon interjected. "What's he doin' with a snake?"

"No, Charon," Sally smiled. "A Viper is a sports car. A beautiful, powerful sports car."

"Well," Fred growled, "he'd better treat you right, and if you have any kids, I hope they look like you, not him."

Sally pinched his ear, and that seemed to end that part of the conversation. Anyway, Fred had something else to talk about.

"Purple lights in Butler's basement last night, again," he said. "They weren't natural."

"After midnight, as before?" Hobbes had managed to regain his composure. He didn't believe in anything supernatural, but Fred had said he thought maybe Hobbes could under the right circumstances.

"Mebby about two o'clock in the a.m., I went out for a look. I could smell something sweet in the air, too. Heavy, like lilacs. They got a witch living there; you know who I mean."

Yeah, I nodded silently. I'd talked to her this morning.

"She does things," he added. "Something bad is going to happen over there."

"Could you see where the purple light originated?"

Fred shook his head. "I couldn't get close enough to look in the basement windows because of the damn motion detector lights."

"I see. Are you often up at two in the morning, Fred?"

"Yeah," he said, "But mostly not.

"What got me up the first time a couple nights ago was that light from their basement comin' through my window. I went out to look around and ran into Abel. He'd heard something, he said. Sounded like a cat being tormented, so he came out to look. He saw the purple light too. Only lasted for a coupla minutes, but this makes three nights in a row."

"Always at two a.m.?"

"Always at two, Chief," I put in. "We used to call it the witching hour."

"Apparently, you found nothing."

"Not yet. Not even a cat."

"We shall investigate tomorrow night, Abel. We could begin tonight, except for the party."

"Good enough, Chief. One more night won't make a difference. Besides, we have to get ready. What about the refreshments? If Fred won't make baked beans, or anything else, you're going to have a lot of hungry people here."

At that moment, the back doorbell rang.

"That will be the caterer," Hobbes said, answering my question. He had already known what Fred's response would be.

He had decided a couple of weeks ago to have a New Year's Eve party. This would be a first for him — but he wanted, he had said, to get better acquainted with the neighbors. I think he just wanted to show off his giant projection screen TV.

Chapter 4

Tonight, the world would change for everyone at the party — for some more than others. At the beginning, though, things seemed about normal.

At nine a.m. our first guest, Forrest Green, who was and still is a reporter for the *National Echo*, pounded on the front door. At a skinny five-foot-four inches, he talks with a phony Irish accent and tries to look like an overgrown leprechaun. He brought with him a bottle of crème de menthe. Its color matched his clothes. I couldn't have asked for a better opening picture than that for the brief catalog of visitors that would be coming and going that night.

"And a Happy New Year to you, Abel, me boy." He tossed me his fedora and coat, and went on to the great room.

"Not until tomorrow," I called after him.

"May not be one!" he answered over his shoulder.

I might have said something else but more guests arrived, and I had to let our next–door–to–the–east neighbors in.

Clyde Butler looked pale and tired, but he gave me a warm handshake. He pushed his glasses up on the bridge of his nose, and squinted slightly as if the hallway light bothered him. He said, "New glasses are driving me crazy." Then he added, "Thanks for asking us over; I couldn't have faced it at home."

"Our pleasure," I said, not sure what he meant.

Rich seemed happy to follow his dad inside, although I thought he might rather be partying with kids his own age. But, maybe not. He looked somber and apprehensive.

"The holiday getting to you?" I asked.

He shrugged, and grinned slightly.

Linda, Clyde's wife, smiled as she crossed the threshold. Not much more than thirty, and with striking blond hair and clear blue eyes, she possessed beauty — a startling, alarming, frightening beauty. Her skin had a golden glow. Her teeth were white and perfect. That kind of beauty. Seemingly unaware of her effect on men, she managed to both attract and repel them. Whether Clyde was the luckiest man alive, or the unluckiest, I couldn't tell.

She kissed me on the cheek, as if we were old friends, and said, "Abel, Happy New Year!" Then she added, "Of course, you know my brother Luke?" In contrast to his sister, Luke had dark brown hair and brown eyes; eyes with boyish features that I supposed some women would find attractive. He had come to spend the holidays with his mother. She had already been here several months, so Rich had told me, and wouldn't be leaving until the middle of January. Rich didn't sound too happy about those arrangements.

I nodded and shook his hand. His grip was strong, and for some reason, he put a lot into it. My knuckles began to pop before I could twist my hand in his and return the pressure. For a moment, we had a test of strength. I squeezed pretty hard without being obvious, and then so did he, a thin smile pulling his lips apart. I gave him more than he could handle, and his smile disappeared. He dropped my hand. Then, suddenly his smile was back. "A power athlete," he said. "There aren't many of you around."

"Astronaut training," I replied. "Started when I was a kid. You never know when they'll call you." I didn't usually tell people about that part of my life, but the handgrip seemed to call for an explanation.

Linda tugged on his arm, but he wasn't quite finished. Apparently, he didn't like losing the hand-squeezing game. A hint of derision emerged in his voice when he answered me.

"That's right; you were in the program, weren't you? And you washed out. Takes more than a handshake to be an astronaut, doesn't it?"

"Luke," Linda chided. "Please come on."

He ignored her. "They don't give second chances, do they?" His smile still didn't reach his eyes. I decided I didn't much like him.

He brushed his sister's hand off his shoulder. "What about that fog this afternoon? Strange, wasn't it?" He lowered his voice. "You don't know what a fog like that can hide."

"Yeah," I said. I'd almost forgotten it.

"An omen?" he asked.

I changed the subject.

"Is Mrs. Ransom coming?"

"She didn't feel like going out," Luke said.

"Too bad," I lied. I tried to not let my relief sound obvious.

He smiled again. This time, his eyes participated. "I heard from Mother that you and she had a long talk this morning. Someday, you'll have to tell me how you survived." I nodded, and he moved on with his sister.

The other two, Kelly Decker and Lemuel Dathan, had been invited at Rich's request. Lemuel, same as Kelly, had one of the small upstairs apartments in the old Butler house; neither had any place to go for New Year's Eve. Rich said he felt sorry for them.

Kelly Decker was pushing forty, but she looked older. Brown hair and eyes had no help from the rest of her face, the way Luke's did. She managed to look mousy and unassertive, but the look she gave Linda's back wasn't exactly what I expected. Come to think of it, I'd never seen a look quite like that. It was touched by curiosity, envy, anger, maybe hatred, maybe jealousy. There were more aspects to that singular look, but I couldn't place what they were. Maybe later they'd make sense.

Sally made an unaccustomed entrance through the front door instead of through the kitchen, but that was because she wasn't alone. Last spring, she had met Greg Frazier at Jane Butler's funeral — his adopted father and uncle were the funeral directors for the Frazier Brothers' Funeral Home — and they had become friends. They found they had a common interest in old cemeteries and ancient tombstones.

They had gotten together a dozen or so times since then, but had not been dating — unless you called tonight a date. When they came in, Greg was carrying a ragged and stained journal that looked to be fifty years old, at least.

"I found it in the Home's attic," he explained after shaking my hand. "It was in one of great grandfather's trunks. It's real history. Everyone that he buried from 1940 to 1950 is recorded in here, some of them with quite personal notes. Part of it, you and Hobbes might find interesting, like the identities of three or four murderers along with their victims."

"Yeah?" I said.

"I'm loaning it to Sal. She'll have it if you want it. Just ask for GGF's journal."

I raised an eyebrow, but Sally interpreted, "GGF is Great Grand Father, Silly."

Sally tugged on his arm and they went on in to the great room where I supposed they would spend an exciting New Year's Eve sitting on a sofa reliving some of Great Grand Father's experiences. And why not? The forties had been the decade of WW2 and The Bomb and their ancestors had survived it. There could be lessons in there; teaching us how to survive ours.

Next was Lemuel Dathan, who Rich had said was twenty-three. He wore thick glasses and mumbled a hello. He bumped against the hall's small table, said, "Excuse me," and then wandered absently on toward the great room.

I was still at the door when a familiar blue Mercedes roared down the street, made a sharp U-turn, bumped over the curbs, and stopped in front of the house. A woman about my age and with bright red hair climbed out and looked across the top of her car. "Is this the home of Mr. Paranormal Snoop?"

My heart started beating a little bit faster. "My friends call me P.S. Who might you be?"

"I am the tolerator of really goofy things — but then you've met my family."

Marilyn Borden had driven down from Chicago on New Year's Eve, an act some folks might consider recklessly suicidal. But she was an anthropologist who had visited many remote tribes around the world, and the idea of danger was something she'd dismissed years ago. For this weekend, she was my guest and I was just a little bit nervous about it. There was a question I'd practiced asking for the past two weeks — *The Question*. You know what it was. I just didn't know what her answer would be.

Maybe that was why our first kiss in the foyer was a little reserved. She gave me an odd look before we walked into the great room, where she smiled at both Hobbes and Green, and gave them a better kiss than she'd given me. Forrest Green caught my eye and winked, but I ignored him.

A few months ago, Hobbes, who loved movies but hated going to the theater because of his wheelchair, had bought an eight-foot projection TV system. It covered almost the east third of the north wall. It was tuned to CNN where New Year's celebrations were being broadcast from parts of the world where the New Year had already begun. Even though this was not any special year — like the year 2000 — the gloom and doom folks still predicted global catastrophes. Nothing had been reported so far, but the night was just beginning.

Sally jumped up from the sofa when Marilyn and I entered the great room, and for the moment abandoned Greg and GGF's journal. She danced around the furniture and the guests, rising to her toes, pirouetting, curtsying, and making them feel either welcome or alarmed, depending on how well they knew her. Eventually, she sat back down next to Greg and began watching the fireworks on the giant screen. "Abel," she called out in delight, "Come watch with us!"

I shook my head and said, "Later, Sally. I've got company."

The doorbell rang again. I made a quick head count and it looked like everyone was already here. With a sinking feeling, I guessed who it was. Hobbes had, for reasons of his own or out of pity, had invited someone I had barely learned to tolerate.

I opened the front door. I was right.

Chapter 5

"Hello, little man. The life of the party is here."
Lieutenant Kyle Murphy from Chicago Homicide
didn't shake my hand, but he slapped me on the back
and followed me into the great room.

Forrest Green stood up and clapped his hands.
"Murphy, me boy! Glad it is I am to see you! Mr.
Hobbes didn't say ye'd be coming. The party was
getting dull!"

"Yeah, runt. Probably started going downhill the
minute you showed up." Friendly sarcasm was the best
that Murphy could manage. At least he was in a good
mood.

"And what might ye be doing in this little town,
Laddie?" Forrest Green asked.

"Ask Hobbes. He invited me to the party, and then
called my boss and asked him to send me down here."

That wasn't quite right. Hobbes had talked to
Captain Kowalski of Chicago Homicide a couple of
days earlier, and somehow Murphy had been invited
to Hobbes' party. My guess was that Chicago just
wanted him out of town.

Hobbes merely said, "Glad you could come,
Lieutenant. Help yourself to food and drink." He
gestured toward the buffet that the caterer had set up.

Murphy made his presence known, all six-feet-six-inches and 260 lean pounds of him, as he crossed the room. He stopped in front of Greg Frazier and held out his hand. "Name's Lieutenant Murphy, homicide. I bury murderers. Haven't seen you before. What do you do?"

Frazier shook his hand cautiously, expecting a squeeze, and said, "I'm Greg Frazier. I bury anybody."

Murphy went on to the bar. An hour-and-a-half passed easily enough, though to tell the truth, I didn't spend much of that time in the great room. Marilyn and I took advantage of the mild weather to walk down by the river, where Charon — who was in charge of Hobbes' boathouse and rowboat — offered to take us out. Marilyn turned him down with a smile and gently touched his long white beard. "Maybe tomorrow," she said.

I had decided to wait until one minute after midnight to ask The Question, which turned out to be a mistake. The waiting, I mean. The question was all right. But by twelve-oh-one a.m., something else would have our attention.

We rejoined the party at a quarter to eleven, Chicago time. When we entered several puzzled faces looked back at me. Something was going on, but I'd missed its beginning.

Hobbes enlightened me. "Mr. Butler believes the world will end tonight."

"At least part of it will." Clyde's voice was weak and raspy, as if he'd been putting too much effort into saying what he'd had to say. "Midnight, New York

40

time. When the end begins. When the dying starts." He looked directly at Hobbes. "Maybe you can stop it, some of it." Midnight, New York time, was fifteen minutes away.

"Dad..." Rich had his arm around his father. Clyde brushed him off. Across the room, Linda shook her head.

"She told me," Clyde had turned to me, "Jane, I mean. I saw her last night. She told me to warn Rich. Especially Rich." He rubbed his left shoulder, "God, that hurts."

I couldn't think of anything to say. Jane was his first wife, but she had been dead for almost a year.

He pointed at the TV where the broadcast had switched to Times Square. "In ten minutes, when the ball drops." His skin took on an ashen color.

For three or four minutes, the only sound was from the television.

"We'll know soon, me lad, now won't we?" Forrest murmured.

I wished I'd heard everything Clyde had said while Marilyn and I had been out walking.

"Linda," he was suddenly calm, "fill this, will you?" He held out his glass. She took it and walked to the buffet. I couldn't see her face as she poured a little brandy for him, although I could see the bottle and her hands. Her shoulders shook as if she were crying.

Clyde took his glass and walked to the center of the room. He watched the oversized screen — the traditional count down was about to begin. He removed his eyeglasses and tossed them into the fireplace. One of the lenses cracked, but the glasses themselves fell safely away from the gas fire. "I won't need them anymore." He sounded greatly relieved.

He held his glass high. "To endings and beginnings. May every ending lead to a better beginning. Somewhere." He said it as if he were talking to himself, barely loud enough for everyone to hear. He waited for a moment as we raised ours, and then emptied his in one long swallow.

"Hear, hear!" Forrest Green said, and in a gesture unusual to him, joined in the toast.

The countdown started. "Ten, nine, eight," a glass dropped to the floor, Clyde's glass. "Seven, six, five..." His face lost the rest of its color and he gripped his left arm with his right hand. Then, he reached out to Linda; "Hold my hand. It hurts! It hurts all over! I can't stand it! Oh, God!"

Linda took his hand in hers, and I could see the pain on her face at Clyde's grip.

"Linda," he called out softly, as if he wasn't sure where she was.

"...Two, one." The Times Square ball slowly drifted down. We watched as it reached bottom.

Linda gripped Clyde's hands tightly. Her face had turned as pale as his. A few seconds later, his legs gave way, and he crumpled onto the floor. Linda whispered, "No!"

Fred, the ex–fireman, rushed to the fallen Clyde and began CPR while Rich knelt by his side and Hobbes called 9-1-1.

Even though it was New Year's Eve, this was still Mercater, rural north central Illinois. Not much in the way of late night celebrating went on. Hadn't for years. In this town, people stayed indoors as midnight approached, although not many would say why. Few cared to talk about the town's history of strange things happening in the late night around the holidays, but they remembered them. People tended to stay home and stay sober, and make frequent checks on their kids in their bedrooms.

So, there were few accidents and the ambulances were seldom busy. One was there in two minutes. It didn't do Clyde Butler any good.

The EMT's took over for Fred and tried to resuscitate Clyde, but nothing, not the paddles, nor the long needle that pierced his heart, nor anything else helped. At 11:50 pm, Chicago time, the ambulance rushed him to the hospital (I went along at Hobbes' request) and at 12:01 a.m., Jan. 1st, the emergency room doctor officially pronounced Clyde dead.

Doctor Robbins, who was interning, and a lot younger than I thought he should have been, shrugged apologetically when I asked him what had happened to Clyde. "Heart attack; massive heart attack. Pretty obvious clinically, but the coroner will have to give the final report, probably early tomorrow."

I remembered that I hadn't asked Marilyn The Question.

By 12:30 a.m., I was back at Hobbes' place.

I made the brief announcement, but nobody was much surprised.

Rich sat in numb silence as Car'l Hobbes talked quietly to him. Luke Ransom put his arm around Linda who was crying softly, and led her to an upholstered chair near the fireplace. Kelly and Lemuel sat on a couch in front of the big screen, occasionally watching the fireworks. They appeared uncertain about what they should do. Sally sat stiffly next to Greg, who tentatively put his arm around her shoulders. Murphy opened a can of beer, but seemed to study everyone in the room.

Chicago's midnight had come and gone, and it was almost one a.m., but no one had left.

Finally, Kelly got up and walked over to Hobbes. In a voice so low that I could barely hear her, she asked, "Can we talk privately?"

Hobbes squeezed Rich's shoulder briefly, nodded to her and rolled his wheelchair out through the short hallway and into the computer room that sometimes served as a private office. I followed as usual. He parked at the writing desk. "Please take a chair, Miss Decker."

She sat down uncertainly. "I need to know first, how expensive are you?"

He raised his eyebrow a millimeter, and drew his hands down the ends of his moustache. "Moderately."

"I don't have a lot of money."

"My fees are not always exorbitant."

"Then I'd like to hire you to investigate Clyde's murder."

"Murder? Dr. Robbins said he died of a heart attack."

"Yes. A heart attack caused by that thing he said was Jane's ghost."

Hobbes narrowed his eyes as he considered his reply. "Indeed. Then you would have me investigate Clyde's death as if it were supernatural in origin, although the coroner's report will say he died naturally?"

"That's right. The coroner and the doctor will agree on that. But I'll tell you this, Mr. Hobbes; Clyde was scared into dying. Directly or indirectly, whatever it was he saw convinced him he was going to die; so die is what he did."

"And claims involving the paranormal are what we investigate, so you want to hire us to find the supernatural cause of his death, if there is one." He indicated I should lean close so that only I could hear him. "Abel, how big is our debt to the Butlers?"

"It is my debt, sir. But it is big enough."

"A commitment to Kelly would be in conflict with the one I have with Mrs. Kelch. Should I turn them both down?"

"No sir," I said. "You are already committed. That person would be offended if you changed your mind."

He turned back to Kelly, "I have already been hired to investigate certain aspects of the Butler and Ransom families. That investigation is certain to involve Clyde's death, so I must refuse to take you as a client. I will, however, solicit your cooperation, and you can save your money."

For a moment she looked annoyed, but then she said, "I hoped I could pay you to start tonight."

Hobbes nodded. "I've already begun, Miss Decker, if only by habit. Before the New York countdown to midnight began, I met and talked with each guest. After Clyde's collapse, I observed their reactions. With the exception of Richard, I could not tell if any one reaction was sincere or bogus." He put his hands on his wheels. "Clyde was a friend. His death, if it was murder, will be avenged."

"Can I make a suggestion," she said as Hobbes turned his wheelchair to go back to the great room.

"Yes."

"Talk to Linda first," she said. "Find out how she met him."

He shook his head. "Perhaps sometime tomorrow, but more likely after the funeral. I would rather start with you."

"Good. You can start this minute."

"No. That would be inappropriate and tactless, and I am tired. If you can come back about ten in the morning, I will have questions for you."

She frowned slightly, but nodded her head. "I guess that will be soon enough. Thank you, Mr. Hobbes."

Back at his desk, he raised his voice a little and spoke to everyone. "It's late, so let's call it a night — nothing more can be done right now, anyway. However, I would like for us to meet here tomorrow at, say, one o'clock, if that's not too inconvenient. Clyde's sudden death needs to be explained and, perhaps, put behind us."

Everyone murmured agreement. Luke put his arm around Linda again and walked with her to the hallway, found their coats, and led her out the door. Lemuel followed in near-sighted closeness, excusing himself to a chair. Kelly said, "Goodnight."

Forrest left for the hide-a-bed in the small office. Murphy said he had a good enough place at the Crazy Eight. Fred went downstairs to the basement room he'd fixed up a few months ago when Hobbes had outlawed any kind of smoke that didn't come from the kitchen. Greg left and Sally went up to her attic rooms, and Charon went to his small apartment in the boathouse. Rich alone was reluctant to go. Hobbes looked across the room at him; the boy was just beginning to come out of shock.

"Can I stay here tonight, Mr. Hobbes? I'll sleep on that couch." His eyes were red, but they held something more than grief hidden in them, more than the apprehension he seemed to have had when he had first entered the house behind his dad. Was it fear? Had he seen Jane's ghost too? It was almost easy to forget that Jane had been his mother, and that his loss was as great as his dad's.

"The couch is yours, Richard. You should call your stepmother, so she will know where to find you if she needs you. Abel will get some blankets and a new toothbrush for you. We'll talk more in the morning — or tonight if you wish."

"In the morning." The words were choked, bitter, and tired. "In the morning will be best."

Marilyn was sitting on the bottom stair waiting for me. She looked up at me and grinned wryly. "Wasn't the most romantic way to spend an evening, was it?"

"Could have been better." I took her hand as she rose to her feet, and we walked up the stairs; both of us lost in our thoughts. I realized that I just couldn't ask her tonight. When we stopped at the door to the room, she put her hands on the back of my neck and pulled my head down and kissed me. It wasn't a long kiss, or a passionate one. It was simply a goodnight kiss, and with it she said, "We'll talk in the morning, Abel." She went into her bedroom, and I went down the hall to mine.

"Yeah," I thought to myself. "Could have been better."

Fifteen minutes later, I was in bed. Two minutes after that, I was asleep.

In my dream, Jane Butler lost her grip and tumbled a hundred feet down the side of the cliff at Starved Rock. Clyde Butler cried at her funeral. Linda, whose last name was still Ransom at that time, stayed close to Clyde and offered him what comfort she could. I woke up angry and frustrated. The clock said four a.m. Clyde and Jane had been good people. It wasn't fair. Fifteen minutes later, I fell back to sleep. In my second dream, I found that Linda was somehow responsible for both deaths, but I didn't recall the details or have any proof.

Chapter 6

"...Forty-nine, fifty." Fingertip pushups were finished. So were the hundred sit–ups and the workout on the second–hand Universal Machine that Hobbes had bought for the basement. I admit I was doing more than usual, but a guest in our house — a friend and neighbor — had died only eight hours ago. The excess was therapy — a way to get rid of some of my anger, and get on with my life.

I heard the squeaking of Hobbes' electric banister lift as it carried him and his wheelchair down the stairway and deposited them on the basement floor. The wall clock said eight a.m. –– Hobbes' usual time. His exercises were mostly upper body, and his routine only lasted twenty–five to thirty minutes, except for the three times a week when a therapist came in and worked on his legs to keep the muscles from atrophying. He had felt a tingling in his toes a few times and was convinced that someday he'd regain the use of his legs. The doctor said the tingling was from phantom nerve endings and originated from wherever the nerves were pinched. Hobbes refused to accept that, even though the fall that had crippled him had happened over twenty years ago.

Usually, when the lift came down, I left by way of the basement's cellar door; Hobbes preferred to work out alone.

"Abel," he called before I could put on my jacket.

"Morning, Chief." I waited for him to get off of the lift and wheel over to me.

Without preamble, he asked, "How secure is the Butlers' house?"

"You mean, is it safe from housebreakers?" I shook my head. "From amateurs, yes. From professionals and ghosts, I doubt it."

"As concerned neighbors and professionals, we should test that security when the opportunity arises. Ghosts should not be allowed free access to that home."

"Not the kind Clyde saw, anyway," I agreed. "But timing will be difficult. I doubt if the house will be empty before they leave for the wake on Tuesday. I'd hate to be caught by you-know-who."

"You'll have to wait until that harridan has left the house."

"Maybe you can invite her over for lunch."

He shuddered. "A preposterous concept — a woman I cannot stand eating a meal prepared by Fred. Do you think cold mashed potatoes, green beans, and tapioca would improve her disposition?"

"Then, how about coffee?"

He ignored the suggestion, and I left.

New Year's Day; the sun was shining and it was forty degrees outside. It was more like March than January. Usually, my run with its warm-up and cool-down totaled about three miles. This morning, I added a little. I opted to circle around by way of the river so I could see the back of the Butlers' huge old house — the next one east from Hobbes'. From my brief visual check of the windows, doors, and shrubs, I could see that if Hobbes expected me to find an easy way in, he was going to be disappointed. There were no bushes covering the windows, although there was a fairly tall blue spruce at the front corner; motion detector lights stood silent guard above the doors. Clyde had protected his family.

Two driveways and about twenty feet of grass separated the two houses. I didn't want to be too obvious in my spying, so I walked down by the river before cutting across their back yard, and came back up between their house and the vacant one to its east. Everything, as near as I could tell, was closed and locked, including the basement windows.

As I passed the front of the house, Harmless, that huge tawny male cat, leaped out from under the porch. I was certain that he was the one that had run into me yesterday morning; there couldn't be many that big. He stared at me, arched his back and hissed, then jumped sideways toward the street, his head jerking back and forth. It was as if something was after him — but the neighborhood was quiet. The only sound I heard was the soft hum of a van that was coming in from the west.

Harmless bounded across the sidewalk and into the street. He turned to face the blinding rising sun and lurched a dozen feet forward. He stopped and looked back at the house, his hair standing on end. He mewed anxiously, then stood up on his hind legs and swiped frantically with his paws. His ears were laid back flat, teeth bared in desperation. I looked at the house, then back at the cat; what did he see that was so terrifying? Did he sense something that I couldn't? Did he see something supernatural, like the ghost of Jane Butler?

I watched the animal gone wild as he sparred with his invisible adversary, and then I looked back at the house hoping to see what he was seeing. Nothing. The cat turned again and this time screamed at something behind me.

Even if he could somehow have told me what frightened him, he'd never have the chance to do so. Glancing over my shoulder, I saw the eastbound van, an old, rusty, whitish monster, picking up speed and bearing down on us, the driver no doubt blinded by the early morning sun. I made a mad scramble back to the curb and onto the sidewalk. The cat wasn't so lucky. With a mechanical lack of intent, the speeding van took whatever lives the cat had left and tossed the remains violently back toward the house. I doubted if the driver even saw him, or noticed the small bump.

It was already a corpse when I reached it. The sight of the twisted body was depressing. There were probably hundreds of stray cats in Mercater, and many were easy prey for the coyotes that often ventured across the open acres of Mercater State Hospital — MerSH for short — I really hate to see them hit by a car.

A man's voice startled me. "A waste of catgut," it said. I looked up to see Lemuel Dathan nervously peering at the dead animal through his thick glasses.

"I'm sorry, I didn't mean to startle you. But people think violin strings are made from catgut. They're wrong. They're made from sheep's gut or pig's gut. At least those on my violin are."

He glanced down the street at the disappearing van, already several blocks away. "I think that van tried to hit you."

"Tried to hit me?" I shook my head; that was an unlikely concept. Why would someone try to hit me? But all I could think to say aloud was, "You play the violin?"

"I play second violin in the Mercater orchestra. Did you know that was Katya Ransom's, I mean, Mrs. Ransom's cat? She called it Harmless. Odd name for a giant sized cat, wasn't it? I think she should have called it Harmlesszebub, you know? A cross between Harmless and Beelzebub. She'll be very upset. It was acting strange, wasn't it? Do you ever come to our concerts?"

I felt as if I had received a shotgun blast of short disconnected sentences. I told him I had but I didn't remember seeing him there, and yeah, the cat had acted strangely, and was he sure it was her cat?

"It's got a yellowish sort of brown fur, a black muzzle, black socks and a black tipped tail. Besides, it was one of the biggest cats I ever saw. I'm sure it was hers."

"It sounds like you knew him all right." I didn't bother to take another look.

He jumped subjects again. "I'm sorry. I didn't mean you should have been going to all the concerts. I've only been in town four months; I don't know what questions to ask." His voice faded away. After a silent moment, he turned the cat over with his toe. "Dead. Completely, undeniably dead. We can't leave it lying there. Do you want to help me?"

"Help you do what?" I had a momentary vision of somehow trying to salvage the cat's guts just in case he was wrong about using them to string violins.

"Why, bury it. Him. Before Mrs. Ransom finds out. I think it will be easier on her if she thinks he just ran away. Did you know it was a boy cat? I'm sorry." He took his thick glasses off and wiped his eyes. "No animal should be left like that. We can get a spade from the basement and lay him to rest in the garden." He put his glasses back on as I nodded agreement, and then he led the way.

As we passed the porch, I asked him to wait for a minute. I got down on my knees and tried to see through the crisscrossed lattice that hid the open space under the porch. I couldn't see anything until I crawled in back of some evergreen shrubs and found a two–foot wide opening, one big enough for a man to crawl through. I stuck my head inside long enough to recognize the scent of lilacs. Remembering the cat, I took a couple of quick sniffs of the air, but there didn't seem to be anything unusual. I crawled back out into the bright sunlight.

I stood up and waited for a few minutes, looking back at the cat. Suddenly, the forty-degree temperature dropped to zero; cold chills ran down my back.

Lemuel shook my shoulder. "Are you okay, Abel?"

"Yeah, sure," I said. I was looking for something. It was dangerous and frightening. I looked around. What was it?

"Abe, Abel," Lemuel said anxiously.

Then, as abruptly as they had come, the feelings disappeared. The cold faded and everything was back to normal. It wasn't the first time I'd felt that chill; it had come before on other cases. Hobbes had said it was my subconscious working, putting things together. I had replied, no, it was the presence of evil.

I shook my head to clear it, and finally said, "Good idea about that spade."

Lemuel seemed undecided about whether to say anything else, then apparently satisfied that I was okay, led me around to the back of the house.

Still a bit shaken, I wondered if that feeling of intense cold was what had scared the cat? Had we had some sort of telepathic moment? Somehow, I'd have to find out. It took me a few more minutes to recover, and then I couldn't quite recall what had happened. It was a good small mystery to figure out later.

As in Hobbes' house and in many other older houses, the basement to the Butlers' was accessible by outside steps. Without a key, the door could be unlocked only from the inside. To get in, we had to go through the kitchen and down the narrow inner back stairs.

"We have laundry privileges, but we're not supposed to mess with any of the other stuff," Lemuel said as he turned on the light. "I'm pretty sure no one will mind us borrowing a shovel and a bucket."

"One person might, especially if she knew it was her cat we were burying."

"Yeah," he agreed. Then he looked at me a little uncertainly. "Did I call you Abe and Abel out front?" He found a galvanized pail and a spade, and then hesitated. "I hope I'm not being too personal. I can call you Mr. Houston if you want."

"Abel's my name. I'm not old enough to be called Mr. Anybody. And if you were thinking about calling me 'sir', forget that too. Fred and Charon, and sometimes Hobbes, are the only men in that house who meet the age requirement or have enough respectability to be called 'sir'."

Dathan muttered something like, "The devil's most devilish when respectable..."

I said, "What?"

"Nothing really," he said. "I once taught Elizabeth Barrett Browning."

"You must be a lot older than you look."

He looked at me for a couple of seconds, then he laughed, "Ha, ha. That is funny. You were being funny, weren't you? She died a hundred and forty years ago. I like to quote her."

He bumped the pail against a chair someone had stripped of varnish and grabbed the chair to keep it from falling.

"Excuse me," he said to the chair, and looked at me sheepishly. He turned quickly back to the door, causing a corner of the spade to hook on my pant leg. A small three–cornered tear appeared.

"I'm sorry." His face turned red. "I can mend that."

A flowerpot had been placed on the ledge above the door — maybe it had been there for years. I don't know how he knocked that over, but it missed me by several inches. "Sorry," he said automatically.

I wondered if he had to practice apologizing when he got out of bed in the morning.

It was time to change the subject.

"What do you do besides play in the MSO, Lemuel?" The orchestra was non-profit, and he had to make a living somehow.

"You can call me Lem, if you want to. Do you know what the name Lemuel means? It means, 'All the smart things I know, I learned from my mother.' I don't know if she knew that when she named me, but if you knew her you'd wonder if she ever had any smarts to spare.

"But you want to know what I do to make a living, don't you? Well, among other things, I write books about genealogy. I've had articles published in The Genealogist's Quarterly. I think it's important to know where you came from."

58

He turned the inner latch that unlocked the basement door and pushed it open. I followed him up the outer steps and around front to the dead cat. Two crows had already started their flybys impatiently waiting for the animal to become food. They flew up to a telephone line and cawed angrily at us. Lemuel lifted the cat by its tail and dropped it into the bucket, and we walked back to the small garden that Clyde had cultivated.

Secure between the house and garage, the garden had produced well; Clyde had shared the bounty with his neighbors. With him gone, the garden was probably finished. I'd miss everything except the zucchini.

"Do you believe in ghosts?" He asked as he dug a shallow hole. December had been so mild that the ground hadn't yet frozen.

"I've never seen one."

"Neither have I." He tilted the pail and let the cat slip gently into the small grave, its passing marked by faint traces of blood on the galvanized metal of the pail. Lemuel shoveled a little dirt over the corpse and tamped it down lightly with his foot.

Chapter 7

We walked back down the stairs and into the basement. He rinsed out the bucket in a mechanic's sink and dried it with a paper towel. It gave me a brief chance to look around and see if anything had changed since the last time I'd been in there with Clyde. That was before he had married Linda, and little had changed. It looked unused, except for the laundry area. Neglected was the better word. If there were ghosts in this house, they would have felt comfortable down here.

"I saw an open window when I looked under the porch earlier, Lem. Let's take a look at it."

"Go ahead; I don't think I should go there, but you can." He leaned on the spade and watched me as I walked through the basement on my self-guided tour. I didn't think he'd notice my special attention to things that might affect my unauthorized visit.

The basement was divided in half by a paneled wall that began just to the left of the outside door and extended the length of the basement. Double doors a third of the way down that opened into Clyde's workshop reminded me that I still had some of his tools. I guessed I'd give them to Rich at some more convenient time.

An ancient gas furnace and a water heater stood near the center of the basement; a utility area in the far corner was host to a washer and dryer. The window that opened to the underside of the front porch was open, but two iron bars would have made it impossible for a man to crawl through. A cat wouldn't have had any problem. A box fan sat on the window's ledge, plugged in but turned off.

At the back end and to the east of the cellar door was a cistern. As in many old houses, it had been converted to a storage room, though this one had a padlocked door. I'd look at that later, if I had the opportunity.

Several fluorescent fixtures were recessed between ceiling joists and two light switches had been mounted near the outside door. One was a three-way, so the lights could be turned on either there or at the head of the stairs leading up to the kitchen. The other was switched ON and labeled DO NOT TURN OFF. I assumed that switch was for the motion detector that controlled the outside lights.

"Clyde said he saw Jane's ghost," I volunteered when I came back to Lemuel.

He started to answer when the spade slipped on the concrete and he lost his balance. The fall wasn't too bad but the bucket hit a jack post and made an alarming racket. He jumped to his feet, red-faced, grabbed the spade and bucket, and put them back where he'd found them.

Before we could make our escape, the door at the head of the stairs was thrown open. "What's going on down there? Speak up! I have my phone here. I'll dial 9-1-1 and send the pit bulls down. I have three of them!"

"It's just me, Mrs. Ransom," Lemuel answered. "I... I kicked the bucket!"

"Hah!" she said. "We should be so lucky." She lowered her voice a little and said to someone up there, "It's just that clumsy young idiot from upstairs. Someone should put him out of his misery. One day, he's going to set the house on fire or blow it up. Mark my words; he's as stupid and useless as that Houston next door. They should both be..." Mercifully the door slammed shut and we didn't hear what we both should be.

"I'm sorry, Abel," Lemuel began his apology.

I held up my hand to stop him. "Three pit bulls! Where does she keep them, under her bed?"

"No," he said, and suddenly added, "In her bed."

The image became irresistible. I almost choked trying to keep from laughing out loud. Tears came. Lemuel had the same problem.

Finally he said, "If we're not careful, she'll be down here to see what's so funny."

"Yeah. That would be as bad as the pit bulls." I said.

Worse," He said.

But the humor was gone.

It was time to go back to work.

"You started to talk about ghosts, Lem," I prompted him.

"About the one Clyde saw. He saw something, all right, but I don't know if it was a ghost. Is Mr. Hobbes going to investigate?"

"You'd have to ask him that," I said. "But he's always curious about anything to do with ghosts, and I know he wants to find out more about Clyde's death. He'll probably want to talk to you."

"All he needs to do is call me. I'll be watching football this afternoon or maybe I'd come over on my own. I've got a thirteen-inch TV. I have to sit this close to see it." He held his hands a foot apart.

I laughed at his not so subtle hint. "Come watch it on his big screen, then. You can talk during commercials."

He bumped into the door casing on the way out, and said an automatic, "Excuse me," and stumbled up the steps to the back yard.

Since I was right behind him and the last to leave, I checked the lock on the basement door as well as the outdoor lights' switch.

He followed me around to the front of the house, stepped up on the porch, and sat down on the old wooden glider that Clyde had built many years ago.

"Make it about one o'clock." I said. He rocked back almost recklessly, barely clipping a plant stand. A potted plant tilted dangerously toward the picture window, but somehow Lemuel caught it. I took that as my cue and told him I should get going.

He nodded sheepishly, and then I began warming up for my morning run.

He never had said what other things he did for a living.

I walked west on River Street to Main as part of my warm up, then ran south across the bridge toward the entrance to MerSH, reversed directions and ran back to the River and Main intersection. At one time, an old boarded-up house had stood on the southeast corner. It had been replaced by the golden arches of McDonalds. I went inside and picked up the order waiting for me. I had a friendly arrangement with the manager; they would watch for me to begin my run and then fill my order just before I was due to finish it, so the McMuffins and pancakes were still fresh and hot. "Eat your heart out, Fred," I said to myself and walked that last quarter-mile home.

After breakfast, I told Hobbes about the curious death of the cat and repeated my conversation with Lemuel Dathan. His response was to close his eyes and rock slowly back and forth in his wheelchair. After a moment, he wheeled to the patio door and looked out across the river at the distant tower clock. Sunlight reflected off his bald head and formed a sort of halo that contrasted with his long, angular face and pointed ears — I had always thought horns would fit him better than the ears.

"Can you get into that house this morning?" he asked me. He sounded as if he already knew the answer.

"Only if I'm invited. Even then, I'd have a tough time searching the place. They'd have to be gone or sleeping."

"It is unlikely that Katya Ransom will leave that house for any reason other than the wake or the funeral, and that won't be any earlier than Tuesday afternoon. Evidence of a manufactured ghost may be gone by then, if it's not already gone."

I sighed. "I'll see what I can do, Chief. But I can't see going over there before one or two a.m. Wednesday morning."

"I suppose that will have to do," was his response. He didn't sound too happy.

Chapter 8

At ten o'clock, Kelly Decker sat down in a swivel chair across from Hobbes. He studied her from his side of the small desk at the north end of the computer room, and I watched both of them from a chair near the door. I was far enough away so I wouldn't be a distraction, but close enough to hear everything that was said. We were meeting there as a courtesy to the other guests — Marilyn, Forrest, and Rich, who were settled in the great room watching the big TV, or trying to.

He leaned back in his wheelchair. "Are you comfortable?"

The lighting must have been different in the computer room. It gave her face the illusion of being crisscrossed with dozens of faint, tiny scars. They seemed to crack into small shards when she spoke. "There are certain questions I will not answer. I want you to know that up front. Some things are too personal to talk about."

"Very well." His eyes slowly closed to slits. "Tell me what you can. We'll proceed from there."

She straightened herself and gripped the arms of her chair. "I told you last night that Clyde was murdered, and that he was driven to it by a presence who called itself his dead wife, Jane."

Hobbes expression didn't change. "A presence? An odd choice of words, Miss Decker. Why not call it Jane's ghost, as Clyde did?"

"Because... because Jane alive or Jane dead would not deliberately have caused him harm. She would not have terrified him, knowing the condition of his heart. If it really has been her, then she was coerced."

Hobbes glanced at me briefly, then turned back to Kelly. "Coerced? How does one force the dead to do something?"

"I don't know, but I saw her myself."

Hobbes and I both sat up straight. "What did you see?" His voice was sharp.

"I saw her talk to Clyde the night before last. She whispered things to him, but I could still hear parts of what she said. She frightened me."

"She talked? What did she say?"

Kelly looked puzzled, "I know I heard her whisperings. I just can't remember them. Isn't that odd? I think they were what Clyde said about everything coming to an end. Later, when she spoke aloud, I could hear everything."

"When you saw Jane's ghost," he said slowly, "how clear was the image?"

"Clear, I suppose. Maybe a little fuzzy."

"I see," Hobbes said, after taking a few minutes to give her time to elaborate. Then he asked, "Miss Decker, are you sure you know my position where ghosts are concerned?"

"I know you don't believe in them."

"More than that. My job is to prove that such claims as yours are hoaxes or frauds, or the result of them. If we continue and your case is solved, I assure you, there will have been no ghost."

"I know what I saw," she said. Her gaze into Hobbes' eyes was unflinching.

Hobbes stroked the ends of his moustache. "You may feel differently in a few days."

She shook her head. "Jane was with him two nights ago. She told him he would die on New Year's Eve.

"Twenty years ago, Mr. Hobbes, she took Clyde away from me. She did it again last night."

"From you? What claim did you have on him? He was married to Linda, and before that to Jane."

Her voice rose, "Linda had no right to him either, but she was here when Jane died, and I suppose he found comfort with her. They were married before I knew what was happening. She should never have come to Mercater." Kelly twisted her hands together in a tight knot of fingers and thumbs. The air around her seemed to become charged with electricity, and her eyes flashed at Hobbes. "If I told you the truth about Linda, you would... No, that's not relevant."

The outburst ended as quickly as it had begun. She grimaced and said, "You wanted to know what happened when Jane appeared, not how I felt about Linda. I'm sorry."

"I understand," Hobbes said. "Perhaps you could give us more of the details. How it began, how it ended. What happened twenty years ago?"

"Of course." She took a deep breath. "But I won't go into... into what happened between Clyde and me twenty years ago. That was too painful.

"What matters now is the night before last. It was past midnight. I had just come in and was standing at the bottom of the stairs. Clyde was in the great room, which was to my left. The air suddenly became warm and I could smell lilacs — that was one of Jane's favorite scents. A glow appeared to come through the east wall and he stepped back from it. A woman's face took shape within that glow, and started whispering to Clyde, as I told you. Later, when she was talking aloud, I knew the voice. I'd known it for years."

She gazed up at the ceiling. "Jane told Clyde she was waiting for him. It wouldn't be heaven until he joined her; but, she said, she could wait. She wanted him to take care of Rich, to warn him of the end of things. She lowered her voice and I couldn't hear her for a while. Then Clyde walked away, toward the dining room, and Jane sort of faded out. I went after Clyde, and found him staring into the fireplace like he'd been sleepwalking. I took his hand, but he just stood there. I don't think he really saw me."

Tears formed in Kelly's eyes and ran down her cheeks. "He said, 'It can kill us all if it wants to. It starts with me.' I asked him what he meant by 'it' but that was all he would say. Instead, he brushed me aside and went to his bedroom."

"Undoubtedly, the apparition had a profound influence on him." Hobbes murmured. "We shall see. For the moment I have other questions."

Hobbes continued. "Four months ago, Clyde converted the second floor of his house into two small apartments. Do you know why? Jane was supposed to have been adequately insured. He would not have needed rental income."

She shook her head. "He started remodeling the upstairs more than a year ago while Jane was still alive. After she died, he finished it because it was something for him to do. Even then, the apartments sat empty for two months. When he married Linda, he put them up for rent. He gave one to me, and offered the other to Lemuel.

Chapter 9

"You said you had known him for twenty years. Is that why he rented one of those apartments to you?"

"I knew Jane for twenty years. Clyde, I knew much longer — I went to high school with him," said Kelly.

"Indeed. How well did you know him then? Was he a boyfriend? Did you date him? Go to the prom?"

"I knew him well enough, but Clyde Butler hardly noticed me. His love interest was Linda Ransom." The words had an edge of bitterness to them.

"Linda Ransom? Yet he didn't marry Linda first, but chose Jane instead. Do you know why?"

Kelly hesitated before answering. "No, but I do know that the Linda Ransom Clyde recently married is not the Linda Ransom he knew back then." It seemed an odd way of saying that — maybe it was just that her voice had lost all inflection.

"Where is the first Linda now?"

"There is a headstone in a cemetery with her name on it. It says she died before her twenty-fourth birthday."

Hobbes turned his wheelchair back and forth, an inch each way, and then said. "A very long time ago. Do you know the cause of her death? Or how it affected Clyde?"

She shook her head. "I don't think he knew about it. But that's one of those things I don't want to discuss. I have already said more than I should have about the past. Ask me about the present."

He looked at me and raised an eyebrow. I shrugged; if we needed to know more about Linda, Sally could probably dig it up, so to speak.

"As you wish. Where did you live before you came to Mercater?"

"Kankakee."

"What did you do there?"

She smiled wryly. "You would not approve."

"There are many things I don't approve of. They are generally illegal, unethical, or immoral. Which is yours?"

"All of them, or none. It depends on your point of view."

"Then, you could have been a politician or a prostitute, a lawyer or a faith healer." The corners of his mouth went up a centimeter, for him a broad smile, "Or none of them. You were something else. What were you?"

"A spirit medium. I communicated with the dead."

She might as well have said she was a reincarnated vanilla wafer as far as Hobbes' response was concerned. His smile increased a millimeter. It might have been a genuine surprise, but then he glanced briefly at me and I wondered if he had already known. Maybe he did. He had been on the phone when

I came back from my run. Few things really surprised Hobbes.

"You did that for money?"

"People sometimes paid me, but only when I was successful."

"How often did you fail?"

"More often than not. Sometimes, it took several attempts; occasionally contact was never possible."

"Were you a fraud?" he asked suddenly.

"I know you think I was. It's your job to be cynical, but you are wrong. I have been a conduit since I was twelve years old." She stopped suddenly, and then added, "I know a spirit — a ghost — when I feel one."

"Lemuel Dathan moved into the other apartment about the same time you moved in to yours. He also came from Kankakee. Is that a coincidence or is there something about you and him I should know?"

"All I can tell you about Lemuel's past is he was a music teacher in Kankakee. He came here to teach history at Mercater High School."

"Did you know him in Kankakee?"

"Most people I associated with were interested in the recently dead. His interest was in the long dead. He has written an extremely dull book on genealogy. He spent his spare time in courthouses and graveyards, not in séances."

I grinned at Hobbes — Lemuel sounded like our Cemetery Sally. I'd have to be sure they were more formally introduced to each other.

Hobbes continued to question Kelly until almost noon, then he said that was enough for the time being. He invited her to stay and eat with us, but like most people who knew Fred's reputation as a cook, she declined. Who knew what he would have for a New Year's Day lunch? Hobbes assured her that today Fred would have nothing to do with it, and the food would be catered and acceptable. Sally, he said, had talked to each of last night's guests, and they all would be here. Kelly finally said she would come, too.

As it turned out, lunch wasn't that bad. After Fred had told Marilyn what was on his menu, she had taken over the kitchen, ordered him out of it, and then used the telephone to find a delicatessen that would prepare a small New Year's feast on short notice. She had picked it up, herself, in her Mercedes.

Marilyn sat the food out buffet style with sturdy paper plates and clear plastic glasses, honest-to-God silverware from somewhere in Hobbes' kitchen, and TV trays. She said we could watch the Bowl games while we ate.

"She's after my cooking job," Fred muttered.

"You have a cooking job?" Sally smiled in her sweetest way. "Where? I know funeral directors who lay out a better spread than you do."

"They get paid better too."

The doorbell rang and Sally sang out, "I'll get it!" and danced her way to the front door. A minute later she returned with a slightly embarrassed Greg Frazier in tow. "Greg didn't have anything planned for today, so I asked him to come over. He can eat with us." She squeezed his hand and he squeezed back.

Her attitude changed suddenly, and she said, "He has been preparing Cly... Clyde's body for the funeral."

Frazier shook his head. "For the cremation, actually. Mrs. Butler said he wanted his ashes taken to..."

"No, he didn't!" Rich abruptly cried out. "Dad wanted to be buried next to Mom. You can't cremate him! You can't!"

"I'm sorry, Rich," Greg said, obviously pained, "but the spouse has the right to choose the method of interment."

"Is it not too late, Laddie?" Forrest Green spoke up, rising to his maximum height. "It would be bad for the boy if that were happening."

"Well," Greg began. "It's not too late, but..."

"It would make good copy for the National Echo, me boy. Front-page story, Boy's Life Turned to Ashes! Or something like that." Good for the paper. Not so good for public relations and the funeral home."

"Well," Greg said. "We want what's best for the family. Let me call Linda and I'll see what I can do."

"Ye'd best call the crematory first, before ye've waited too long."

"Yes, of course," Greg said. "Excuse me, please." He took his cell phone from its belt clip, and walked to the far side of the room, near Hobbes empty desk.

The doorbell rang again. It was Lt. Murphy. I let him in.

"I was supposed to give this to Hobbes last night," he said as he followed me into the great room. He tossed his brown Indiana Jones style Fedora onto a chair near the buffet, and then reluctantly added, "Couldn't find it when I unpacked before coming over here. If you want to know the damned truth, it was laying on the car seat when I came out this morning, like I might have left it there last night." He handed me a white business size envelope. It was addressed to Carl — without the apostrophe — Hobbes, Mercater. The envelope lacked both return address and stamp.

I took it to the kitchen where Hobbes was watching real food being prepared using his kitchen equipment. It was a rare experience, even though most of it came ready to eat from the super mart deli.

"Murphy brought this," I said and handed him the envelope. He opened it and took out a single sheet of paper. He read it, frowned, and then read it a second time.

"I think we should go to the small office," he said; Murphy and I followed him into the computer room.

He waited until we had found places to sit, and then he handed the letter to me.

It was simple, short, and to the point.

"Captain Kowalski," it said, "Abe Houston, a psychic detective for Hobbes' Investigations here in Mercater has foreseen a murder on New Year's Eve, or New Year's Day. It will take place at Carl Hobbes' home here in Mercater. Carl has requested police help, the kind I don't have. If you have a homicide detective free and you can loan him to us for a few days, we would be grateful. — Bull."

"Well?" Murphy asked.

"Left the apostrophe out every time," I said.

"Is this a photocopy?" was Hobbes' response.

Murphy shrugged. "Kowalski copies everything."

"Have you read it?"

"Hell, no," Murphy said without rancor. "I figured if you needed my help, you'd show it to me."

"Then, tell me what you think of it." Hobbes handed the paper to Murphy.

Murphy read it, and then like Hobbes, reread it.

"Well. I'll be damned," he said finally. "Abe is a psychic. I knew he wasn't a detective, but I never thought he could see in the future."

"If I could do that, I'd tell you who's going to win the ass-kicking contest, you or me."

"Yeah?"

"Yeah!"

"Yeah?"

"Yeah!"

"Enough," Hobbes said mildly. "Again, Lt. Murphy, tell me what you think of the letter?"

"It's a pile of crap," Murphy said. "It was written after Butler died and then put in my car so it would look like it was written yesterday. A trick to get me out of town for a few days. I'm heading back home. Something's going on there that I don't know about."

Hobbes said, "One minute, please. The letter is right in one aspect. There was a murder in my house."

Murphy didn't seem surprised, even though we had let everyone think that Clyde had died from an ordinary heart attack, one brought on by stress and alcohol. Kelly had been the only exception. "Then, who do you think wrote that letter?" was his response. "It sure wasn't Bull Dickerson."

He didn't get an answer because that was when Marilyn called us to lunch.

Turkey and dressing, mashed potatoes and gravy, cranberry sauce, and so forth took our attention for an hour, then we settled down to relax.

Some of us started to watch a pre-game show, but without much enthusiasm. Clyde had died in front of that TV, and the ghost of his passing, if not his real ghost, seemed to haunt it. Choosing to ignore the TV, Lemuel Dathan — who had accepted my invitation — asked Hobbes if he knew much of Hobbes' family's history, and the two had gone to the big desk at the other end of the room. After a few minutes, I followed them, and soon Sally and Forrest joined us. Greg was on the phone, again. Fred and Charon stayed with Rich, who had placed his chair over the spot where his father had fallen. The expression on the boy's face was unreadable.

Dathan was saying that the key to successful genealogy for Hobbes would start with the father.

"Ye may have a problem, me boy," Forrest Green volunteered. "Many of the souls who have entered that door have suggested that Car'l never had a father."

Dathan looked puzzled behind the half-inch thick glasses. "But everyone has a father. It's a biological necessity."

"Aye, you're right enough, lad, but they were just saying he didn't know who his father was."

"But..."

"The word that describes the condition begins with 'B' and has seven letters to it."

Dathan stared at Green for a long moment then suddenly said, "Oh, I get it, ha ha. It's a joke." His laugh needed practice.

Forrest sighed and looked at Sally. "Would ye care to join me in the kitchen for some coffee, Lass?"

"Don't mind if I do."

I wanted to follow them, but Hobbes shook his head slightly.

"You're a teacher?" he asked Dathan.

The young man nodded.

"Do you get on well with your students?" he asked.

Dathan' face brightened. "Some of them find history as fascinating as I do, the better ones anyway. The others find more satisfaction in the present."

"Why did you leave Kankakee?"

"The young people there had little interest in good music. Class enrollment declined and they no longer needed me."

"Good music?"

"Yes, the very best music. Brahms, Bach, Beethoven — I guess I was too advanced for the common student."

"No doubt," Hobbes agreed. "Tell me, did you know Kelly Decker when you lived in Kankakee?"

Dathan shook his head slowly. "Decker, Decker, Decker. There was a Decker Park near Central elementary school, I think. It had a big playground. High school kids went there to buy drugs, until the police closed it down. I don't know what Decker Park's first name was."

Hobbes shook his head as if to clear it. "Playground? Drugs? What does that have to do with Kelly Decker?"

Dathan looked around slyly, then laughed again. The laugh was better this time. "That was a joke. I was pretending to misunderstand you." He sighed, and added, "I thought you might laugh. Well, anyway, Kelly Decker was supposed to be a fortuneteller, but I never met her until I moved here. I had heard of her, that's all."

Hobbes reached into his pocket as if he was reaching for a cigarette, then frowned and withdrew his hand — he hadn't smoked for ten years. "She told us she saw Jane Butler's ghost the same time Clyde saw it. Do you believe her?"

"Maybe part of me does; I don't know. She talked to me about it yesterday, but Clyde was still alive then and I didn't pay much attention. Now he's dead. Makes a guy wonder, doesn't it?"

The discussion went on in that fashion for ten minutes, with Hobbes asking questions and Dathan skirting the answers, until Hobbes put both his hands up, palms forward. "Enough. You talk while saying nothing. Watch the game. I'm going to the kitchen. Abel, come with me."

As we entered the hallway, Dathan said, "Excuse me," to an armless chair and started bumping his way to the TV. That was followed seconds later by the sound of a lamp crashing to the floor. Even in the kitchen we could hear his voice muffled by the walls. "Uh, pardon me," Dathan said. I studied the back of Hobbes' ears. They were an unusual shade of red.

He rolled to the fridge, took out a beer — a Desmond's — and wheeled to the table. He popped the lid and took a long swallow, then closed his eyes for a moment. A slight wrinkle on his forehead told me he didn't like the stuff — all I could figure about the cheap beer was that he drank it to make a point. He took another drink, emptying the can, and asked, "What is your impression of Mr. Dathan?"

Chapter 10

"If you look in the dictionary under 'hopeless,' you'll find his picture."

"No doubt," he said. "You may also look up 'guile' or 'conceit.' That man cannot be what he pretends to be. No one could be that obtuse and survive as long as he has."

I sat down figuring Hobbes had come up with some great insight.

"Then what is he?" I asked.

"I don't know," he growled. "But if knowing becomes necessary, I shall take great pleasure in finding out."

He drank a second beer and smiled sardonically — the corners of his mouth widened slightly — and said, "In the meantime, while he is in this house, he bears watching."

Lt. Murphy's roar suddenly penetrated the wall between the kitchen and the great room. "You damned squirt, Dathan. Do one more thing to my hat and they'll carry you home in buckets!"

Later we heard that Lemuel Dathan had, one, sat on Murphy's hat; two, stepped on Murphy's hat; and three, spilled mashed potatoes on Murphy's hat. Murphy hadn't liked any of it.

Two hours later, Linda Butler called and quietly told me the arrangements. The wake would be Tuesday from four o'clock to eight at the Frazier Brothers Funeral Chapel. The funeral would be at eleven a.m. Interment would follow at the Oakwood cemetery. There would be no cremation. I passed the information on.

A little while later, Rich asked if I was busy. His eyes were red and puffy, but he seemed to have reached some sort of acceptance.

I said, "Waiting for Fred to broil the T–bones and bake the sweet potato casserole, Rich. Might take a few minutes though."

"Yeah," he agreed. "Maybe a lot of minutes." He allowed himself a faint smile. He knew of Fred's aversion to cooking, of course. It was a well-known joke among even the infrequent visitors to the old house on River Street; and there were times recently when Rich had almost lived here.

"Something I can help you with?"

"I need to get outside and get some air. Want to come shoot some hoops with me?"

Several years ago, Clyde had put a backboard above his garage door along with a standard hoop at the regulation height. It wasn't a very good imitation of a basketball court — the blacktop drive wasn't level, nor were the markings accurate. But it had been good enough for Rich and Clyde and some of Rich's friends to practice on. Once in a while, he would ask me if I wanted to try to guard him, and I'd say yes. Foolishly.

I caught Green's eye and made a gesture like I was shooting a basketball, then pointed in the general direction of Rich's back yard.

He nodded and said, "I'll get me jacket, Laddies."

Marilyn said, "You'll need a fourth, won't you?" and followed us.

Outside in the neighbor's back yard, we began playing two–on–two. For some reason, Rich chose Forrest Green as his partner, and I was stuck with Marilyn — who could play basketball as well as she could dance.

Rich and Forrest were small and quick. I was taller and slower, but I had reach on them. Gradually, Green and I loosened up and began hitting our shots, and Marilyn was delighted when she made her first basket. Rich, though, seemed to get tighter as the minutes went by and his shots went wild, bouncing off the rim, missing the backboard, one nearly going over the roof of the garage. I called time and asked him if he was okay.

He didn't look at me, but instead studied the backboard. "Dad built that for me," he said slowly, "While he was alive."

He caught the basketball and started dribbling it around the blacktop. "But he's still around. I know he is." Rich took a twenty–foot shot and it rattled its way through the hoop. "See that, Dad," he said softly.

An answer came, brutal and sudden, but it wasn't from Clyde.

"You're wrong, you stupid, ignorant child!" The cold sharp voice of Luke and Linda's mother, Katya Ransom, cracked the growing darkness and stopped our shooting. "Your poor father's dead and likely gone to hell, Richard. He's nowhere around here!"

"Grandmother Katya," Rich began, but he didn't know what to say.

"You want to see him again, don't you? You'll have to die to do that, and then you'll spend eternity looking for him." She raised her voice, "But maybe God will answer you." She stepped out of the shadows around the back porch — a slender hawk-eyed sixty-year old woman rigid as a broom handle, "But He won't give you what you expect. You don't believe anything about the true God, do you?"

"I go to church."

"Bah! A church that knows nothing about Him," she spit the words out.

"You're wrong, Grandmother," a little fire crept back into his words. "We believe in God."

"Then don't waste your time playing childish games with these foolish men and that harlot! Get down on your knees and ask..."

"Stop it!" Rich yelled. He picked up the basketball and threw it hard against Green's chest. The little man caught it, glared at the old woman, and then tossed the ball to me. I passed it to Marilyn and she flipped it over her shoulder in the general direction of the hoop. It thunked against the backboard and fell through the basket.

"Game," she called out. "We win!"

Katya Ransom turned and stalked away.

Rich burned a lot of energy after that, more like his old self. It was a good sign.

We played another fifteen minutes then went back inside. Forrest and I were winded, but Marilyn, who had been trying to defend against Rich, was flat–out exhausted. Rich whistled a short tune as we walked down the hallway. It was something I'd heard his dad whistle many times.

"I think I might dig a big hole in the front yard and cover it with sticks and dead grass, just in case she tries to come over here again." I said to Rich.

"It wouldn't hold her," he replied.

Forrest Green concurred, "Aye, me boy. You'd need a moat with a Loch Ness monster to stop her."

"She's just a crazy old woman," Marilyn said, unusually sympathetic. "I've seen worse."

"So have I," I said, remembering Molly Beecher who had spent forty years hiding in the tunnels under Mercater State Hospital. "A lot worse."

The leftovers we had for supper were only about ten times better than what we usually ate, and I found myself feeling relaxed, if not downright mellow.

Marilyn snuck up behind me and slipped both arms around my waist, "Do you think Charon's offer for a boat ride is still open?"

"Maybe. But it is January," I said, "and it's still gonna be cold out on the river."

"Then you'll have to think of some way to keep me warm, won't you?"

As it turned out, we couldn't find Charon, either in his small apartment in the boathouse or in the kitchen.

"Try the Dam Tap," Fred suggested. "Or Captain Joe's, or the River Rat."

Marilyn smiled. "Let's go dancing, instead."

I reluctantly agreed –– not because we'd be in a crowd and I wanted us to be alone, but because she was a truly lousy dancer. During the academic year, she taught anthropology at the University, but in summers, she traveled to obscure African countries and studied primitive cultures. I think that's where she learned the one–and–a–half step.

Nobody could dance it like she could.

She also always wanted to lead.

After half an hour on the dance floor, we went to a movie. That was a definite improvement.

At least it was until Charon sat down beside us.

"Fred says you be lookin' for me," he said in a stage whisper. Half a dozen people turned their heads and said, "Shhh."

So we watched the movie. My problem was, my mind kept drifting as it tried to explain Clyde's dying. Different explanations hovered nearby, but none made any sense.

When we returned to the house, it was past midnight. Marilyn asked me to come into the hallway for a minute. She sat down on the bottom step of the stairs, and patted the carpet with her hand indicating I should sit. I sat.

"How goes the case, Mr. Snoop?"

"I dunno yet. Listen, Marilyn, I'm sorry that all this happened." I wanted to say more, but I was at a loss.

She took my hand gently. "Don't worry about it. I never could compete with the paranormal or with a murder investigation. We can try again when your time is your own, and you can give some of it to me.

"As for me, Abel, I'm going back home. You can keep me posted."

"You're not going now, are you? It's the middle of the night!"

She stood up. "Best time to travel. Won't be much traffic. I'll be home in an hour."

She went upstairs, picked up her suitcase, came back down and kissed me; and just like that, she was gone.

I watched at the door until her Mercedes was out of sight. I resolved to make it up to her somehow, but she was right; she couldn't compete against this kind of a situation, and I couldn't ignore it.

Hobbes called from the hallway and said he wanted to go over some plans for Sunday. I followed him into the kitchen where Sally and Fred were drinking coffee, and Charon was gazing out the window at the river.

"Not much moon tonight," Charon seemed to be speaking to himself. "There's the clock tower across the way, but you can't see nothin' of the grounds. Can't tell if anyone's wanderin' around there or not."

"Should there be?" I asked.

"Nope. But I thought I saw something a while ago. A flashlight, or a reflection maybe. Don't see it no more."

I shivered at some memories about the place. Even a guess that someone was moving around there at midnight was more than I wanted to hear.

Hobbes wheeled up to the table and took the cup of coffee Sally offered to him. "It's late, so I'll be brief. Sally, is there any way you can, on a Sunday morning, get some background on Lemuel Dathan, Kelly Decker, and the Ransoms?"

"Of course," she smiled brightly. "But it won't be a lot, and I may have to drive to Kankakee."

"We all got to make sacrifices," Charon murmured.

"What do you want me to do, Boss?" Fred asked. "So long as it ain't cookin' or nothin' like that."

"I want you to watch the front of the Butler house while Abel is inside, and to alert us if you see anything that could pose a threat."

To me, he said, "It's late enough, and the downstairs lights in that house are all darkened.

Nevertheless, you should assume that at least one person is awake."

I grinned; that was his way of telling me I could sneak into the Butlers' house, if I wanted to. "And we never mention her name out loud after midnight. Right, Chief?"

Even though the last light to go out at the Butler house did so at 1:15 a.m., it made sense to me to wait an extra half hour before going in. Call it my comfort zone, but this was more than just looking around; if the cops caught me, it could mean my license and maybe some time in jail. That didn't bother me so much, though; the rush I got from the risk more than made up for the danger.

Our house became quiet too, with everybody but Fred, Hobbes, and me having gone to bed. The extra wait was for the other house. Seven people had lived next door until last Friday evening. Now there were only six, and if you didn't count Rich, who was staying with us until he felt ready to go home, there were still five; Katya, Linda, Luke, Lemuel and Kelly. I wanted to be sure they were all asleep, especially Katya Ransom.

It was about a quarter to two when I turned off the circuit breaker that controlled Hobbes' outside lights and motion detector, and went out the back door. It was cold enough to remind me it was still January, but not cold enough for a coat. Anyway, I was wearing a black sweater, jeans, gloves, and a dark gray ski mask. The quarter moon and the distant streetlights gave a feeble illumination. That was all I needed.

No outside lights came on as I crossed the back yards and slipped down the stairs to the Butlers' basement door. It opened easily. The door had remained unlocked and the light switch turned off the way I had left them when I followed Dathan out of the basement yesterday.

I stepped inside, closed the door, and listened. The quiet hiss of the pilot light on the furnace was all I heard. The darkness was virtually complete — murky, sinister, and slightly claustrophobic. The only hint of light came from under the door to the old cistern. It was faint, and unmistakably purple. I twisted the head of my pocket flashlight to turn it on and then twisted it some more to fan out the beam. The darkness withdrew only partway, but that was okay with me. I went to a window that faced west to Hobbes' house and briefly flashed my light, and saw Hobbes flash his in return. If he saw anything happening around the house, he would dial my pager, which was set to vibrate instead of ring audibly, and I would get out immediately.

The door to the cistern was secured with a decent brass Yale padlock. I could probably open it with the tools I had brought along, but that might take a while. It could wait.

Chapter 11

The west half of the basement was enclosed in paneling, and had been Clyde's workshop. I didn't bother opening the double doors –– I'd seen the inside several times with Clyde. He'd been proud of it.

Of more interest right then were two large wooden crates about four feet long by two wide and maybe ten inches tall, that I hadn't seen yesterday morning. They were nailed shut, and didn't have an address or packing slip on either one. I could imagine the noise I'd make trying to open one, and shook my head. Maybe later.

In the meantime, the smell of lilacs had become stronger as I walked toward the front of the basement. It brought me to the barred window that was hidden below the front porch and had been left open.

That window was where Harmless the Cat had emerged from yesterday morning. Inside and along the wall was the usual clutter of stored junk: boxes, a table and chairs set, and a folded stepladder that leaned against the table. I flashed the light around, but I didn't see anything that explained lilacs or the open window.

Suddenly, something brushed against my leg and I jumped back almost knocking the stepladder over. I caught it before it fell, and steadied it with one hand while I flashed the light down with the other. A giant yellow cat stared up at me like a stunted mountain lion, a twin to the one I'd seen die yesterday. I was amazed that there could be two of them, exactly alike.

"Harmless?" I said tentatively.

It meowed once loudly, jumped onto the table, then to the window and disappeared outside.

I leaned the ladder back and then stopped; it was an odd place to store a ladder. I turned my light onto the overhead joists. The section of aluminum duct that connected to the cold air return register had been removed. I opened the ladder, climbed it and looked through the grillwork. Apparently, it was near the front door. The streetlight shining through the great room windows above was enough to show part of the great room in a pattern of dim contrasts, but the angle of the grill opening made it difficult to see very much.

This would be a good place to bring hypnotic gas or the aroma of lilacs into the house, if that was what had been done. I quickly scanned the area around the ladder for any kind of apparatus that might be operated by remote control, but I didn't see anything. Of course, it could have been too obvious to leave sitting around.

Then, I heard rapid footsteps coming from one of the bedrooms at the back of the house, muffled slightly by the heavy carpeting. They stopped in the great room and Katya Ransom called out, "Harmless? Harmless? Is that you? Are you back?" She stumbled against something and then found a light switch and turned a floor lamp on. I belatedly turned my flashlight off. Mostly what I could see was the upper end of the stairway, and once in a while, Katya would walk past in her ancient, dingy nightgown and robe.

"Harmless, Harmless," she called again. For several minutes she maundered around the great room, slowly, dreamily. She started crying.

A few seconds later, an upstairs door clicked open and someone came to the top of the stairs.

"Mother, dearest," Luke called out. "What's wrong?"

"I heard Harmless," Katya said. "I heard him call me."

Luke came down the stairs, stepped across my register, and put his arm around Katya. I could see them both. "He's dead, Mother. Killed by a car. Lemuel buried him. Another minikin will take his place. Maybe that's what you heard." He glanced downward, and for a moment I thought our eyes locked, but I was positive he couldn't see me. He lit a cigarette that looked like it had been hand-rolled and offered it to Katya. "Sit down and rest here, Mother. Smoke this. Relax. You have your glasses? Good." He led her to a chair almost on top of me. "Read this magazine for a while. When you are relaxed, go back to bed. Okay?" He dimmed the light, and went back to the stairs.

Katya took three or four deep drags on her cigarette, then snuffed it out in an ashtray. I heard her chair squeak and guessed she was setting the ashtray on the floor. She thumbed through the magazine, but I doubted if she took time to read anything; it was as if she was waiting for something. A few minutes passed, and I was getting tired of standing on the ladder.

Unexpectedly a white light appeared on the east wall. I heard Katya take a deep breath. "Linda," she said. "My Linda."

The light took shape. I twisted around trying to see it, but it was out of my line of vision. The basement suddenly seemed cold.

Whatever it was spoke to her. "It is I."

"Not you, not a minikin," Katya cried softly. "I want my Linda."

"You have your Linda," a soft voice answered her. "Be content. Be content."

The light faded.

A few minutes later, Katya returned to her bedroom. I climbed down from the ladder, folded it and leaned it against the table. I walked back to the other end of the basement, stopped, and stared at the door that led up to the kitchen. Was it worth going after that cigarette butt? I was pretty sure Hobbes would say no; I was also pretty sure it wouldn't be there tomorrow afternoon.

Besides, I had a little plastic bag with me that would be perfect for transporting it.

I avoided the two squeaky steps that I had noted when Dathan had led me down to the basement. I stopped on the small landing at the top of the stairs and listened before pushing the door open and stepping out into the kitchen. Again, all seemed quiet. I took a moment to visualize the layout of the first floor. I'd have to navigate it with almost no light. That wouldn't be too difficult; on the east side of the house were the kitchen, dining room, and living room, all lined up along a central hallway. On the west side, offset by their own short hall, were two bedrooms, Katya's and Rich's. A few steps further north were the main bathroom and Linda's bedroom. It was a straight shot from the kitchen to the front room.

Unfortunately, I waited too long. The large furry body slipped between my legs and darted through the kitchen and down the hallway. Harmless, if that's who it was, was answering Katya's call. I had to wait, poised to get out if anyone heard the cat and came to investigate. Minutes passed and nothing happened. What the cat was doing, I could only guess.

Well, I thought, I could run pretty fast if I had to and I was getting tired of waiting, anyway. Quietly, listening for any sound that didn't belong, I cat-footed it, pardon the expression, through the kitchen, dining room, and living room to the front entrance. I stopped on top of the cold air register that I'd looked through a few minutes before, and studied the wall that had been out of my sight. Even in the near darkness, I could see the two small holes where the projectors had projected their images.

There was only one cigarette butt, but I couldn't see well enough to locate it on the gray carpet. I got down on my hands and knees and felt around near the chair Katya had sat in, but I couldn't find anything. The cigarette loomed in importance. I felt more and more each minute that finding it was essential.

I took my flashlight out, took a deep breath, and turned it on. I saw the ashtray immediately Katya must have kicked it when she got up, and it was about four feet closer to her bedroom. I flicked the light off — it had been on less than a second — and grabbed for the single butt in the ashtray.

Even as I closed my hand around it, the air suddenly was filled with ear shattering screeching and howling as the cat attacked Katya's door, scratching and throwing itself against it with a terrible ferocity. I heard her door open almost immediately and the hallway was instantly flooded with light. At the same time the cat settled down with a simple plaintive meow. I couldn't actually see what was happening because Katya's room was down that short hallway and out of the line of sight. Fortunately, she couldn't see me either. Yet.

I couldn't do much but crawl frantically into the dining room and roll under the long table, hoping the table cloth hung down enough to hide me.

"Harmless! Harmless!" she cried. "Oh, my dear, look at you! You're filthy. Where have you been? You look like you were buried alive!"

Linda came out of her room, and almost at the same time Luke came running down the stairs. The two met Katya at her door.

Luke swore loudly, "How did he get back inside the house?"

For the moment, I couldn't see them, and that meant they couldn't see me. That wouldn't last. I tensed my muscles, ready to make a surprise, to them, run for the back door.

That damned cat. Why did Katya find it necessary to keep him? He had been against me from the first time I saw him. He caused nothing but trouble. I repeat; damned cat!

At that very moment, when I was sure I would be found out, Dathan called out from the middle of the stairs, "What's happening down there?" I could barely see him as his feet tangled together and he stumbled the last few steps to the bottom of the stairs, landing on his knees. He grabbed the doorknob to pull himself up, and the door swung open several inches. He let it go and fell to the floor. Luke, Linda and Katya rushed past me without looking in my direction.

"Klutz," Luke growled at him. Then, he saw the open door. "Here's where your mangy cat came in, Mother dearest. Someone failed to close the door properly. Right, Lemuel?"

Dathan nodded his head, and his eyes briefly glanced in my direction. "Went for a late walk, was all. I didn't want to be locked out."

"Yeah," Luke snorted. "Next time, be more careful." He turned and stalked up the stairs, followed by Dathan. A minute later, Linda returned to her room. Katya picked up her cat and said, "You filthy creature. Before you come into my room, you will be clean. Understand."

The cat purred in answer.

"My, my. Where did the blood come from?"

They went into the bathroom and closed the door

As soon as I heard the bathwater running, I rolled out from under the table, got to my feet and walked as quickly and silently as I could back to the kitchen and down the stairs, closing the door behind me.

I stopped in front of the cistern door and waited for my heartbeat to return to normal. I opened my hand and studied the cigarette butt. Surprisingly, it was still intact. I found the plastic bag in my pocket and put the butt in it, and then stuck it back in the same pocket.

It took me about two minutes to pick the lock, but then the cistern door swung out with a maddening squeal. More damned noise! Luckily, I stopped it before it went very far, but it had been loud, or maybe it just seemed that way because it was half past two o'clock in the morning. I waited again for someone to come busting down the stairs, but nothing happened.

So. It was time to check out the cistern.

Until city water became common, cisterns were big storage reservoirs made of concrete, maybe eight feet square. They were used to capture rainwater that ran from the roof through gutters and down to the basement. When they were no longer needed, they were torn out, or converted to something else.

This one had become a greenhouse. Lilacs and tomatoes grew along one wall; herbs and unfamiliar plants grew on benches along two other walls. A pair of UV lamps made everything purple. I stepped inside and pulled the door almost shut behind me. I took four flash pictures with my small camera. I was thinking about picking a tomato in January — when my pager vibrated against my hip. Time to get out!

Before I could turn around, the door slammed the rest of the way shut. Then I heard the ominous click of the Yale padlock. I was caught as simply as that. Like a stupid rabbit in a stupid rabbit trap. Maybe Katya had been right about my intelligence. I braced myself for the sound of the phone being dialed, for a voice saying the police were coming.

But all I heard was the receding footsteps of someone walking away. Why hadn't he (she?) said something? It had been a perfect chance to gloat. Apparently, he had other things on his mind; at least he went up the stairs to the kitchen. It occurred to me that he was going after a gun.

A year ago, I would have broken out in a cold claustrophobic sweat. Not now. Now, I was just angry. Mad. I put my shoulder to the door and heaved. The padlock held; the cheap hasp didn't. The wood screws came out, the door opened; I stepped out, closed the door, pushed the hasp and screws back into place by hitting it with my fist, and went quickly to the outside door. I set it to lock, but then changed my mind and unlocked it again, and pulled it shut behind me. I ran across the backyards to Hobbes' house, waved at the man in the wheelchair during that mad dash, and then went inside and headed for the kitchen, I took off the mask and gloves, and then sat down to wait. A minute later, Fred came in and sat down with us, shaking his head,

"I assume you saw nothing, and you are disappointed," Hobbes said to Fred.

"Nothin', unless you want to count a couple of kids tryin' to make out in an old van, but they was half a block away. They scooted out soon's I flashed a light down their way. You probably heard their tires squealin',"

"You saw them well enough to tell they were kids?'

"No, but there is always some kids parking close to the river."

Hobbes said, "Well done, Fred. I have coffee ready."

"Thanks, Boss. It got a bit cool out there. Is it as good as what I make?"

"Yeah," I offered my opinion. "At least."

"You ain't tasted it yet."

"That's right," I said.

Hobbes had turned the lights off when I went next door, but he knew his way around the kitchen well enough. A minute later he put a cup on the table in front of me. "Whenever you're ready," he said.

Chapter 12

"I had to break out of that cistern," I began. "Whoever locked it will have called the cops by now."

Hobbes shook his head, "That is unlikely. Look at their house."

I did. It was completely dark. If they were going to report a burglar, at least one light would have been on.

"Then they don't want the police looking around. Did you see who locked me in the cistern?"

"No, Abel. Someone came down the stairs with a flashlight. I couldn't tell whether it was a man or a woman, but he or she may have thought the cistern door had been left open, and simply shut it."

"Why come down in the first place?"

He shrugged. "Maybe he'd gone to the kitchen for something to eat, heard a noise from the basement, and went to check it out. I'll have a better idea after I hear your report."

I took the plastic bag from my pocket and handed it to him. Then I told him, in detail, everything that had happened over there. It took thirty-five minutes.

Hobbes sat silently for a while, sipping on cold coffee, and then stroking the ends of his droopy moustache. "Was Dathan's clumsiness deliberate?"

"With him, it's hard to tell. It was convenient, though."

"Odds?"

"Maybe three to one; maybe one to three. I'd have to know him better."

"No doubt, we both will get to know him better. In the meantime, we have other mysteries — two large unmarked and mysterious wooden boxes, and a cat that may have returned from the dead. They tease the imagination, Abel."

"I know live from dead, Chief. The cat was dead when we buried it."

"Yet it appeared to be the same cat. How did you describe it — tawny, black muzzle, black socks, black tipped tail?"

"Yeah," I admitted. How could there be two cats that looked like that?

He raised his right eyebrow a sixteenth of an inch, but dropped the argument.

"And the boxes?"

I shrugged. "Find out tomorrow, I suppose. Do you know what time it is?"

He nodded. "Sleep well." He slipped the plastic bag into his shirt pocket and wheeled himself into his bedroom, which was four feet from the kitchen. I went upstairs to the bathroom and brushed my teeth, then to the northwest corner bedroom, which caught the sun in the afternoon but never in the morning, just the way I liked it. In three minutes, I was undressed, in bed, and asleep.

I dreamed of a shallow grave and a yellow cat scratching its way out. It took great gulps of air, gathered itself and made a desperate lurch, pulling itself free. It staggered from side to side shaking the dirt off, then lay down and started licking its fur. Dirt and blood disappeared. Suddenly, it turned and stared at me with yellow cat's eyes that slowly turned red. It arched its back and hissed at me. It whispered a warning; "We will be after you, if you come after us. We know you. You know us. Remember?"

I woke up covered with sweat. It was almost six o'clock, a.m. A window was open. I got out of bed and closed it, then crawled back into bed. It took ten minutes this time before I fell asleep. Yes, I remembered them. But the cat was dead. I knew the cat was dead. I was positive the cat was dead. Almost positive.

The old house on River Street that I called home had seven phone lines — one for Hobbes' Investigations, one for the computer, another for the fax machine, and one for each person who lived there, except for Charon, who refused to talk on any telephone, ever. Hobbes, Sally, and I also had cellular phones, although Mercater, Illinois was one of the worst reception areas in the country.

I would have been happy if the telephone had never been invented. The electronic ring woke me at 8:30. It was the second night in a row that I didn't get my sleep out. I sat up in bed and looked at the Caller ID; it said *Lemuel Dathan*.

"Hello, Abel," he spoke quickly when I picked up the phone. "It's gone."

I knew what he was talking about, but I had to ask him anyway, "What's gone?"

"The cat. From where we buried it. It wasn't dead, Abel. We buried it alive. It got out and went to Katya's door in the middle of the night. I saw it! You gotta come see where we buried it."

"It was dead, Lem. It got ran over by a van, remember?"

"Just come and see," he insisted. "Then tell me if it's dead."

I took a deep breath and let it out slowly. The backs of my hands had started to itch. "Ten minutes." Itching hands; my version of a sixth sense. They meant someone was watching, or something bad was about to happen. When I had asked Hobbes about them, he had said they were a cross between imagination and coincidence; I had said that they were right half the time. What about the other half, he had asked? Do you just ignore them? I never ignored them, I said. Maybe the watcher had quit watching me before I figured out who it was, or perhaps the danger had just disappeared because I was looking for it. In either case, I never ignored the itching hands.

I shaved in four minutes, got dressed in three, and was in the Butlers' back yard two minutes after that.

Lemuel Dathan was striding back and forth, clearly agitated. "L—look at the grave! Look at it, and t—tell me what you th-think."

I knelt down near the small grave. It was empty, of course. That didn't surprise me. If someone had wanted us to believe Harmless had revived and escaped his grave, it had to be empty. Harmless himself had shown us last night that he'd been the one buried, although I had ignored the evidence of my own eyes, as well as what Dathan had just said on the phone.

No, it wouldn't have taken a lot to dig up the small body, and until this very moment I had just assumed that the dead cat hadn't been Harmless, but was a look-alike come from somewhere. Why someone would dig it up, I hadn't a clue.

The grave changed my mind.

It is surprisingly easy to tell the difference between a grave that's been opened from the outside and one that's been opened from the inside, once you've seen it. The difference is profound. Maybe it's the paucity of dirt moved, or the claw marks left behind, or even the hollow in the ground —— but it's unmistakable.

He hadn't been taken out. He had crawled out by himself.

"Harmless," I murmured, "has come back from the grave."

"R-r-resurrected, you mean. I know he was dead. You said so, too, remember?"

"I must have been wrong."

"Both of us wrong?" Lemuel shook his head. "Not both of us."

"You said it went to Katya in the middle of the night. Did you see it?"

"Yeah. It yowled, screamed, and scratched on the door until the whole house woke up."

I really was at a loss. Hobbes had always contended that everything had a rational explanation; that was the purpose of his firm's existence. I had argued that he hadn't been able to explain everything; that many cases had loose ends left hanging around. He had said there wasn't enough time to find all the answers. We usually left the argument there -- neither of us satisfied.

"What are you going to do about it?" Lemuel said suddenly.

"I don't know," was the best answer I had.

"Lemuel!" Luke Ransom interrupted us, but we weren't getting anywhere anyway. He had come out on the back porch and acknowledged me with a wave. To Lemuel, he said, "Are you going with us?"

"Yeah, sure, in a minute. I have to wash up first."

Luke smiled briefly. "Don't be too long. Mother doesn't like to be kept waiting."

Lemuel nodded, and said to me, "St. Paul's having a Mass for Clyde. Katya got everybody up and even had Linda call Rich home so we could go as a family."

"That doesn't sound much like Katya," I said, "going to a Catholic church."

He nodded. "It was what Clyde believed in. She said we owed that much respect to the dead. How about you? Are you coming?"

I shook my head. "I'll be at the wake, though."

He murmured, "House won't be the same, empty like that. Gotta run." He tripped on the edge of the sidewalk, but didn't quite fall. He stumbled again on the stairs, and looked back at me apologetically, then went inside. I listened for the sound of something breaking, but all was quiet.

I went back to talk to Hobbes. My morning plans had changed.

The Butlers owned a two–year old Chrysler minivan. Luke drove; Katya sat next to him, rigid and inflexible, staring straight ahead. Linda and Kelly took the middle captain's chairs, neither speaking to the other; Lemuel and Rich sat in the way–back seat.

I watched them through the front window as they drove away. They would be gone maybe an hour and a half. Plenty of time to inspect the rooms that had contained people when I was there last night.

Sally volunteered to come with me. We'd both check the basement, then I'd do the main floor while she went upstairs. We wore pagers, and Hobbes and Fred were going to watch the house as before, ready to call us at if it looked like someone was coming. We also wore latex gloves, and had ski masks ready to slip on just before we went inside. I didn't think there were any surveillance cameras in the house, but why take a chance?

The basement door was still unlocked, so we entered without breaking.

Two things had changed since night before. Critical things.

First, the door to the cistern was standing open. The lilacs and tomato plants were still in place, but the herbs and such were gone. Even the pots they'd been growing in were missing. The UV lamps were turned off.

Second, the wooden crates had vanished.

"They had to take them out before dawn," Sally said.

"But after four o'clock," I added. "They had three hours in which to do it."

"Charon gets up at five; he might have seen something."

"We'll ask him later, Sally. Let's hope nothing else is gone."

Someone had been busy down here; the ductwork had been put back together, the window closed, and the ladder placed by the stairs. Everything appeared to be arranged as Clyde would have left it.

I almost didn't check his workshop, but Sally shook her head when I ignored it and started up the stairs.

"You'll regret if you don't at least take a quick look."

She was right. Strange things had happened in this house; why should Clyde's workshop be an exception?

It was locked. That was out of character for the old Clyde. Even though the lock had come with the door, in the half–dozen times I'd been there, it had never been used.

"How long since you've seen what's inside?"

I thought that over; it was a good question. "Not since Clyde married Linda." That was many months ago.

As if she were reading my mind, Sally said, "He changed a lot, didn't he?"

I nodded, took out my tools, and started working on the lock. Four minutes later, I gave up and put the tools back in my pocket. "I'll try it again on the way out, Sally. Let's go upstairs."

She put her hand on my shoulder. "Are you okay, Abel?"

I said, "Sure. Fine." But my hand was shaking, and a cold sweat was trickling down my neck. Somewhere beyond that locked door, something was growling; faint and threatening, like an animal.

She stared at the door. "Is there something inside there?"

"Don't you hear it?"

"I don't hear anything. Give me your lock pick."

"But..." I didn't know how to explain it. A change in the atmosphere — door knob suddenly turned ice cold — something growling behind the door... Yet Sally seemed unaffected by any of it.

"Now, Abel!" She held out her hand.

I reluctantly handed her the small pack of tools. Thirty seconds later, she pushed the door open.

"Me first, Sal," I said, trying to push her aside.

She ignored me and stepped into Clyde's workshop. I was right behind her.

I found the light switch by the door and turned it on. I don't know what I had expected to find, but I was ready for at least something. What we saw was a complete surprise.

It wasn't so much that there was anything wrong as it was that there wasn't anything wrong, if that makes any sense. Everything, from the six−foot wood lathe and table saw at one end, to the drill press and shaper at the other, was immaculate −− dust free, even. It looked like a show place for The Modern Woodworker.

He'd once told me it was his "home within his home." At that moment, Clyde's workshop looked like it had never been used −− not once.

"Clyde gave Mr. Hobbes an umbrella stand for Christmas, Abel." Sally was as puzzled as I was. "Shouldn't we at least still smell the varnish?"

"Yeah," I said. The chill in the air had faded. "Rich said he and his dad made it together, right here."

There didn't seem to be anything else to say about the place; I'd already convinced myself that my imagination had been overactive. It had happened before. This time it was probably because of the cat.

But, why was the shop so clean? Maybe Katya had gone into a cleaning frenzy after Clyde died. Maybe Clyde had done it himself before New Year's Eve, believing he was dying and not wanting to leave a mess for Rich. There could be a dozen explanations.

"Let's go," I said, turning toward the door.

She stopped me. "Look at the calendar."

I should have noticed it myself. It hung on the wall, one of the first things you'd see when you entered. It had a picture of pumpkins and cornstalks — a Thanksgiving scene. The month it showed was November. If Clyde had been here in December, he would have changed the calendar. It wasn't a big thing, just another part of the puzzle that Clyde Butler had become. I wondered what had he been doing, instead?

Chapter 13

I turned the lights off and closed the door behind us, making sure it was locked. We took the stairs to the kitchen, went quickly through the dining room and living room, and stopped at the front entrance. I pointed at the shelf high on the wall where two hand–painted Japanese plates looked out of place. "They weren't here last night; now they're covering something."

By standing on the second step, I could just reach the one on the left, and pulled it toward me.

"What do you see, Sally?"

"Nothing," she said. "Just a peep hole in the plaster. What's behind this wall?"

"A closet in Clyde's... I mean, Linda's bedroom." I pushed the plate back in place and stepped down. "I doubt if we'll find anything there, though. Too late. Now that Clyde's gone, whatever they used back there will be gone too."

"They may have missed something. People usually do," she assured me.

"I'll check the downstairs bedrooms, Sally. You can do Luke's room. It's at the top of the stairs to the left. I don't think we need to check the apartments; I doubt if Lemuel or Kelly has anything to hide."

"Sure," she said. "Just watch the time. We've got thirty–five minutes."

I felt embarrassed when I first entered Linda's bedroom. The king–sized bed hadn't been made; a nightgown and robe were carelessly thrown on a chair; underclothes were scattered around the foot of the bed.

Nevertheless I made a pretty thorough fifteen–minute search. I hadn't expected to find any equipment in the closet, and I wasn't disappointed. All of Clyde's things were still there –– more of his than hers, actually. I stood in the middle of the room and turned slowly all the way around. The room didn't feel right. Something was missing; it took me a few minutes to identify what it was. Personality. The room had none. At least, Linda's touch wasn't there. Other than her clothes, almost nothing stood out that marked it as a room shared by a man and a woman. Only two three–by–five photos were on her dresser, both of them pretty old.

The first one was of much younger Katya Ransom and a man I hadn't seen before, probably her husband, Frank. The other picture was of an older woman. It was fuzzy and out of focus, but the eyes appeared to be blue and the hair may once have been blond, but was now mostly white. Even in the blurriness of the hurry-up picture, she was an unmistakable relative of Linda. She wasn't smiling at the photographer, but her expression was strange, as if they shared a secret. Two days ago, I wouldn't have known who she was. Now, I wondered why the woman who had become Linda Butler kept a picture of her biological grandmother next to that of her spiritual mother. But the picture of Grandma Agnes Kelch offered no answer.

I didn't bother with Rich's room, which was down the other short hallway, but opened the door next to it.

Katya's room. Katya and Luke had come for the holidays, and were supposed to leave about the ninth of January. At least, that is what Clyde had told me three weeks ago. Judging from the closets and the dresser, Katya Ransom had moved in to stay.

She had brought more clothes with her than Linda had in all of her walk-in closet. Dozens of pictures — mostly of Linda and Luke, but some of her and the same man I had seen in the photo in Linda's room — covered the tables and dresser. I glanced at them briefly; my mind was on more important things than pictures. I might have ignored them completely except for one of Katya and, I assumed, Frank. They were lounging against a '64 Ford and a girl about three years old was sitting on the hood. She had been laughing at something. Curious, I slipped the photo out of the frame and looked at the back. Penciled in were the date, June 1, 1964, and three names: Frank, Katya, and Linda. The little girl didn't look at all like the Linda who'd grown up and married Clyde Butler. I put the picture back and looked over the rest of the room.

A score of cats lay around on the floor. Life–like cats. Cats that had once been alive, but when they had died, had been restored by a skilled taxidermist. They lounged around, stretched, yawned, rubbed against a table leg, stared at the door; and like most real cats, ignored me. A big yellow that looked remarkably like Katya's Harmless had a mouse cornered, and they were watching each other, although the mouse appeared to be uneasy. The taxidermy was flawless. It had perfectly captured the ancient cat and mouse game.

Suddenly, the cat's paw swept out and pinned the mouse to the floor, and I realized that I'd been fooled. It was Harmless, all right, the cat I'd helped bury; the cat who'd been dead and was resurrected. He glanced at me, then bit down on the struggling mouse's tail, picked up the small creature, and walked casually into the hallway. He stopped there and looked back at me, as if he wanted me to follow him. So, I followed. He led me through the dining room and living room, and to the front door where he stopped and waited again, not bothering to look back.

I opened the door and he walked past me, crossed the porch, and went down the steps. He gently lowered the mouse and let go of its tail. The mouse darted under the porch, out of sight. Harmless came back into the house and ambled casually down the hallways and into Katya's room. He made himself comfortable on Katya's bed, disregarded me, and went to sleep. I finished my search without finding anything important and then went to find Sally to see if she was ready to leave. Our time was about up.

She met me in the living room. We'd been in the house for forty-five minutes; we should have had another thirty. "Time to go, Abel?"

My hands were suddenly itching. "Yeah."

We started to head for the kitchen, but Sally stopped and put her hand on the pager fastened to her belt. "Got a call," she said. She held it up so that I could read it with her. "Nine–one–one." The pager allowed the caller to leave a number up to ten digits long. It was a simple way to send a message. 9-1-1 in this case meant, "Someone is coming to the back door." 9-1-2 would have meant the front door. We heard a car enter the driveway, coast past the side of the house, and stop in front of the garage. A second car was parking on the street.

Mine vibrated against my hip, and I held it out to Sally. "Nine-one-three," it said; the code for, "Too late to get out. Find a place to hide."

"Basement?" she asked.

I shook my head. I suddenly wanted to find out why they had come back so soon.

Sally grinned at me. "Kelly's apartment?"

"Rich's room."

Car doors were slamming even as we hurried down the short hallway. There, we were met with a real surprise.

The bedroom door was locked. And not with a simple privacy lock that could be opened with a small screwdriver; it couldn't have been that easy. No. It was an exterior doorknob assembly that required a regular key.

In the distance, the kitchen door opened and I could hear Katya's strident voice coming from the back of the house. "They think a Mass will get him to heaven? The misguided fools!"

I felt in my pocket for my lock pick tools, then recalled that Sally still had them. I whispered, "The tools," but she shook her head and pushed me aside.

"I'm better at this," she whispered back. She started working the miniature picks.

"God has his plans, Mother," Luke was saying tentatively. "No one can really know them. The Catholics could be right. Everyone could be right."

"Everyone?" she answered derisively. "The Mormons? The Buddhists? The Jews? All of them right? What about all the other religions? Thousands of them? Idiotic. How could you — a son of mine, my flesh and blood —– be so stupid?"

Linda interrupted with, "What do you believe in, Mother?"

"Not what you believe. Not what any of you believe. But my prayers are answered. They are always answered. You know that, Linda. You've known that for twenty years. I am right! If I hadn't been right then, you wouldn't be here now."

Sally continued picking at the lock. She looked at me frantically and shook her head.

"Then let me try," I whispered.

She gave me the tools, and I went to work. It was the most difficult lock I'd ever tried.

"Make some coffee, will you?" Katya changed the subject, "No, not you, Linda, your coffee is an abomination. Luke will make it. You can get me a chair to sit in." I heard a chair slide across the linoleum, and Katya sigh as she sat down.

The front door opened and two people went upstairs. Two more went into the living room where one of them said, "I'm glad I met you, Grandma." The voice belonged to Rich. "That chair is the best one we have." How long would it be before he came to his room?

I was becoming frustrated. The lock just wouldn't give up its secret.

Suddenly, Katya's voice came from the kitchen. It was deliberately loud. "Did that old woman come into this house? I will not be in the same room with her. She's a lying...."

"Mother, she's Kelly's guest staying upstairs with Kelly," Luke cut in. "She's here for the funeral. She'll be leaving Thursday. That's just two days."

"Very well. But that will not excuse her foul tongue. I'm going to my room. Bring me my coffee there. And some donuts if you can find any in this pig sty."

Her chair squeaked as she stood up. I looked at Sally.

She shrugged, and said quietly. "Get ready to run."

Katya's footsteps moved slowly through the kitchen. As soon as she stepped on the carpet and looked down that short hallway, nothing would keep her from seeing us.

But then, their phone rang. Katya stopped and waited, as Linda answered.

"Butler's." Then with a puzzled expression in her voice, she said, "It's for you, Mother."

"Who is it? Never mind. No one calls me except for telephone solicitors," she said with a sudden eagerness. "I'll make short work of him." She took the phone from Linda, and said sweetly, "Katya Ransom speaking."

At the other end of the house, Rich was saying, "Excuse me for a minute, Grandma, I need to use the bathroom."

"I'll wait here. I'm close enough to that woman already."

In the kitchen, Katya sounded annoyed. "Mr. Hobbes? I'm a busy woman; make it quick."

Hobbes must have been able to see Katya from the window in his bedroom. The call was to give us more time.

We were caught anyway. Rich stepped into our hallway and stopped with his hand on the bathroom doorknob. He was surprised, but only for a second. I put my finger in front of my lips, then pointed at the locked door. He glanced back into the kitchen, then reached into his pocket and took out a small key ring. He took two quick steps to the door, put the key into the lock, opened the door, withdrew the key, and returned to the bathroom. Sally and I slipped into his room and closed the door quietly. We locked it from the inside.

We could still hear well enough — Katya slammed the phone down, said, "I'll be in my room!" and stormed out of the kitchen, her angry footsteps thump–thumping down the hallway. She muttered as she opened her door, "What does he think I am, some common hussy? Coffee in his house likely just the two of us. Hah!" She slammed the door behind her, and went to be with her cats.

We took deep breaths, and let the air out slowly. Rich had saved our butts, and had done it as if finding two burglars in the house was a normal, everyday experience. Later, he'd want to know why we were sneaking around and not asking him for help. I'd be glad to tell him. I had a question for him, too. About that lock...

Sally nudged me with her elbow. "Look." She pointed at the far end of the room, on the other side of Rich's bed.

The two wooden crates waited there, one on top of the other.

The room felt like the inside of an icebox.

I wished Hobbes was here.

Chapter 14

I shivered. "Does it feel cold to you, Sally?"

She shook her head. "I'm burning up," Sally kept her voice low, but her face was flushed with excitement.

I seemed to be the only person in Hobbes' household subject to shivers and chills. Hobbes, in one of his more annoying judgments, had said mine was a subconscious response to a perceived threat, real or not, and the perception was based on the complex sum of my experiences growing up. When he said it, it seemed to make sense. When I repeat it, it sounds pretty dumb.

Was my subconscious fooling around with me? If it wasn't, why didn't Sally feel the cold?

"I'll check out the crates. You wait here," Sally said. She took two short steps toward them before I grabbed her arm and stopped her. "Wait, Sal. Listen." A growl like I'd heard down in the workshop came from the crates.

The growl and the cold. She wasn't aware of either one.

"We have to see what's in there, Abel." She brushed my hand off.

I was almost amazed when Sally reached the crates and nothing happened to her. She lifted the end of the top one. She motioned for me to come over, and I yielded reluctantly. The cold and the growl disappeared when I touched the other end of the crate, and I grimaced self–consciously. Nothing happened. Maybe it really was just psychological.

Together, we lifted the top crate and sat it on the floor. It could not have weighed more than fifty pounds; the other one, when we raised it up slightly, weighed about the same. Anyone in the house could have brought them up from the basement.

We still didn't have any way to open them, and to be honest, I wasn't sure I wanted to.

"Let's put them back the way they were," Sally said. "For now."

We did so, tilting the top crate unintentionally. Something inside slid from one side to the other, and hissed angrily. At least it sounded like a hiss. But, again, when I asked Sally if she had heard it, she said no.

I hadn't wanted to search Rich's room. It seemed like a violation of trust, somehow. Sally wasn't bothered by such a simple reservation; she went to the closet and slid the doors open.

One suit, in a cleaner's plastic bag, some dress pants and matching shirts, a hooded winter coat, several flannel shirts, and everyday jeans did not crowd the closet rod at all; nor did a skateboard and roller blades, a pair of dress shoes, and some old Reeboks take up much floor space. Sally looked at me quizzically; "Not much stuff for a kid, is it?"

Before I answered, I slid the drawers on his dresser open and quickly closed them. Socks and underwear—and a lot of empty space. "Nothing like you might expect." A picture of his mom and dad was centered on top of the dresser. Otherwise, the room had very little personalization. It reminded me of Linda's.

Except for a compact stereo system in one corner and a computer desk in another, the room could have been one in any number of hotels. It was not a normal fifteen–year old boy's room, any more than the workshop was the way Clyde would have kept it.

"Well, Abel, how do we get out of here?"

I checked my watch; it said ten-forty. More than three hours remained before the wake would begin.

At that moment, the door opened and Rich came in. He quietly pushed the door shut, and then put his finger in front of his lips. He crossed the room and turned on his stereo, cranking up the volume.

Almost instantly, Katya began pounding on the adjoining wall, screaming, "You useless, worthless, brat of a boy! My cats are sleeping! Turn that monster down, or I'll bring an ax to it!"

Rich slowly turned the sound down until the pounding and screaming stopped, but kept it loud enough to cover up our talking. "Her cats are sleeping all right. All but that big yellow devil. They're never gonna wake up, no matter how much noise I make.

"Her Majesty, Queen Katya doesn't really care about the music, anyway," he added. "It's just something for her to complain about. She'd have my head if she could, you know. She hates me. She'd be happy if I fell over dead, like Dad."

He sat on the edge of his bed, and studied both of us. "He really was murdered, wasn't he? That's why you're here, isn't it, to find proof?"

"We think your dad was murdered, Rich. We're convinced of it. But finding proof may be pretty tough. We were looking for answers to that question when you caught us. That's quite a lock on your door."

He nodded his head slightly. "Dad put it on when Katya started searching my room. She did a lot of strange things the first few days she was here that I didn't really mind, but I didn't want her coming into my room. Today, she was really weird; she didn't like Mass, so she told the priest what she thought right in the middle of it." He grinned slightly. "They threw her out. Did you find anything? Basement, upstairs, anywhere?"

"We found those crates," I said. "They were in the basement yesterday. Do you know what's in them?"

He aimed his finger at them as if it were a gun. "They were outside my door this morning." He jerked his hand and said a sharp "pow," letting the imaginary gunshot decay slowly. "I don't know who put them there, or why, but I brought them in here before I left for Mass. I want to open them."

"Let's do it!" Sally spun around and danced her way to the crates.

"Not here, not now," I said quickly. "Too many people in the house. We can come back this afternoon when everyone has gone to the wake."

"The crates won't be here that long. Luke knew about them. I think they were supposed to go in Katya's room, but something got messed up and I got them before she did. Luke didn't like that at all. He told me to leave them alone and that he'd get rid of them after Mass. He's going to take the way-back seat out of the van, load up the crates and take them somewhere. I think he's doing that either for Linda or for Katya."

"When?"

"Pretty soon, I think."

"Then we need to get out of here," I said.

"I've gone in and out of that window," Rich pointed at the one closest to the wall between his room and Katya's, "but it's been after dark. If she's looking out, she'll see you. If you use the other window, you might be seen from the street."

"We'll take our chances with the street."

The house was old, but the windows were new. The bottom sash was designed to pop out from the inside for easy cleaning. In a few seconds, Rich had the window and screen out of the way. I went first, dropping the few feet to the ground; Sally was right behind me.

We had made our escape.

Well....

Almost.

Two driveways and about twenty feet of lawn separated the Hobbes' house from the Butlers'; a minute earlier or a minute later and that short distance wouldn't have mattered. But Murphy's Law the original, being what it was (if anything can go wrong, it will, and at the worst possible time), we were seen.

Murphy's Law version two, came to Mercater courtesy of Lieutenant Kyle Murphy of Chicago homicide. It was his own version of the law; mainly that it superseded all other human types of law enforcement. It was Murphy's Law. His law. He was big, tough, obnoxious, and a human bulldozer, and he generally got his way.

It was he who pulled into Hobbes' driveway just as I dropped from the window to the ground, and he who touched the siren just long enough to get our attention.

A big, broad, muscular man, he opened his car door and climbed out. His closely cut red hair, the smile that didn't reach his eyes, and the undisguised sarcasm in his voice clearly identified him as the Chicago plain–clothes cop we had dealt with before. He had had dinner with us yesterday and we'd been civil to one another. Now, he was back and on police business. Politics had gotten him his job in Chicago, and he boasted that the law he used was his own law, and superseded anybody else's. Murphy's Law. His own Murphy's Law.

"Well, little man," he said, "I come to investigate a murder and find a private detective and his girlfriend breaking and entering. That's even against your law, or are you too dumb to know that?"

Inside his room, Rich cranked his stereo up loud enough to shake the windows. The uncertain lyrics of The Devil's Home Planet effectively drowned out Murphy as far the household was concerned, and the cop's expression said he was clearly annoyed.

We could barely hear Katya's renewed beating on the wall, but her vile and graphic threats somehow rose above the noise until the music abruptly stopped.

By that time, Sally and I had crossed over to Murphy's car, and I was looking him up and down, eye to eye.

"You need new glasses, Lieutenant. In the first place, we didn't break anything; and in the second we were leaving, not entering; and third, this isn't Chicago. You're out of your jurisdiction."

He ignored the jurisdiction reminder completely. "Maybe I should drag you up to their front door and ask 'em what you were doing; what do you think they'd say, huh?" He started to grab the front of my sweater with his hammy fist, but I had my hand on his wrist before he could finish his move. He had me by six inches and seventy pounds, but it wasn't enough — his hand didn't quite reach my sweater.

He wasn't accustomed to physical resistance. His face turned red. More from embarrassment than exertion, I thought.

"They'd say that you're an idiot," Sally interjected. "Wait here. I'll go knock on the door and you can hear it for yourself!"

"Never mind," Murphy said. He dropped his hand, "I got more important things to do. You and Houston probably got them trained to roll over and fetch, anyway. Besides, little girl, I came to talk to Hobbes, so you might as well go to the kitchen and do the dishes, or whatever you do. Houston, you come with me –– I know Hobbes won't talk business unless you're there."

"Did he know you were coming back this morning?" I asked the question because it was what I would normally have asked, and I didn't want to appear rushed. I did want to get out of sight of the Butler's house.

"Yeah, I called him."

"Okay, then." I nodded to Sally and preceded them up the front steps. On my last glance to the east, I thought I saw the curtain to one of Katya Ransom's windows move. Maybe it was the cat.

The boss was sitting behind his desk in the great room when Murphy and I entered. He leaned back in his wheelchair and studied the cop for a full ten seconds before saying, "Take a seat, Lieutenant."

The Chicago homicide detective pulled up a straight-back chair, turned it backward and straddled it. "Can't you just send Houston across the room so we can talk privately, like real policemen?"

"You know the answer. He is my colleague as well as my bodyguard and witness."

"Yeah. Well, as long as you don't call him a detective."

Hobbes glanced at me briefly. I kept my face straight.

He said, "Today is Sunday, the first one of the new year. It's a day that people traditionally spend with their families. One might think you would have a better reason to be here on this first Sunday than to impugn my associate's ability."

"Impugn?" Murphy snorted. "My ass. All right. Forget it. You know why I'm here."

"Specifically and at this moment? No, I don't."

"Yeah. Well, your Chief of Police Dickerson sent an email to Captain Kowalski, who I still worked for as of this morning, wanting to know why I haven't caught the murderer. He sent this one to Kowalski's home. The captain called me at my motel, wanting to know what the hell was going on."

Hobbes leaned forward — clearly surprised. "Murderer? Officially Clyde died of a heart attack, so there is no murder and thus no murderer for you to apprehend."

"Look," Murphy calmed down a little, "Friday, the captain pulled me off a goddamned case that would have busted the mayor's office wide open, and sent me down here. Now, you say it's not a murder? My ass!" He stared hard into Hobbes' eyes, trying to read my boss. I could have told him he was wasting his time. Hobbes' eyes never gave away anything he didn't want them to.

"I know nothing of any murder investigation undertaken by the Mercater police." Hobbes said flatly.

"This says different." Murphy pulled a folded paper from his coat pocket and tossed it onto the desk.

Hobbes picked it up and read it, then handed it to me.

It was dated January 1, at 9:13 p.m.

Captain Kowalski,

I know you're interested in the death of James Larsen four years ago, and that of Oscar Fields two years ago, both of which happened in your jurisdiction. A similar death occurred last night at midnight, at Carl Hobbes' home in Mercater. Mr. Hobbes and I would welcome the assistance of a qualified homicide detective.

Thank you,

Lloyd Dickerson

Chief of Police, Mercater, IL

It had been forwarded to Lieutenant Murphy at the Crazy Eight at 8:15 this morning.

Chapter 15

Murphy added, "Kowalski called me when he got it. He said he hadn't heard of any of those men, but he checked to see if they were on file, and they were, but they were marked *inactive*. That's all he could tell me."

"Remarkable," Hobbes said. "According to this, I have asked for your help in connecting three deaths, two of which I know nothing about. What is the nature of the connection I'm looking for, Lieutenant?"

"You don't know? Really? Then, why is your name there?"

Hobbes ignored Murphy, while I found the number in the phone book. I repeated it to Hobbes and added, "Lloyd Dickerson."

"A moment, Lieutenant, and I shall have your answer."

He pressed the speaker button, dialed the number, and waited as the phone on the other end began ringing. On the sixth ring, it was answered.

"Listen, dammit!" someone yelled into the phone, "If you've got an emergency, call the police department!" and abruptly hung up.

Hobbes looked at me, then at the picture on the wall. When he spoke, it was to Murphy: "Dickerson was promoted to Chief of Police only a few months ago, and is still new to the job. Apparently, he is suffering the trials of adjustment."

He pressed the redial button. Apparently, Dickerson didn't have an answering machine, or it was turned off. Anyway, this time the phone rang eleven times before he picked it up. "Who is this? If you're one of those damned kids who thinks ruining a football game is funny, you'd better think again!"

"Chief Dickerson!" Hobbes said sharply, "This is Car'l Hobbes. I am not a kid, and I offer my apology for interrupting your game. I do, however, need a moment of your time."

"Hobbes?" Dickerson's anger faded. "Hobbes. Sorry for the way I answered the phone. My wife taped two of the Bowl games for me yesterday. I've been trying to avoid hearing who won by not listening to the radio or the TV, but those damned kids keep calling in and trying to tell me how it ended. It would be funny if I hadn't spent half of yesterday afternoon in the morgue trying to get something out of the coroner."

"Because of Clyde Butler?"

"No, because of that damned email you sent me."

Hobbes was silent for a brief moment, then he murmured, "I sent you nothing, Chief Dickerson."

"The header says it came from you, or at least from your computer. You don't know anything about it? Then someone's screwing with both of us. What if I send it back to you, and then you call me and we'll talk it over?"

"Agreed," Hobbes said. He switched the phone off.

"Abel?"

"Be right back."

I went to the computer room and waited about three minutes, printed out the message, read it, and took it back to Hobbes.

The time of transmission was given as 3:15 p.m., Jan. 1st.

Chief Dickerson,

I believe that Clyde Butler was murdered, the same way and for the same reasons that James Larsen (four years ago) and Oscar Fields (two years ago) were murdered. Captain Kowalski of homicide in Chicago has been investigating those first two cases, and he would be eager to work with us on the last one. As chief of police, you can request his help. Please do so.

Carl Hobbes.

"He keeps forgetting the apostrophe in Car'l," I said. "A lot of people were here at 3:15 yesterday. It could have been any one of them."

Hobbes closed his eyes and leaned back. After a minute, he opened his eyes, glared at the painting on the wall. "Who sent it is obvious. The reason is obscure.

"Lieutenant Murphy, you have been sent to work with me; now would be a good time to begin. Can you get me the files on Larsen and Fields, or at least copies of them?"

"Yeah. Might take an hour. You got a fax machine?"

I showed him where it was. As he was picking up the phone, I thought that it was time for Sally and me to give Hobbes our reports on the morning's search, while Murphy was occupied. It didn't work out that way. Instead, the doorbell rang.

Rich Butler stood on the front porch in his t–shirt and jeans, shivering. He was pulling on a sweatshirt even as he stumbled over his words.

"Abel, I thought you oughta know. They're taking the crates out right now. I'm gonna follow them on my bike."

"Hold on a minute, Rich. Who's taking them?"

"Luke and Linda. I just wanted to let you know, in case something happens."

I heard a car engine start. I shook my head. "They'll spot your bike right away. I'll get one of our cars out. We'll go together."

"Ain't got time, they're coming around now." He dropped down behind the porch railing as the Chrysler minivan roared backward out of the next–door driveway, its tires squealing as it turned onto the street and braked, switched gears, and headed west toward Main Street.

I could see Luke's face, angry in its concentration as he went by. Linda seemed to be hugging the door, as if she couldn't wait to get away from whatever was in the back of the van.

"See ya!" Rich yelled. He took the steps three at a time — even as he slipped his headphones in place—grabbed his bike and raced off after them.

He was right; I didn't have time to get one of the cars out of the garage. But another one was already in the driveway, if I could borrow it.

The computer room where Murphy was waiting for the fax machine to start coughing out documents was just west of the main hallway. I opened the door, stuck my head in and said, "Hey, Murph! Keys to your car; it's in my way. I need to make a run before lunch."

He fished a key ring out of his pocket and tossed it to me.

I caught it, and then hesitated as if a thought had just occurred to me. "Since I'll already be in your car, why don't I just use it?"

He clapped his hand over the mouthpiece, "Suit yourself, little man. Don't bother me with the small stuff. I got to straighten out the whole damned Chicago police force just to get those files for your boss!"

"Thanks," I said, and casually withdrew, closing the door behind me. Then, it was a breakneck dash down the porch steps and over to Murphy's car. I could still see the minivan, but it had already reached Main, turned south, and crossed the bridge. Rich was pedaling hard half a block behind them. "Too close," I said to myself. "Luke'll see him in the mirror." As if the boy had heard me, he slowed down, ran his bike up on the sidewalk, and sped up again.

The unmarked police car was a gray Mercury Grand Marquis with only a Chicago sticker revealing that the car wasn't local. The bullhorn and red light, with its magnetic base, had been carelessly tossed on the front passenger seat, and I wondered how often Murphy used them. The siren was probably somewhere under the hood, but I didn't take time to look for the button that controlled it. I even managed to ignore the computer screen in the middle of the dashboard, although it kept flashing a message for Lt. Murphy to log on.

I backed out of the driveway, shifted to drive, and pushed down on the accelerator. Whatever engine he had in that car, I decided I wanted one. Two black streaks followed me for thirty feet before I could let up on the gas.

A minute later I crossed the bridge. At least two blocks ahead of me, Luke had already turned into the main entrance of Mercater State Hospital, and Rich wouldn't have been far behind them on his bike. I drove as fast as I could, but when I followed them onto Lincoln Avenue –– the main street through the heart of MerSH––they were already out of sight. To make matters worse, when I stopped at the four–way just inside the gate, there were three directions they could have gone –– each of them a winding road obscured by evergreen trees and the hospital's endless brick and stone buildings.

I could take Lincoln straight on into the central administration complex. I could turn right onto Jackson South and circle most of the residential areas and eventually return on Jackson North, the street on my left. Or I could go left on Jackson North and come back on South. Either direction on Jackson would go past hospital buildings, cottages, residence halls and dormitories; most of which were unused but still had places to park a car and not be seen.

I had no way of telling which way they had gone. I mentally drew straws and the short one said to go right. I spun the steering wheel clockwise and gunned the engine.

Once again the squeal of spinning tires and the smell of burning rubber filled the air, and I had to let up on the gas to get traction. I wondered what kind of engine Murphy had in this car. It was overpowered for searching the narrow winding streets, but for the moment at least, I envied him.

The search turned out to be annoyingly slow. There were at least three miles of paved streets on the hospital grounds, and if I expected to see Luke's van, I might have to drive down all of them. It was too big a place for a quick search.

Construction of the sprawling hospital had begun in the 1870's; it had been designed to be self-supporting. Had the project been completed as planned, it would have had its own 120-acre farm with barns, livestock, and everything necessary to operate in isolation from the nearby communities. It had been meant to care for several thousand residents, but political scandals and so–called "mad doctor" rumors had almost closed it. Closed–door politics, threats and the untimely suicide of a senator who had opposed closing the hospital had kept it open. A replacement facility had eventually been built in nearby Kankakee (Eastern Illinois Hospital for the Criminally Insane) and that became the major mental hospital in the Midwest.

Even though Mercater State Hospital remained open, it had faded into obscurity. Less than a fourth of the original eighty or ninety buildings were in use, and never more than three hundred residents lived there at any one time.

I hated the place. When I was twelve years old, I had been kidnapped and taken through the underground tunnels to a secret chapel where a coven worshipped Satan. I had been meant to serve as a sacrifice. I had narrowly escaped, thanks to Hobbes and two of my friends, and it had been my intention never to return to any of the tunnels.

But here I was, in Murphy's car, right above them.

I followed the road as it circled the first complex of four two-story dormitories built around a central hub –– it was called the Eight Hundreds because the building numbers went from 800 to 804. As far as I knew, they had never been occupied, but the underground tunnels reached each one of them, just as it did most of the other eighty buildings.

I drove as fast as I dared, past the Number Six dormitory which had been an orphanage for the past forty years –– where I'd lived until I was six years old.

I circled the Five Hundreds complex, followed the road as it turned north and cut through the East Ten cottages (for relatively independent residents) passed the gymnasium, the library and the chapel as I continued north, almost to the Illinois river. I became annoyed with myself as the road turned west and I hadn't yet seen either Luke's van or Rich and his bicycle. I should have turned left when I first came in. Wasn't hindsight great? I sped up. The northernmost road was relatively unused with a high cyclone fence between it and the river. The only building of any size in the vicinity was the ancient, decaying guard tower. The road turned south and divided the West Ten cottages into two sets of five, and then continued south until it took me back to the main entrance, where the incoming Lincoln Avenue had split three ways.

I turned the Mercury left onto Lincoln Avenue, and drove into the Administration and Management area. Lincoln provided access to the hospital and X-ray buildings, the first aid office, and the central kitchen; then, it circled the massive administration building that was the heart of MerSH. The admin building housed the fifth floor clock tower and the infamous third and fourth floors, where medical experiments had once been performed on certain patients. Those experiments, performed to benefit mankind, so the offenders had pleaded, had led to the downfall of MerSH and to the replacement facility by the Kankakee hospital.

Scanning the grounds, neither the van nor the bike were anywhere to be found. I headed back toward the entrance, figuring that if they hadn't already left, I'd see them on their way out.

I pulled off the road, well short of the main intersection, and waited. At last, after what seemed a small eternity but really wasn't, the Chrysler Minivan came down Jackson North. I stayed where I was, as the van left the grounds and turned right onto Main

Street. As before, Luke was driving and Linda was the only passenger, or at least the only one visible.

I waited two minutes, but there was no sign of Rich. With a sinking feeling, I started the car and turned onto Jackson North and tried to see where they might have been. I drove a third of the way around Jackson. Nothing stood out; there was no Rich, no bike.

I turned the car around. I intended to stop at the abandoned old guardhouse and then go to the cottages, but I changed my mind when I saw the privet hedge that grew close to the cyclone fence. I remembered it well —— it had surrounded and concealed a manhole that I had entered many years ago. Now the hedge had grown wild and dense, but a person could still get through it. Could Rich be in there? It was worth at least a quick look.

I stopped the car, got out, and jogged over to the hedge. At first it appeared to be impenetrable —— six feet high and a yard thick. But I saw the faint path that seemed to go right through the hedge. It was a place where the hedge had been thinned just enough that a man my size could push his way in without too many scratches.

"Rich!" I called out. I really did not want to go inside that circle of hedge. The back of my hands started itching at just the thought of it.

The Necessary Cat

Chapter 16

No answer. Well, I hadn't expected one. I took a deep breath and forced my way in. It was worse than I had expected. Weeds, mostly thistles, hogweed, and sunflowers three to four feet tall had grown in wild abundance in that small wilderness. December had turned them brown, but old spider webs with their husks of dead flies were still intact. They attached themselves with a wild eagerness to my hair and hands, and I tried brushing them off as I took a quick look around. No one had been here recently, that was pretty obvious. There wasn't any padlock on the manhole cover, and for a second I considered opening it. A quick look for old times' sake? "Don't be stupid," I whispered. "Get out of here!" There were other places to look for a boy and his bike.

I stood for a minute in front of the car brushing the spider webs off, and letting my pulse slow to normal. I hadn't liked being that close to certain memories.

The old guardhouse was the next place I could check. There was a drive up to it, but no place to park a car. I doubted that they would have gone there, so I skipped it for the time being.

I drove on to the West Ten cottages and parked in the West 1–5 lot. Five cottages on each side of the street were joined together by a long enclosed porch. I remembered from many years ago that each porch had access to a two–room utility unit between the second and third cottages, and that each utility unit had a green door that led to a stairway going down. The door was kept locked.

There were supposed to be two men to a cottage, a total of twenty men in the West Ten. I didn't see anyone around.

Time suddenly seemed precious. I felt it slipping away. Quickly, I walked around the first five cottages, then crossed the street and checked the other five. From the outside, everything looked normal.

I looked across the street in time to see the curtain in one of West–3's windows move slightly. "Hey!" I yelled as I ran back across the street, jerked the screen door to the porch open, entered, took two long steps, and pounded on the door. No answer. Hell, I'd probably scared him. I'd forgotten that the residents were here at least partly because they couldn't cope with real world stress.

My pounding changed to a light knock, and my yell to an apology; "I'm sorry if I startled you, but I'm looking for a boy on a bike. Have you seen him?"

At first, there was no response; I listened for a back door to open, but it was silent. I knocked again, "It's very important; he might be hurt."

Half a minute passed before the man inside pushed the curtain open. He cautiously pressed his forehead against the window and stared at me through unblinking milky eyes. His grizzled unshaven face and wild fringe of gray hair reminded me of someone, but I couldn't think who.

"Have you seen him?" I repeated.

He tapped on the window twice and then twice more.

"Twenty–two?"

He shook his head slightly without moving away from the window, and tapped again, this time only two times. Then he pointed across the street.

"Number two over there?"

He blinked his eyes once, then stepped away from the window and let the curtain fall. Apparently, that was the answer.

"Thanks," I said. I crossed the street again and stepped onto the porch, (the screen door was missing here) and knocked on the door of the second cottage from the end –– really number seven in the West Ten cluster.

"Anybody in there?" I called out and knocked, but not too hard. No answer. I called and knocked a little louder and harder. Nothing. I glanced back at that first cottage –– the old man had gone to his porch and opened the screen door, and was watching me. I pointed at the door and raised my eyebrows. He raised a thumb to me.

I tried the doorknob and the door swung open in front of me. I stepped inside. The bike was there, tossed on the floor and abandoned. Rich was not. I went through the cottage quickly. There was no sign of him anywhere.

The old man crossed the street and stepped in hesitantly, his eyes more wary than fearful. He looked at me, then at the bike, then back at me.

"Friend," I said, "Do you know what happened to the boy?"

He picked up the bike and tried to spin the front wheel. It was bent and jammed after a quarter of a turn.

He cupped his hand over his ear, as if he was listening, and put his finger in front of his mouth. His milky eyes were bright and questioning.

I listened with him, holding my breath. I could barely hear the tinny sound of headphones. "Where's it coming from?"

Still carrying the bike, he motioned for me to follow, and led me into the utility cottage. He leaned the bike against the wall, then looked from me to the radio and back again.

Rich's headphones –– the self–contained kind that had the radio built in –– lay on the floor near the door to the stairs.

I picked them up and held them a foot away from my ear. They were loud enough. The radio was tuned to an oldies music station. I listened for a few seconds. There was a lot of irony in the song from the Fifties; they were playing *Green Door*.

The singer wanted to get on the other side of that door after midnight. I couldn't imagine anything worse.

Unless it was going in there right now, alone.

I put my hand on the doorknob. It felt like ice. The backs of my hands started to itch. I tried to turn it; it was unlocked. The door opened. A stairway leading down into darkness welcomed me.

Something huge and silent seemed to be watching me from that darkness below. Its shadow filled the bottom of the stairway; yellow cat's eyes reflected the light behind me. It slowly moved away.

A hand touched my shoulder.

I jerked around and caught Rich as he started to fall. He had blood on his forehead and on his sweatshirt. Dried blood.

I lowered him to a nearby chair and looked around for the old man, but he was gone.

"I crashed my bike," Rich said. His speech was halting, but not slurred. "They'd slowed down and I was trying to ride where they wouldn't see me. How bad do I look?"

He had a cut above his right ear, but it had stopped bleeding. "Not bad, but you might need a couple of stitches and a tetanus shot. We'll have to get you to the hospital."

He nodded slowly.

"They brought the crates in here and took them down the stairs. When they left, I dragged my bike into the cottage next door to hide it, then I came in here and waited in the back room for you. I knew you'd come. We can go down there together. Right?"

"Yeah," I agreed. "Down into the tunnels. After we get you taken care of and talk to Hobbes, we'll come back."

He shook his head. "We gotta look at those crates now, before they get hauled off. I think.... I think there's other people coming to get them."

"Yeah?"

"Yeah. Look, when I saw Luke drive the van into the parking lot, I got off the road and tried to hide in a clump of trees. I ended up getting my front tire stuck in some roots and spilled my bike." He gingerly touched the cut on his forehead and winced, "I must have clunked my head against a tree because the next thing I knew I was laying on the ground way up there and they were standing down here, outside the door. The crates were gone, and they were arguing about what to do next.

"'We can't leave them down there unguarded. It's too risky.' That was Luke talking, but Linda said, 'Her cats will be there. No one will dare touch those crates with them around.'"

Rich stood up, a little unsteady at first. "I think she was talking about Katya. Would cats be smart enough to guard those crates, Abel?"

I said I didn't know, but I added, "I can think of one that might."

"Not Harmless," Rich shook his head. "He wouldn't hurt a mouse. Besides, he's my friend. He comes to my room when Katya's not around and listens to my music."

148

"Maybe," I said doubtfully.

"Anyway," he continued, "Linda said they didn't have any time to spare. They had to get ready for the wake."

"So do you, Rich. And we still need to get you to the hospital."

He shook his head, "It's just a scratch; the blood'll wash off. I want to look down there, Abel, before they move those crates."

He walked to the head of the stairs, "You coming?"

I took a deep breath. "I'm coming."

The cold air wasn't unexpected. It filled the staircase and crept inside my clothes as we climbed down steps made of ancient two–by–twelves that felt mushy from age.

The door at the bottom was open, and Rich stepped through and into the darkness. I followed close behind, dreading what we might find. The tunnel wasn't pitch black; the light from behind us helped a little. Beyond that immediate illumination was nothing but darkness, damp and musty smelling.

I felt along the wall and found a light switch; it turned on a single light bulb far to our right, but nothing to our left, although I guessed that that way led under the street to the other set of cottages. That single dim bulb added to my sense of foreboding. Even Rich, who was only a few feet ahead of me, shivered; otherwise, he was apparently back to normal. He took off toward that light, his footsteps echoing along the concrete floor. We both brushed annoying spider webs out of our hair; spider webs full of dead flies and other things we couldn't see. If I hadn't been preoccupied with my loathing of the tunnels, I would have known what those undisturbed webs were telling me. As it was, I just followed the leader.

The light brought us to a three-way intersection. We could go straight or turn right again. In either case, we would end up stumbling along in darkness; the light ended there.

"We need flashlights," Rich said, frustrated. "You got any in your car?"

"I don't know. I'm driving Murphy's."

"Then let's go see."

It was a relief to turn around and retrace our steps. Outside, the cool January air somehow brought warmth back to my chilled skin, and I repeated to myself, "Never, never, never, will I go back down there." That was wishful thinking; in my heart I knew better.

Murphy had two five-cell flashlights in the trunk. The batteries were dead in both of them.

"We can get some batteries at the Food Mart," Rich said.

I shook my head. "We'll have to come back later. We need to get cleaned up for your dad's wake."

"Yeah," he said. "Dad's wake." He said it as if he'd forgotten about it. A few minutes later, he laughed. "We were going the wrong way anyway."

"How do you know that?"

"Spider webs."

I thought about that for a few seconds, and then laughed with him. The webs wouldn't have been there if someone had gone that way ahead of us. The moment of laughter was good for both of us.

We drove Murphy's car to the ER at Mercater's small hospital, where a nurse cleaned him up and a doctor examined him, ordered a tetanus shot, and added three stitches to his scalp. The whole visit took less than half an hour, a gift of the holiday season.

Back home, I parked Murphy's car on the street so it wouldn't be in the way when we got ready to leave for the wake. I wasn't sure I could keep those thousand or so race horses respectable and under control.

Before we got out, Rich asked me, "Have you met Grandma Kelch?" I nodded my head.

"Grandma Katya hates her." He looked toward his house. "I think they've known each other for a long time. Grandma Kelch showed up at Mass, unexpected. That's partly why Katya lost her temper and we had to leave."

"If feelings are that bad, why did Kelch come here anyway?"

"She said she knew Dad since he was a kid, and that she'd known Linda since she was a baby. She said it was about time I learned about the past, but she wanted to wait until after the funeral. Kelly had already said she could stay in her apartment."

He opened the car door, "I wish she had been my real grandma." He got out and looked back at me. "After the wake, the tunnels?"

I nodded. What else could I do? I didn't want him going back by himself.

With a little reluctance, I left Murphy's car and started walking up the sidewalk. Halfway to the house, I said, "What the heck," returned to the car and popped the hood. I just wanted to know what its power plant looked like. I was impressed by the size of an engine that crowded the firewall and both fenders, and by a label that said it was 8.0 liters, 32 valves, and turbocharged. It was definitely not a stock engine; it had a stripped–down look that made me suspect illegal changes had been made to the pollution controls –– changes that a manufacturer wouldn't want his name associated with. It told me a lot about Murphy, but nothing I didn't already suspect. I closed the hood and returned to the sidewalk. Again, I saw the curtains move in Katya's window.

I stuck my head into the computer room intending to toss Murphy his keys, but he had leaned back in an upholstered chair and put his feet on the desk. He was snoring lightly while the fax machine was quietly pumping out a document already several pages long. I decided to let him sleep, and laid his keys next to his shoes which were still on his feet, and which were probably scratching the finish on my desk. But, it was an old desk, so what the heck.

Chapter 17

I still hadn't reported to Hobbes about the visit next door, and I needed to tell him about the quick trip to MerSH, but he wasn't in his office. I chased Fred down in the kitchen, and he said the boss was in his room changing into a dark suit for the wake.

After a minute's consideration, I decided the reports could wait until that evening, and that I needed a shower after the brief sojourn into that tunnel. Besides, I wanted to be at the wake; funeral homes were good places to observe people. That was probably why Hobbes was already getting dressed —— he wanted to get there early, same as me.

Later, after I had changed and while I was waiting, I met Murphy on his way to the office. He was reading over the fax he had stapled together for Hobbes. "Interesting stuff," he said, not offering it to me. "That crippled egghead you call a boss will thank me for it." His eyes glinted, waiting for me to ask what it said, so that he could tell me it wasn't my business until Hobbes said it was.

Instead, I asked him about his car; where did he get it?

"Mercury dealer in the precinct. Why?" He eyed me suspiciously. "You think I stole it? Funny. Ha-ha."

"No, because it's got a jet engine in it, and I might want one for myself. So, was that a special order?"

"Not from me. I got it off the lot."

"Street legal?"

"It's a cop car, Houston. My car. That makes it legal."

That, of course, was part of Murphy's Law.

Hobbes had chosen his new dark gray suit, light gray shirt, and the Italian silk tie with the orange sunset. The tie had been a gift from Clyde a year ago.

He took the fax from Murphy and put it on his desk without looking at it. "Will you be going to the wake, Lieutenant?"

"I go to them when I have to. This one, I'll skip. I didn't know the man or the family."

But, I thought, he knew that this man was Clyde Butler, whose death was his reason for being here.

"Nothing personal," he added. "I see enough dead people as it is."

Hobbes said, "Well, we'll be gone for several hours. You can stay here if you wish; Fred will keep you company."

"Thanks, but no thanks. It's early, but the bars are open," he winked at me, "and there may be some lonely women out there."

"Then, I thank you for the files and I wish you good luck; although I think you'll find the pickings pretty slim."

"I'll do all right –– my name ain't Houston."

"Yeah," I said. "We can all be thankful for the small things."

Hobbes waited for Murphy to leave, then picked up the report. "Bring the Lincoln around, Abel, and remind Sally that it's time to go."

"Sally?" That was something of a surprise. She spent most of her spare time in cemeteries gathering information from headstones and putting it into her computer database, but she hated funeral homes. Cut flowers made her cry. Sally had come to work for Hobbes seven years ago, when she was nineteen or twenty, with no memory of her past except for a dream of three coffins. She was convinced that some cemetery, somewhere around Mercater, held the answer to her past. But to go to a funeral home that would be loaded with cut flowers was out of character.

"Yes. Keep an eye on her, Abel."

Ten minutes later, Hobbes wheeled down the ramp and locked his brakes next to the open door of the Lincoln. He gripped the custom hand bar at the edge of the door, and then swung himself in –– his overdeveloped arm muscles making it look easy.

I folded the wheelchair and put it into the trunk. If we'd taken the van, he would have ridden the lift up, locked the chair in place, and transferred to the driver's seat; but, for the wake, he preferred the formal look of the Lincoln.

Sally was already in the back seat, her head held low, handkerchief in her hand. Hobbes asked her how she was.

She shook her head without looking up.

"You don't have to go," he said.

"Yes I do," she whispered. "He was a friend."

"Then, stay no longer than you must. Abel will bring you home."

I backed the car out of the driveway and drove west on River, then north on Main. The funeral home was across town, so we had some time to talk, but Hobbes rode in silence. I knew he had looked at the files that Murphy had given him, and he knew I wanted to know what was in them, but he didn't volunteer anything. I glanced sideways at him. He had his eyes closed and his lips compressed, fingers drumming on the armrests.

"Sir?"

He had wanted me to call him Car'l for years, but I had never felt right about it. Depending on my attitude at the moment, I would call him Chief, Boss, or Sir. He was Chief in ordinary conversation, Boss when I was halfway kidding him, and Sir when I was in a formal mood, or when I was irritated with him. When he ignored me as he was doing now –– eyes closed, lips compressed, and drumming his fingers on something –– it meant he was putting things together. Now, that really irritated me.

What things? Except for the fax Murphy had provided, I knew everything he did. More, actually; I hadn't given Hobbes my report yet.

He opened his eyes slightly. "I will explain after the wake, Abel, if you haven't figured out what is going on before then." He was silent the rest of the way.

When I parked the car at the funeral home, Sally got out first and waited for me to get the wheelchair out of the trunk, and for Hobbes to get settled into it; then she stood up straight and began walking stiffly toward the entrance. We followed close behind.

Sally's only link to her past was the memory of three coffins, but she knew those coffins had been buried somewhere in that distant past. Once, when I'd asked her whom she thought was in them, she had said, "My parents, and maybe me." Her search of the countless cemeteries had been for headstones that would suddenly break those memories wide open. I didn't know how she would react to this coffin, but I intended to stay close to her.

The Chrysler minivan that belonged to the Butlers was already in the parking lot, so we weren't the first ones there. But two cars and an old Ford pickup pulled in while we were unloading. Kelly drove one of the cars with Lemuel as a passenger; the chief of police drove the second car. Grandma Kelch sat behind the wheel of the pickup, having chosen not to ride with anyone else today. She backed it easily into the parking spot next to the minivan. I waited at the door to the funeral home long enough to see what she looked like dressed up for a wake. She looked okay, dressed in a gray suit with a pink frilly blouse. She was a big person —— almost my height, and maybe seventy pounds heavier —— but the way she walked reminded me of a cat; not a tomcat, but a housecat, light on her feet and independent. I'd seen her twice before –– once Friday morning in Hobbes' office, and once today in a picture on Linda's dresser. Grandma Agnes Kelch. She waved at us and smiled, and I waved back, then I followed Hobbes and Sally into the funeral home.

The young man in the dark brown suit who met us at the door was Greg Frazier, adopted son of one of the Frazier brothers. His smile was subdued and he spoke softly. "Mr. Butler is in chapel one, just to your right. Some of the family is already there."

To Sally, who was on a first name basis with almost everyone in Mercater who knew anything about graveyards, and whose distress was obvious, he said, "If I can be of assistance, Sally, please let me know." They had become friends about the time Jane Butler had died. Frazier Brothers had managed that funeral, and Greg and Sally had gone out two or three times a month since then, although she refused to call them dates.

She gave him a brief glance, barely acknowledging his offer, and then followed Hobbes into the viewing room.

I wasn't sure how she'd react to all the flowers around the casket –– all of the cut flowers, anyway, but she did all right. After one quick desperate look around the room, she gripped my arm and closed her eyes. "Take me to him, Abel."

I led her down the side aisle and across the front of the room. I think she tried not to see the twenty or so flower arrangements that flanked the open casket. Nor did she look at the front row where Linda and

Rich Butler, and Katya and Luke Ransom were sitting, or at the twelve rows of twelve cushioned folding chairs behind them.

We stopped in front of the coffin. "We're here, Sally," I said as gently as I could. Linda and Rich Butler left the sofa and stood at the right side of the casket to talk to her, but Sally seemed unaware of them.

I watched her carefully as she opened her eyes. She didn't look at any of the flowers, or even the casket, only at Clyde. She reached out and touched his forehead, then withdrew her hand. She whispered to me, "He's not there, is he?"

I shook my head, "Only the clay, Sally."

She looked up at me, "We'll find out who killed him, won't we?"

"Hobbes will," I promised.

I led her back to the foyer, tilting my head toward Kelly and Lemuel. The older woman hadn't come this far yet.

Gregory Frazier had apparently been watching us. He gestured toward an upholstered chair, "Some water, Sally?"

She sat down on the edge of the chair. "Yes, please."

He filled a paper cup at the water fountain and brought it to her. "He'll be interred at Oakwood, next to Jane. It's almost at the top of the hill under the twin oaks."

Sally seemed to see him for the first time. "I know where that is. The Cunningham's family plot is just to the south. Twenty-four of the Cunninghams are buried there —— they go back five generations. It's a good location."

She turned to me. "I think I'll go home now, Abel."

"Sure," I said. "I'll get the car."

"No," she shook her head. "You should stay here. I can walk."

Greg Frazier touched her arm; "My uncle will be here in a few minutes and he'll take over as the Home's representative. If you can wait until then, I can give you a ride."

She hesitated, "Will you go past Oakview?"

"I can show you the new mausoleum." I hadn't noticed before, but Sally and Greg were about the same age. Both were single. I guess there were worse places to start a romance.

"Tramp!" Katya Ransom came up beside me and stage–whispered the word, nodding in Sally's direction. "The man's body isn't cold yet. Couldn't she wait until he was in the ground before she looked for someone else to sleep with?"

Sally jerked her head up and stared at the old woman. She straightened her shoulders, and fire returned to her eyes. "I know you. You're the crazy woman who came to visit the Butlers and stayed to make people hate you."

"They hate me because I tell the truth."

"Then you should learn the truth before you speak," Sally said with deceptive mildness. "Clyde was my friend. He was faithful to his wife. You're the witch aren't you? Did you bring your cat?"

Katya snarled and raised her hands. Her fingernails were like claws. She took a step toward Sally.

It had gone far enough.

I grabbed Katya's shoulders and forced her to face me. I didn't know exactly what I was going to say, but I felt like shaking her as I said it. Sudden anger flashed across her bitter face and she brought both hands up, claws extended, lunging at my eyes. I dodged and grabbed her wrists. It wasn't hard to imagine the damage those claws could do.

Fortunately, Luke intervened. He stepped between us. "Mother, dearest. Come sit with me." He wrapped both of his hands around hers. To us he said, "You'll have to excuse her. She's under a lot of stress apart from the funeral. One of her cats nearly died and she hasn't gotten over it. You know how old women are with their cats, and this one was her favorite."

"He's not dead yet!" Katya protested. "They tried to kill him, but he's not dead yet! He can't die! He won't let him die. I have to have him for the..."

Luke interrupted her, "Hush, Mother, or people will think you really are crazy."

"I'm not crazy," she said emphatically. "He answered me before. He'll answer me again!"

I suddenly had the feeling of walking down an old familiar road. I knew who she was talking about. Something made me look around for Rich Butler. I relaxed when I saw him by the casket.

Luke spoke urgently, "People are coming in, Mother. We'll have to get in the reception line to greet the mourners. Now please, please, don't say anything. Okay? Let people come and go. Promise?"

She took a deep breath and pinched her lips together. She exhaled through the nose. "Okay," she muttered. Luke led her back into the chapel, toward the casket and its receiving line of Linda and Rich, but he apparently changed his mind about letting her join them. Instead he ushered her to an upholstered chair near the wall and insisted she sit there.

"Not good enough to be with them, am I?" Her voice was loud enough to be heard in the foyer. Luke whispered something in her ear, and she looked at him in alarm. "I'd better go now!" she said.

"It'll keep 'til tomorrow."

"What if she finds it?"

"She won't."

Katya lapsed into silence but her eyes roamed suspiciously from person to person. She stared for several seconds at the three people standing in the back of the chapel, but only Agnes Kelch stared back. Kelly and Lemuel appeared to have other things on their minds; at least they had their heads close together and were talking quietly to each other.

Luke admonished Katya to stay seated and went to stand by Linda and Rich. After a moment he moved to the left side of the coffin so that he could watch his mother.

Chapter 18

The first two of the several hundred people who would come into the chapel spoke to the family, then paused at the coffin to contemplate the mystery of death.

Their comments were the soul of what people said at wakes:

"He looks good, doesn't he?"

"So natural. You'd think he was asleep."

"He is asleep."

Several more people came in and a line slowly formed as they spoke to the family, then shared a few moments of silence with Clyde.

One of the senior Frazier brothers arrived and talked to Greg for a few minutes. Shortly after, Greg and Sally left by a side door.

Hobbes had parked his wheelchair near the organ in the far left front corner of the chapel. He wasn't totally inconspicuous, but he didn't stand out much either. I found a chair and pulled it up beside him.

The grandfather's clock in the foyer struck four times. The wake had officially begun and would last until eight o'clock –– that was four hours from now. A long time to sit and watch people.

"Have you gone up there yet, Chief?"

"Briefly, while the family was watching Katya. It is incumbent on us to say farewell, but there is no need to stay long. Little can be gained from looking at the husk of a man."

"Yeah," I said. "I'll be right back."

I took my turn in line and shook hands with Rich. There seemed nothing to say. Linda wouldn't let her eyes reach mine, so I moved on to the casket. I surprised myself by whispering, "See you later, Clyde."

I walked back to Hobbes and sat down beside him.

"Back to business, Chief?"

He nodded. "We are a day behind in reports. Sally has given me hers, but I need yours."

"And I'd like to know what was in Murphy's fax."

Hobbes raised his eyebrows slightly. "They're in the car. Later, when people have quit coming in and you have ten minutes, I want you to read them for yourself. You'll find them revealing. In the meantime, you can talk, I'll listen, and we both can watch."

I nodded, "In a minute." Grandma Kelch had started walking down the far aisle. In a few seconds she would pass in front of Katya. I said, "Expect fireworks."

Grandma Agnes Kelch walked slowly, allowing her feet to shuffle on the carpet. Her rubber-soled shoes made a soft shush-shush with each step. She was twice the size of Katya Ransom and reminded me of some ancient behemoth, some predator moving in for the kill. Katya shrunk back slightly when Agnes

165

approached, but she didn't seem intimidated. Instead, she suddenly leaned forward and said loudly, "Bitch!"

"Such a sweet mother," Grandma Kelch replied, and reached her hand out to touch Katya on the forehead. The sharp crack of static electricity discharging sounded like a small caliber pistol going off. Katya jerked back, a vivid red spot appearing where the spark had struck, and hit her head against the chair.

"Very nice to see you, my dear," The older woman murmured. Then she walked on to the head of the line, ignoring everyone, waved at Clyde, said, "See you soon," and then walked back to Kelly and Lemuel.

I wanted to applaud her.

I watched Katya to see how she'd respond, but Luke was at her side before she recovered. Again he whispered to her, and again she stayed in her chair.

A long line of family, friends, and others made the circuit. None stayed very long at the casket and it seemed to me that most of them felt uncomfortable around Linda and Luke. Even so, the majority had a moment or so for Rich, and he seemed to get through the hardest part of his grieving.

Hobbes listened to my reports during the first two hours, fishing for details and observations that I might have seen but overlooked. Finally, he said, "Let me know what you think about the reports Murphy brought us."

Feeling dismissed at last, I went out to the Lincoln, climbed inside, made myself comfortable, locked the doors, turned the dome light on, picked up the faxes which had been separated into two files of six pages each, and began reading. Each file began with a summary sheet; the first was as follows:

LARSEN, JAMES, Born 1948, died Jan. 1, 1998. Cause of death: heart failure.

First marriage was to Nancy Hall in 1969. Nancy drowned in March of 1997 when a boat she and a friend were in capsized.

On August 15, 1997, Larsen remarried. His second wife's name was Linda.

December 16, Linda's mother and brother came to visit for the Christmas vacation. Two weeks later, Larsen died.

A living trust had been set up for Linda in order to avoid probate. Larsen's entire estate (worth about six hundred thousand dollars) went directly to Linda.

A month later, Linda packed up and moved to Watseka, Ill.

I took my time reading page 2 of the first report. Reduced to the basics, it clearly implied that the woman called Linda was responsible for Nancy's and James Larson's death, but provided no proof of foul play.

Pages 3 to 6 described Heidecke Lake near Morris, Illinois, where Nancy had drowned, along with details about its boat ramp access, the ranger station, and safety regulations. All of the information on these pages seemed to have come from state park publications.

The second cover page was similar except for names and dates.

FIELD, OSCAR, Born 1954, died Jan. 1, 2000. Cause of death: heart failure.

First marriage was to Elaine Weller in 1977. Elaine died from snakebite poisoning while on a camping trip April 22, 1999. A friend was unable to get help in time to save her.

On August 18, 1999, Field remarried. His second wife's name was Linda.

On December 17, Linda's mother and brother came to visit for the Christmas vacation. Two weeks later, Field died.

A living trust had been set up for Linda in order to avoid probate. Field's entire estate (worth about seven hundred and twenty thousand dollars) went directly to Linda.

A month later, Linda packed up and returned to Watseka, Illinois.

Page 2 of the second report was the same as the first page 2, except for the names. It, too, implied that the woman called Linda was responsible for Elaine and Oscar Fields' death, but provided no proof of foul play.

Pages 3 to 6 described Kankakee River State Park. I didn't bother to read it. I laid the papers down on the seat, got out of the car, locked it, and joined Hobbes in the chapel.

He tilted his head slightly, and I sat down beside him. "Your opinion, Abel?" he asked.

"Reserved until I hear yours, Chief." I said.

He looked over the few mourners still in the chapel, especially Grandma Agnes, Kelly, Lemuel, Linda, Luke, and Katya. "Like those people, the reports are not what they seem." He raised one eyebrow an eighth of an inch. "I value your opinion, Abel."

"All right," I said finally. "First, they aren't police reports. Second, they have too many similarities to our case to be believable. Third, you already know a lot more about them than I do."

He nodded, "They're obvious fabrications. No records of either man could be found in the files of the National Echo, according to Forrest Green, nor in the accessible obituaries of other newspapers affiliated with the Echo." He paused as the clock chimed seven times, then added. "What do you suppose was the point of sending them to us?"

"I can think of two reasons, Chief. To get us thinking about how Jane died, and to be sure we keep a close eye on Linda."

"There may be a third, Abel. Both reports may depict true events, but with the names of the victims changed. We're being asked to solve those crimes as well."

"Ouch," I said.

"Exactly," he agreed.

Finally the wake was over.

Kelly, Lemuel, and Grandma Agnes left shortly before eight o'clock. Linda, Luke and Katya left promptly at eight. Rich left with Hobbes and me, after he asked to spend the night again.

Clyde had died only forty–five hours ago. The funeral would be Wednesday at eleven a.m. What would happen then? I wasn't sure I was ready for it.

Back at the ranch, Hobbes offered to watch some videos with Rich, and they settled on a couple of the original Star Trek episodes from the TV series.

When eleven o'clock rolled around, I was ready for bed.

I woke up briefly when Sally backed her Bronco out of the garage. My alarm clock said it was 6:30, and I thought it was a heck of a time to go to Kankakee. I went back to sleep.

During the night, a dusting of snow had covered the ground, and I had to wear sweats when I went out to run. It was a fine morning for the third day of January, although the sky was rapidly becoming overcast. It seemed great to be alive. I stretched and twisted to loosen up, taking deep breaths and then emptying my lungs as completely as I could. Ten repetitions and I began to feel a little lightheaded, but I was ready to run, as soon as I was past McDonald's.

But, as I was turning the corner onto Main, a familiar voice called to me.

"Hey, Abe. Abel!" This was followed by the rattle of someone bumping into the Chicago Tribune dispenser and an automatic, "Excuse me."

"Sure, Lem." He hadn't surprised me; I had seen him walking past Hobbes' house a few minutes earlier. "Want to run with me?"

He shook his head. "I'm sorry, I don't do that very well. I'd probably trip on something and break my neck. Do you ever trip? I didn't think so. Let's sit inside and I'll buy us a couple of cups."

A couple of minutes later, we were sitting at a booth. I'd watched him take the lid off his coffee, add cream and sugar, and put the lid back on. I'd expected him to knock it over with his hand, but somehow he'd managed.

He took off his thick glasses and placed them on the table. He squinted as if he could barely see me. "You're lucky. You have two good eyes. I have two weak eyes. That's why I bump into things."

He was silent for a minute, and I just waited for him to tell me what he had pulled me in here for.

He sipped at his coffee, and I sipped at mine.

Finally he said, "Katya Ransom is a witch."

"Yeah? Everyone knows that."

"No, no. I mean a real witch. A practicing witch. She's the head of a flock of them." He put his glasses back on and stared at me. "It's true. I wouldn't lie to you."

He mistook my silence for skepticism, and went on quickly, "It started when I saw her go out by herself at eleven p.m., on the first night she was here. She was gone for so long that I was worried about her, and I almost called the cops. But, she came back before I had made up my mind to do it. That was at two in the morning." He waved his right hand and almost knocked his cup over. I caught it before it could spill.

"That would be a coven, not a flock. Flocks are for birds," I said.

He grinned self–consciously. "Sorry. Anyway, I wondered if she would go out again, and the next night she did. The third night, I followed her. She crossed the river to the hospital grounds, and went through a place in the wire fence that opened kind of like a gate. I stayed back where I could hide in the bushes and watched her; where she went wasn't too far from the street light, and I could see her sneak across the grounds and go into the old guardhouse. I didn't follow her any further that night, but I stayed where I was and waited for her to come back." He paused and took a small drink of coffee.

"You should be talking to Hobbes, Lemuel." I said.

"This is better; I don't want anyone to see me going into Hobbes' house. I think Katya suspects me already. Can I tell you the rest?"

"Yeah."

"Good. Anyway, she didn't come out right away. What happened was, other people from the hospital grounds snuck in there with her."

"Other people? How many?"

"Twelve. An even dozen."

I felt a pit open in the bottom of my stomach as I asked the next question. "How were they dressed? What did they look like?"

He leaned back, then took another drink of coffee. "You would only ask how they were dressed if you thought you already knew. You believe me!" He sounded surprised.

"What did they look like?" I repeated.

"Well, it was hard to see because of the darkness, but some of them looked like cats and dogs."

"And others looked like weasels and rats," I added.

"Could have been, could have been."

I closed my eyes and leaned back, resting my head against the plastic seatback in a Hobbes–like manner. Was the coven back? Not the same people, of course; some were dead and others had left town. But the twelve –– the four trinals –– how could they have reorganized in Mercater without my hearing something?

I took a deep breath and decided that Lemuel needed to know about them. "I think, Lem, that what you saw was a resurrection of a special coven. It was unique twenty years ago, and I thought it had been destroyed, but it may be back with new members."

Lemuel shook his head. "I don't know anything about covens, unique or not."

"The old one -- when I knew it -- was made up of four trinals of three people each. Each trinal took on a single identity. There was the *Cat* which called itself *The Three of the Claw*; the *Weasel* who was *The Three of the Lash*; the *Dog* was the *Three of the Chase*; and the *Rat* was the *Three of the Bite*." I didn't like talking about them, but I added, "They were dangerous, and I was lucky to have survived."

"Yes! Oh, yes. I know what you mean. That first night, I just stayed outside of the fence and watched. The next night, I built up enough courage to go in ahead of her and find a hiding place not very far from the guard shack. I think they suspected something right away. They started sniffing the air as if they were real animals and they'd picked up my scent. They started looking for me, but someone called them inside. I got out as quick as I could, and I've been afraid to go back."

Chapter 19

"Have you thought about going over there during the daytime?"

"Yes," he cleared his throat. "Yes, I've thought about going in the daytime." He lowered his head. "I'ove been thinking about doing it today, now." He raised his head just enough to lock eyes with me. "But I don't want to go alone."

Well, I thought, maybe the guardhouse won't be too bad. "Let's go," I said. "We can be back in plenty of time for the funeral." We had two and a half hours.

We walked. The sky had continued to darken and we were walking almost in twilight by the time we reached the guardhouse.

"Will it snow, Abel?"

I shook my head. The darkened sky seemed like an omen, like my hands itching, only other people could see it, too.

The guardhouse was in the northwest corner of the hospital grounds, and actually had been built to handle the river traffic. Of course that was a hundred years ago when supplies came by way of boat; now it was just another unused building.

Even though it was daytime, there was little traffic on Main, and it was easy to sneak in through the same

opening in the wire that Katya had used that first
night.

The old guardhouse was, in its own way, a
surprise. Instead of brick and stone, it had been built
of heavy timbers and rough–hewn logs. Octagonal in
shape, two stories tall, and with narrow barred
windows, it appeared to have been a military barracks.
I wondered what the military might have been doing
here. On the visible part of the foundation was the date
1901, which meant that this building had been
constructed twenty years after the rest of the hospital
had been built. Somehow, the hospital had received
authorization for that, even though Springfield had
supposedly abandoned MerSH.

The door was locked, which could have been a
problem except that, while I was fiddling with my lock
pick, Lemuel walked partway around the guardhouse
and then called me over.

"I saw this before," he said, pointing to a window,
"but I was afraid to go in by myself."

The hinged window was unlocked and partly
open, as if it had been waiting for us. It was stiff when
I pushed on it with my foot, but it very slowly yielded;
a couple of minutes later, Lem and I were standing on
the floor of a darkened basement. On a normal day,
the window would have let in enough light to see
around us, but not this day. The clouds had seen to
that.

"I have a penlight," Lemuel said. "It's not very
bright, but maybe you can use it to find a light switch."
He switched it on and offered it to me, but it slipped

out of his hand and dropped to the floor. The faint light went out. "I'm sorry," he said quickly and started to search for it.

"That's okay, Lem." A faint reflection showed me where it was. I picked it up and slapped it on the palm of my hand, and again we had light, feeble though it was. I flashed it around but the best it would do was show the way to the basement stairs. That was good enough; it led me to an old rotary light switch that provided instant light. Four naked sixty–watt light bulbs in porcelain sockets mounted on ceiling joists gave the basement a harsh illumination. I half expected to see what was before us, but I was still surprised and revolted.

"Abel, Abel, Abel!" Lemuel stammered. "What is this? What is this?"

Nearly a hundred cats looked down at us from shelves that lined the walls. On the floor under the shelves, fifty dogs eyed us in baleful silence. Not a cat hissed or spat at us; not a dog growled or barked.

But they all watched us through empty eye sockets; dried skins fitting loosely over skull and bones, and somehow held together by wire and glue. Meatless, bloodless, stripped clean, and preserved.

I shook my head. Cats and dogs. Trying to keep my stomach under control, I examined half a dozen of them. All I could tell for sure was that sharp knives had been used. How long they'd been here was hard to guess. Maybe months, maybe years.

Lemuel stumbled back to the window and put his head out. I heard his deep breaths as he sought fresh air. Finally, he turned to me. "Why did they do this, Abel?"

"You know why, Lem," I pointed at the granite table near the west wall. Three feet wide and six long, polished, wiped clean, bare of everything, but with stains that could never be completely removed. Two smaller tables at its head were also barren, but a tall cabinet against the wall opened easily at my touch. Sharp knives and porcelain drinking cups lay on its shelves. It was a sacrificial altar –– one that had been used many times.

And yet, the whole place had an amateurish look to it. Sloppy. Would Katya Ransom be a part of any ceremonies held here? I had to tell myself that I doubted it. There had to be another place, one hidden in the miles of tunnels, and in the scores of basements the size of small theaters. We could search for days, maybe for weeks, and still miss it. I hoped the boss had a way to find out where to go.

"Why?" he repeated.

"Ritual sacrifice," I answered. "At least they've only used animals." Years ago, that other coven had chosen more select victims. I had almost become one of them –– a victim, I mean.

A few minutes later, after the original shock had worn off, Lemuel began wandering around the basement –– a single room forty feet across with six posts rising from the floor to give support to the building above it. He stopped at stairs that went downward. "To the tunnels, I suppose?"

"Yeah, but let's look upstairs first." The tunnels could wait until later. Besides, I wasn't sure that it would be smart to take Lemuel into any place that could be dangerous. If I had to, I could come back alone. At any rate, I wanted to tell Hobbes about this place before I did anything stupid; I'd done that before.

Upstairs was nothing exceptional. Only a path through the accumulated dust showed anyone had ever come there, and that went directly from the front door to the stairs.

"Lem," I said finally, "if we're going to the funeral, we'd better be heading back."

"Yes," he sounded relieved.

I waited at the foot of the basement stairs until Lemuel had crossed the floor and climbed out the window, then I turned out the light and followed, pulling the window shut behind me. Ten feet away from the house, I stopped and took my time looking around as the backs of my hands itched, and shivers crawled up and down my back.

Lemuel waited for me. "Is there something wrong, Abel? Did I do something?"

"No," I said absently. I couldn't see who, or what, was watching me. I stared for a long minute at the old privet hedge that surrounded the manhole to the tunnels, and for a second, I thought I could see someone move inside the circle. Then, suddenly the feeling of being watched disappeared.

"Let's go," Lemuel took my arm and tried to lead me to the fence. "I don't like it in here."

We went.

Not surprisingly, the sky was beginning to clear.

It was almost ten o'clock when Lemuel and I parted. He looked anxiously at the windows of the Butler house, but if anyone was looking out, I couldn't see them. I said, "See you at the funeral,"

"I hope so," He took a deep breath, and in an awkward run, cut across the front lawn and stumbled up the steps. I watched his adventure; it was somehow unavoidable considering who he was. He tripped on the top step and collided with a concrete vase. The vase fell against another one and both cracked and broke into dozens of pieces as they fell to the floor. On that quiet Monday morning, it sounded as if a cannon had gone off.

Lemuel picked himself up and said in a hopeless tone of voice, "Excuse me, I mean, I'm sorry." His words drifted off into silence as he started to pick up the bigger pieces. He stopped abruptly when the front door opened.

"Leave them alone, you idiot, before you knock the whole house down!" Katya Ransom stepped onto the porch and saw me in front of Hobbes' house. "You cretinous mongrel!" For a moment, I thought she was talking to me, but she continued, her icy stare focused on Lemuel, "I suppose you told the nosy neighbor, Houston, everything that goes on here, and now he'll tell that crippled know–it–all, if he's got enough brains in that Neanderthal head to remember any of it." With that she turned to go back into the house, stopping only long enough to add, "We leave for the funeral in thirty minutes." She slammed the door behind her.

Lemuel's face turned scarlet, and he wouldn't look at me. But then, I felt my face turning red, too. Neanderthal head, was it? Well, that had to be a matter of opinion. I had always thought of myself more of a Cro-Magnon type. She was lucky; a Neanderthal would rip her head off.

As I went into the house that I called home, I found myself trying to picture her in that dead cats and dogs chapel. She fit well enough, except for her attitude about her own Harmless and those artfully stuffed cats she kept in her room. Would such a woman, witch or not, be part of a ceremony that cruelly sacrificed cats? Besides, she'd only been in town a few weeks. It occurred to me that she might be a guest speaker of sorts, and that maybe they hadn't had any real ceremonies yet.

Of course, Hobbes was the know–it–all who would have the answers. He was in the big office, and already dressed for the funeral. He had spread out a state map on his desk and appeared to be giving it serious consideration.

"Do you have thirty minutes, Chief?"

He leaned back, "Can it wait until after the funeral? You will need time to shower and change clothes."

"How about fifteen minutes? I can brief you now and give you the details later."

He took a deep breath, glanced at the map, and reluctantly said, "Very well. Sit down and report."

I reported. He listened, and interrupted me only once. "Will my wheelchair navigate the stairs to that basement?"

"No sir. We'd have to carry you and your wheelchair separately."

"We?"

"Lemuel and me, Boss, unless you want other people to know what's in that basement."

He shook his head. "Not Lemuel. I have fallen down stairs once, and look at me now. With his assistance, he, or I, or both of us would be at grave risk to life and limb. Do we have another option? It there access through the tunnels?"

"Yeah," I answered. "Through the tunnels."

I finished my report.

His only comment; "Neither Neanderthal nor Cro-Magnon." He stroked his moustache thoughtfully, and then added, "More like the Piltdown man."

"Piltdown man was a hoax," I said. "Skull fragments. Nothing more."

The corners of his mouth went up an eighth of an inch in his version of a broad smile. "Precisely."

The squealing of tires and brakes at the back of the house, and the slamming of a car door added an exclamation point to Hobbes' final word.

"Sally's back," I said unnecessarily. Her running footsteps echoed through the house.

She was almost out of breath when she took my hand and danced me around the room, then gave Hobbes a deep curtsey.

"Your humble servant returns!"

"And we welcome you," he said. "But now we are pressed for time. The funeral starts shortly."

"A summary then, Chief? Abel? Five minutes?"

"As briefly as possible, Sally."

"Good. Remember, this is just from Kankakee. I'll find out more when I go on down to Watseka where the Ransoms lived before they moved to Kankakee. I think, though, that what I have given us was a decent family skeleton.

"Katya had three miscarriages before Linda was born, and that made her paranoid. She was terrified that something might happen to the baby. She was overprotective to the point of forgetting her husband Frank, and almost forgetting the next baby — a boy born eight years later. This is that boy about fourteen years old, with his sister before she died in that fire. The picture is from the old MIDWESTERN PRESS." She placed a single photocopy on his desk.

I looked at the picture with Hobbes. The boy was unmistakably Lucas, and the girl was no doubt his sister. The family connection was unmistakable. It made her look familiar, especially around the eyes that seemed to me haunted and desperate. She definitely wasn't the Linda we knew.

"She had started having seizures when she became a teenager. At first, she just collapsed and passed out. Later, she began speaking in strange voices that she claimed were dead people speaking through her. That kept up until she was sixteen, when a local boy got her pregnant. The boy apparently never knew of the pregnancy, because her mother sent her away as soon as she found out about it. Linda refused to name the boy or even go back home. Three or four years later, the boy had grown into a man and gotten married. Two years after that, she died.

"Lucas tried to take her place in Katya's life, but she virtually ignored him. That was when he brought Susan Kelch into the picture. End of brief report."

"Excellent," Hobbes said. He tapped the picture with his finger. "What is your secret, Sally? How do you find things like this?"

She only said, "When you spend your time looking for dead people, you meet living people who like to talk."

"Just so," he nodded. "One question; when those living people were talking about the boy who made her pregnant, did they give him a name?"

"There were rumors," she said sweetly, "that it was Clyde Butler."

"Very well." He looked at me, "Abel, we're ready for the car."

I went to the garage, got the Lincoln backed out and brought it around front, honked the horn twice, got out, opened the passenger door, and waited. A few minutes later, Hobbes and Sally came out.

As usual, he put himself into the car and I put his wheelchair into the trunk, and Sally put herself into the back seat.

Chapter 20

I was surprised that she was coming with us. It was one thing to go to a wake, but another thing to go to a wake and a funeral. She usually stayed away from both and that was mostly because of the cut flowers. They depressed her. She believed living things should die a natural death, not be cut down in their prime, as she thought her parents had been.

But today she was smiling and cheerful.

Hobbes commented, "An unusual first date, Sally."

I put the car in gear and backed out of the driveway. "First date?" I asked. "Lemuel Dathan and you must have a lot more in common than I thought."

She kicked the back of my seat. "Not Lemuel, Mr. Piltdown man. Greg Frazier. And it's not a date. We've gone places together a lot of times and none of them were dates. We're just friends. After the service, we're going to take the hearse out to the Kankakee State Park. He says there is a small, ancient cemetery there that I ought to see."

"Frazier, of course," I said. "The real missing link; not just a cross between Neanderthal and Cro-Magnon, but the real thing. Tell us, Sally, does he have a lot of hair on his chest? Do his knuckles ever drag the ground?"

She kicked the back of my seat a second time.

Sally remained in the foyer. She had begun to look a little pale and I wondered for the hundredth time what had taken away her memory and left little more than a revulsion to cut flowers. Years ago, Hobbes had pried a little, gently, but she had been unable or unwilling to tell him anything. She seemed content to search the cemeteries for clues to her past, but as far as I knew, had found nothing.

Hobbes parked his wheelchair near the back of the chapel where he could get a better overall view. I sat down next to him. We watched the mourners —— the family and friends —— as they paid their final tribute to Clyde Butler. Linda, Rich, Luke and Katya were already seated in the front row, although Katya kept looking over her shoulder to the back of the room. She kept her back straight and her neck stiff, as if she would break if she turned too suddenly.

The corners of her mouth turned down when Fred and Charon came in together; Fred in gray slacks and a brown sports coat, Charon in bib overalls, denim shirt, and a fleece-lined jacket. It occurred to me that I'd never seen Charon in anything but bib overalls and a denim shirt. I probably wouldn't have noticed it then if Katya hadn't said in her stage whisper, "No respect for the dead! Pure trash!"

"Hush, Mother," Luke said. "You promised."

She pressed her lips together as if it took a great effort to be silent.

He had heard though; his face and neck were red as he paused in front of the coffin, then moved on.

Charon placed a hand on Clyde's forehead, and nodded to him as if Clyde had spoken. He turned and walked casually to the front row where Katya sat glaring at him. He stopped in front of her and gazed down thoughtfully. They stared at each other for a few seconds, then Charon said gently, "He misses you."

She was startled. "Clyde misses me?"

"Not Clyde, Katya. Your husband. Frank misses you."

Katya was unable to say anything, but Luke stood up and put himself between her and Charon. "Go away, old man. She doesn't need to hear that drivel."

Charon smiled slightly. "And you are the son? He longs to see you again. He waits with much longing."

"Go away!" Luke said, and raised a hand made into a fist, then quickly lowered it. "Just go away."

Charon caught up with Fred and the two walked out together. Presumably they had come in Fred's old Mazda pickup and didn't plan to join the funeral procession. Charon never stayed long at a funeral because, as he had once said, "What is the point of long goodbyes? Nothing ever really ends."

Grandma Agnes Kelch, Lemuel, and Kelly came in just before the priest started the eulogy, and took seats in the last row. Katya watched them, but if she had planned on saying something, she'd changed her mind.

Grandma Kelch stopped in front of Hobbes, however, and with her eyes on Katya, said loud enough for everyone to hear, "Mr. Hobbes, I would like to talk to you in the morning, before I go home. There are things you should know."

He leaned back so he could look up into her face. "Why not today?"

"This is his day," she said. "Tomorrow will be soon enough."

The service finally came to an end, and we left the funeral home to join the procession. Our car was twenty–seventh in line, so when we parked at the cemetery, we were a block away from the gravesite. That was too far for Hobbes' wheelchair, so Sally and I walked together while Hobbes watched from the car.

The priest said the words that asked God to accept Clyde's soul, repeated the twenty–third psalm, and led the people in the Lord's Prayer. He concluded by inviting everyone to meet in the basement of the church, where the ladies had graciously prepared lunch.

On the way back to the cars, Rich called to me, "Hey, Abel! Wait up, I'm riding back with you!"

Katya stopped him by grabbing his shoulder and squeezing. "You're coming with us. It is time for you to learn your place."

He winced in pain, but allowed her to lead him to the minivan. He caught my eye and shrugged.

I reported the incident to Hobbes on the way to the church. It wasn't the most efficient report I'd ever made -- I had to watch the traffic and at the same time try to see his reaction through the rear–view mirror.

Nevertheless, when I was done he leaned back, and locked his hands in back of his head. For a minute he appeared to be gazing at the dome light, then he closed his eyes and took a deep breath. We were nearly at the church before he leaned forward and placed his hands on the back of my seat.

"The future is hidden from me, Abel," Hobbes said, "and it frustrates me. I believe Richard Butler is in danger, but I am not sure from whom. Nor can I guess if it is imminent, or if it is days or weeks into the future."

"My money says it all comes from the old woman, Boss, if you want my opinion."

"Because she is spiteful and hateful? Or because your skin crawls whenever she's around?"

"Something like that. But then you didn't see her bedroom with all the stuffed cats. You didn't see the basement of the guardhouse where cats and dogs had been sacrificed. Boss, she hates everything but that damned cat, Harmless, and her hate isn't just skin deep; it goes all the way to the bone."

"Perhaps, Abel, and perhaps she is the leader of a coven of witches who sacrifice animals to the prince of the underworld; perhaps her cat is a familiar that abides with her, and tells her the secrets of hell. But, ask yourself, has she been in Mercater long enough to regenerate that coven? Surely, it would have taken years to gather such a group of strange worshippers, yet she's been here how long? A few weeks?"

I thought that over, "Then, I guess my second choice would be Linda, depending on how Clyde had set up his will."

"If the estate is to be shared between Richard and her, and if she is responsible for Clyde's death, then, yes, she is a clear and imminent danger to the boy."

Hobbes didn't sound as sure as I felt, so I asked him who else it could be.

"We have three other interested parties, Abel; Luke, Kelly, and Lemuel. Each of them has an interest in this affair that they have chosen to keep hidden. Eventually, we shall find out what those interests are. Until we do, we must protect Richard as well as we can."

St. Michael's basement was already crowded by the time we found the small elevator and went downstairs. It took me several minutes to check out all of the tables and get back to Hobbes.

"Did you see them, Chief?" I was hoping he'd say yes.

"No, Abel. Kelly is here, but not Lemuel. Nor are the Butlers or the Ransoms."

"But we do have Grandma Kelch."

He nodded, "But Linda and Richard should have come before us, Abel. I am concerned. Is there a good reason for them to not be here?"

"Only if they took Katya back home. They could have done that so she wouldn't bite anybody."

"How long would that take? Thirty minutes?"

I shook my head. "If they went straight home and then came directly here, I'd say not more than another twenty minutes."

"Then," he looked at the tables full of food, "we should take advantage of the excellent dinner the good ladies of the church have prepared."

"Or we could wait until we get back home and see what Fred's cooked up."

He raised the corners of his mouth a millimeter — one of his broader smiles, and said, "Microwaved pizza? Ham sandwiches? You may wait and savor his culinary expertise if you wish."

"You forgot the plastic cups of tapioca, Chief." I said, as I followed him to the tables.

Potato salad, baked beans, fried chicken, apple pie. Good food, but I didn't have much of an appetite and it tasted flat. I noticed Hobbes had the same problem; the process of eating quickly became mechanical and detached, his gaze frequently going to the clock on the wall and then to the door.

Fifteen minutes later, Linda Butler walked in. She looked ragged and burnt out. Close behind her was Luke Ransom. He, too, was showing signs of fatigue.

Katya Ransom wasn't with them.

Neither was Richard Butler, although Lemuel Dathan almost seemed to follow them in. He hurried past me and I lost track of him in the crowd.

I crossed the room and stopped in front of Linda. "How are you holding up?" I tried to sound sympathetic, but she was high on my list of murder suspects -- even though so far, there was no real evidence of murder. When she raised her head and I saw into her eyes, I saw pain and sadness. It wasn't what I expected. Getting by, Abel. Thank you." It wasn't the words so much as the way she said it -- there were undertones that I couldn't quite define.

"Where's Rich?" I asked casually, "I thought he'd be with you."

"We dropped him off when we took mother home. He said he wanted to walk. Get some fresh air, you know." She smiled briefly. "He should be here soon -- unless he changes his mind. Boys his age do that you know. Isn't that right, Luke?" She had turned to her brother.

He tightened his lips for an instant, and then relaxed them; it seemed inappropriate in some small way. Still, he said, "That's right, Sis. Fifteen–year–old boys often have strange ideas and do things that adults might not understand. I can vaguely remember how I acted when I was fifteen. What about you, Abel?"

"I remember the summer I turned sixteen better," I said.

"Well, I'm sure you'll see him later today." Luke glanced toward the tables, "We should eat, Sis."

Linda met my eyes then looked at her wristwatch. "By the way, I've told him he won't be allowed to stay overnight at Mr. Hobbes' home any more. He's far too much of an imposition. Tell Mr. Hobbes for us will you?" Saying that, she hurried away. Luke gave me a helpless look, then followed her.

I repeated the conversation to my boss.

"Do you believe them?" he asked.

"I don't know, chief. I think he'd come if he could, walking or riding. He'd see this as the final public goodbye to his father and he wouldn't miss it."

Hobbes nodded agreement. "We have wasted too much time already, Abel. Take the car and go to their house. If Katya opens the door to you, call out his name. If he answers, talk to him. If she's not there, or refuses to answer the door, or Richard doesn't answer you, then find a way in and search the house. If you can't find him, let me know. I will be here with my cellular phone as long as Linda and Luke are here." He flipped it open and said, "At least the signal strength is adequate. When they leave, I will call you. If I don't call, then you should return here. Perhaps by that time I will have devised a strategy."

St. Michael's was at the north end of Main. If Rich was walking from home, his most direct route would have been to go west on River to Main, and then north to the church. So I drove south to River, and east to the Butler house. I didn't see him, but that didn't mean much. He could have walked the side streets.

I parked in Hobbes' driveway, then went to the Butlers' front porch and rang the doorbell. No one answered; I waited fifteen seconds and rang it again. Still no answer; I tried a third time, then knocked on the inner door.

I was about ready to go around back and try my luck on the basement entrance when Katya swung the front door wide open, letting it bump hard against the stop.

"Well?" She demanded; her straggly gray hair was swept up into a kerchief, and she wore a ragged apron. Her hands were covered with something that looked like paste. "What do you want? Make it snappy; I'm working!"

"I need to talk to Richard."

"And you think I might have sweet–talked him into coming here? You don't know him as well as you think you do. I'd tell you something about that boy if I thought you had the brains to understand it."

Chapter 21

Frankly, I was getting tired of her insults. I could feel my teeth grind as I forced myself to be polite. All I said was, "Try me, Mrs. Ransom."

"Try you, huh." She nodded her head slowly. "An intelligent human would know what 'I Ching' is. Do you?"

"Of course," I said, and then took a chance on a little sarcasm. "It's a game kids play with hexagrams."

She narrowed her eyes. "You played it as a child?"

I grinned at her. "It kept the bogeyman away."

"Hah!" she snorted. "Then you know of the Judgment of Youthful Folly?" She stared at me intently as if the question was of unusual importance.

I shook my head, "No."

"Played is right. Well, let me educate you a little. "It's part of an 'I Ching' hexagram." She turned the corners of her mouth down. "The judgment is this: 'It is not I who seeks the young fool. The young fool seeks me.' Do you understand? He comes looking for me, but he never finds me, and he won't find me until I deem him ready."

"Ready for you, maybe, Mrs. Ransom. I just want to talk to him."

"Hah! Lots of luck. I needed his help, but do you think he'd do anything for me? Come along. Let me show you what he refused to do!"

I followed her into the living room, and asked, "Isn't he in the house?"

"Here? Don't be stupid! The maggot insisted we take him to the old guardhouse and leave him there. I was with them. I saw him get out of the van."

"Richard insisted?"

"That's what they said; he didn't say a word that I could hear. If you don't believe me, you can search the whole damned house, but not until you see what little help I asked from him. Not until you see how ungrateful and self—centered he was." She stopped at her bedroom door, and looked at me fiercely. "Now, this is my bedroom; don't you dare touch me! Understand?"

The thought hadn't crossed my mind. "Okay. You're safe with me. You have my word."

She entered; I stepped in close behind her. She went to a table that held the skeleton of a cat that was partially covered with a light plaster. Next to it was an empty skull, and off to the side the skin of a cat. A small pan of water boiled on a hot plate.

"All I wanted him to do was boil the skull clean. It would have taken him five minutes. But, no, I have to do everything myself."

"Some people don't handle dead animals very well. Have you already boiled it?"

"Don't be an idiot! Anyone with half an eye can see the traces of blood and brains that are still on it. Now, get out! I have to finish this myself."

"I'll do it," I volunteered.

"You will boil that skull?" She looked at me suspiciously, "Why?"

"I'm an investigator," I said. "Maybe I'll learn something about taxidermy as well as from 'I Ching.' Better yet, I'll learn something about you and your family."

"Not likely. Do you think I'd tell family secrets to a man that hides in a boy's bedroom? Oh, yes! I saw you and that trollop climb out through his window.

"Now, if you're going to do anything with that skull, use that long—handled wooden spoon to put it in the water, then keep turning it for five minutes."

She watched me pick it up and put it carefully into the boiling water. "Now, stir it, stir it, stir it! That's good, that's good. Do it easy, a cat's skull is very delicate."

I kept my eye on the boiling pot while I asked her, "Did you stuff all of these cats yourself?"

"Of course. There isn't another person in this state who can do that as well as I can."

"How many are there?"

"Forty—seven altogether. But three of them were naughty and are taking a time—out."

"But they're stuffed... I mean, what did they do?"

"They moved the photographs that were on my dresser. Don't stir that so fast; you'll cause the shape to change. The boiling water makes the bone soft. There, that's much better."

"Were all of these yours?" I glanced around at the multitude of cats that had suddenly acquired a half–life. I had the uncanny feeling that they were watching me.

"No, most of them belonged to someone else. They were given to me after their master died."

"Who was that?"

"None of your business who had them, or for that matter, how they died." She took the spoon from me, and said, "Thank you. Now get out. Find that bastard boy if you can."

"You're very welcome. Will you answer one question?"

"If that will get rid of you, and if it's not one of your usual stupid inanities."

"When you meet with the coven in the basement of the guardhouse, are you the high priestess? Or are you just an ordinary witch who sacrifices cats and dogs?"

She lifted the skull from the pan and placed it carefully on the table. "See," she said. "White as alabaster."

Then, for the first time, she locked eyes with me. They glinted like diamonds, and I felt purpose and defiance behind them. "I am not a priestess; I am not a common witch. And I certainly am not a butcher. Do you think those poor creatures in the guardhouse would look so terribly botched if I had wielded the knife?"

There didn't seem to be any good answer to that, so a few minutes later, I was back in the car, and heading for St. Michael's.

I didn't doubt that Rich was somewhere on the grounds of MerSH again, and that willing or not, he was in grave danger. I hoped Hobbes had come up with a plan.

He was waiting in the church, and as it turned out, he had a plan. Sort of. After he listened to my report, he grimaced as he told it to me. "We have very little to go on other than Katya Ransom's declaration that Richard had gotten out of the car at the guardhouse. It is not necessarily a logical assumption that he is there or close by, but it is the only lead we have."

"And you want me to check it out before supper, and then what, search the tunnels?"

His smile was thin. "You may enter the tunnels if you wish. In any case, you should stop at home and arm yourself. I wish you luck."

"Right, Chief." I got up to go and bumped into Lemuel Dathan.

"Excuse me, Abe," he said automatically. "But Kelly and I would like to talk to you and Mr. Hobbes. It is very important."

"Hobbes may have time, Lem, but I have urgent business." I tried to squeeze by him, but he blocked my way.

"Excuse me again, Abel, but you need to hear us out." He took hold of my arm as if he was going to guide me, but let go when he saw the expression on my face. "It's about Richard," he added.

I looked at Hobbes.

He grunted, "It may be worth a few minutes."

"Please come with me," Lemuel said.

We followed him to the corner of the basement that had the fewest people, where Kelly was waiting at an isolated table. She motioned for us to join her.

"I didn't think it would come to this," she said without elaboration. She seemed angry and desperate at the same time.

"Come to what, Miss Decker?" Hobbes asked sharply. "Lemuel said you have something to tell us about Richard."

"Yes, and I'm not happy about it. Ever since Saturday morning, we've been trying to watch out for him. Until today, we had done all right –– today he had said he would ride to the church with you, and we felt he was safe. But he went with Linda instead. They were too far ahead of us in the funeral procession, so we weren't able to follow them when they rushed away from the cemetery. I had Lem bring me to the church and then go back to the house and wait. When Linda and Luke brought Katya home, ten minutes later,

Richard wasn't with them. Lemuel followed them back here."

"Linda said he had chosen to walk," Hobbes said.

"She lied." Kelly's words were hard and inflexible.

"That is possible. She did tell Abel she had left Richard at home, but Katya Ransom said he was dropped off at the old MerSH guardhouse. Was that what you wanted to tell us?"

She shook her head. "You already knew? Well, Lemuel can confirm what Katya said."

"The guardhouse?"

Lemuel answered, "I didn't have much of an appetite after the funeral, so I thought I could park my car in back of the house, and then go upstairs to my apartment so I could watch out of my front window. I guess I also wanted to check Harmless' grave, but it was still the same.

"I saw their minivan when they let Katya out, and Rich was still in it when they left. I could see them turn left at Main Street, so I suppose they were going to cross the bridge and go to MerSH. I couldn't see any more than that because I only had front windows. I went back outside and a few minutes later, I saw them coming across the bridge and heading north on Main Street. It looked like they were coming from the hospital. They were in a big hurry. Before I left, I tried to get Katya to talk. You know what she said?"

Hobbes shook his head.

"She said, 'don't nose around things that aren't your business, unless you want to become a part of those things.' Then, while she stood there looking across the river, Harmless came out from nowhere and jumped into her arms. He stared at me. It was like a threat. I found that frightening. I got back into my car and came here."

Hobbes touched his moustache briefly. "Katya told Abel that Richard had asked to be let off at the guardhouse," he said. "Abel was leaving to investigate."

Lemuel turned to me. "I keep thinking of that cement table in the guardhouse. It was big enough for a man."

I looked at my boss. He nodded.

"As I said, Abel, go by the house first and arm yourself. Perhaps you can persuade Fred or Charon to accompany you."

"I'm going with him, Mr. Hobbes." Lemuel put his hand on my arm again. His grip was firm and steady. "I can help him."

I hesitated. Hobbes had said at one time that Lemuel Dathan couldn't be what he seemed –– maybe he was right. I said, "Yeah, you could be a diversion. Bait."

To Hobbes, I said, "Your car or theirs?"

"We can take mine!" The familiar voice of the Chicago detective brought a quick look from the four of us. He dropped a box of tissues onto our table. It landed with a clunk. "Directional mike. I could hear everything you said from the time I followed Dathan inside. You could use my help more than his."

He held out his hand. I picked up the box and tossed it back to him.

"I got new batteries in my flashlights," he added.

I looked at Lemuel; he nodded without much enthusiasm. "He can come, but not without me."

"Then, we'll see you later, Boss," I said. "Maybe Kelly can drive you home."

The three of us went quickly to the stairs, and stopped briefly to thank the priest, who apparently was waiting for us, or at least for me.

He beckoned me to come closer, and said, a little hesitantly, "I feel compelled to warn you of some danger, Abel, but I don't know exactly what it is. I know you fight the powers of darkness in ways different from mine, but... well... Be careful about whomever you let get behind you."

We'd been friends for several years, going all the way back to the seventh grade. It was never quite clear to me why he became a priest, but like me, he had an awkward and usually unreliable, and annoying, psychic ability. It came and went.

As I said, I'd known him, Jack Turner, since we were kids, and long before he became a priest. He'd grown up Jack, and that's the way it would stay, as far as I was concerned. It took too much effort to call him "Father."

I said, "Yeah? Well, thanks, Jack." I looked at Murphy and shrugged. I had been warned many times over the years. I had ignored most of them. I added this to that list.

Lemuel sat in the front seat of the Mercury and I chose the back. Murphy drove the over–powered car without restraint. Lem's knuckles turned white as he squeezed the handgrips and was pushed back into the seat by the thrust of acceleration. As we pulled into Hobbes' driveway, he grinned at me over his shoulder. "I want one of these," he said as the roar died down.

I told them I'd be back in a minute, got out of the car, ran to the house, went in and up the stairs to my room, got my pistol, glanced out the window, and stopped. What I saw across the river didn't look good. I went back down and out and climbed into the car. "Look across the river," I said.

"What is it?" Lemuel asked.

Murphy said, "Clean your glasses, little man, and see for yourself."

"Oh, yeah. Sorry." A second later, he said, "Smoke?"

I said, "Smoke. Let's go!"

Two minutes later, Murphy parked his car in front of the west number seven cottage and the three of us got out to watch the fire. The guardhouse blazed like a dried out Christmas tree. MerSH's old fire engine was already there; its hoses spread out and connected to a hydrant. Two firemen struggled to control the nozzles, putting the water where it would do some good. The sirens of Mercater's fire trucks could be heard in the distance, but it was clear they would arrive too late.

Five minutes after we got out of the car, the roof collapsed. A minute later, several small explosions destroyed the walls, and forced the firemen to move back. Mercater's tanker pulled in and added its high-pressure water to that of MerSH's.

Eventually, the fire was put out. When the chief felt it was safe enough, he loaned us a ladder and we climbed down into the ruins.

Chapter 22

The concrete table was about the only thing recognizable, and even it had cracked in several places. All of the remains of the cats and dogs had been completely destroyed. Nothing was left as evidence of animal sacrifice.

Neither was there anything to suggest that a human body had been a part of the fire.

We walked back to the car.

"Well, Houston," Murphy sounded pretty subdued, "you know this place better than we do. Any suggestions?"

I shook my head. "All I really know is that they were on this side of the bridge. They could conceivably have been in any one of sixty buildings that nobody ever goes into."

"We could choke it out of Katya," Lemuel muttered.

"She said he was let off at the guardhouse. She'll probably stick to that story. All she could tell us is which building the coven used, maybe even who they met there –– but not where they went."

"Hold it a minute," Murphy said. "How do you know they met somebody?"

"I don't. Not for certain. But Lem and I know there are at least a dozen people who used the old guardhouse basement. One of them probably set that fire. Others could have taken Rich. Linda and Luke had to drop him off and leave. They didn't have time to do anything else."

"He wouldn't have stayed," Lemuel said. "Not voluntarily."

I remembered the drug that Molly Beecher had used on me so many years ago. "No, he wouldn't have stayed if he had any choice."

"So, what do we do, Sport?" Murphy asked.

I considered my answer carefully. I didn't want to say that searching the tunnels wasn't likely to have much success; that it would take the National Guard to do anything like a thorough search. But we had to at least make an effort.

I had roughly mapped out three or four miles of those ancient tunnels in the years after Molly Beecher died, but less than a fourth of those were really explored. Nor had I looked into many of the dozens of basements and cul-de-sacs that were cold and empty, or behind locked doors. Worse were the ones I wouldn't go into on a bet –– a couple of miles of dark and decaying, collapsing –– some of them –– tunnels that gave me a severe case of claustrophobia.

"We can get into the tunnels right here," I pointed at the utility cottage next to W 7. It was the same one Rich and I had stepped into earlier. The door was still unlocked; the old man was not to be seen. Murphy and Lemuel followed me in; the green door to the tunnel stairs stood open as if it expected us.

"We have flashlights," Lemuel said. "Should we go down now?"

"In just a minute," I said, looking around. "I'm missing something."

"Yeah?" Murphy muttered. "If you ask me, you're missing a lot."

"Is it the two crates, Abel?"

I didn't think so, but I couldn't really see anything that looked wrong. Still, something said I should wait and figure it out —— but time was wasting. Who knew what danger Rich was in? So I said, "Could be. Let's go."

I turned left at the bottom of the stairs. The first thing I wanted to see was the exit to the guardhouse, if there was anything left of it.

"Smoke! Smell it?" Lemuel sounded pleased. We walked cautiously about a hundred yards until tendrils of smoke reached out to us from a smaller passageway. A steel door hung open and we passed through it into the smaller tunnel, which in turn, would have a smaller branch passageway that went to the guardhouse. They all carried the stench of burning hair.

"Cat hair," Murphy said, as if he were reading my mind.

The closer to the guardhouse, the worse the smoke became. "No cross ventilation, so it's just hanging around here." I pointed my high-powered flashlight straight through the center of the tunnel. The beam was swallowed up by the slowly moving, twisting grayness. "We can't go into that without gas masks."

"We can get a little closer, I think," Lemuel said.

"Yeah, as long as that stuff stays where it is, we might get to where we can see into the guardhouse turn—off. I went down that tunnel once when I was a kid, and up the stairs, but the door had been locked."

We went ahead cautiously, and stopped at the turn—off. It was one of those entrances that passed through a doorway, but at least the steel door was swung wide open. "May be only fifty feet, but the heat has probably welded the door shut." The smell of burnt flesh added to that of singed cat hair. My stomach began to churn.

We stopped after about twenty feet. "Smoke's getting bad," I said. "Maybe we should turn back."

"You pansies stay here," Murphy growled. "I can hold my breath long enough to get there and back." He pushed his way past us and disappeared down the narrow tunnel.

"Should we follow him?" Lemuel asked.

I shook my head. "Listen."

The sound was unmistakable. The squeal of dry hinges. It was right behind us.

"That's our door!" Lemuel cried out. "Someone's closing our door."

His words were emphasized by a clang, and the faint snick of a lock bar sliding into place.

We ran back, coughing in the growing smoke. We were too late. We put our shoulders to the closed door, but we couldn't budge it. Lemuel and I looked at each other.

"What's going on?" he asked. "Tell me it's not what I think it is."

I shrugged. "If you think someone's trying to kill us with smoke, you just might be right. C'mon. Let's find Murphy."

But he found us. The Lieutenant stumbled out of the smoke. "Hell of a long fifty feet," he coughed out. "Door welded shut, but look what I got."

He tossed the two wooden crates onto the floor. They were both empty.

From somewhere on the other side of that door, the whir of a fan started and slowly came up to speed. Black smoke began churning and spinning around us, drawn by the fan's suction, some of it through the small louvers above the door, but most of it filling the tunnel. Our flashlight beams became like beacons from a fog–hidden lighthouse. The fan shut down after only a minute, but it had finished surrounding us with smoke.

Lemuel was the first to cough. He wasn't the last. In seconds, the smoke had become dangerously thick.

We managed to tell Murphy what had happened; then we had to turn around and go back to the barred door so that he could try it, too.

"What the hell," he muttered in two quick coughs. He had no luck either.

"Get down near the floor, guys," I said, dropping to my hands and knees. "The air will be cleaner there." It was. In a second, they were beside me, choking and gasping, but at least breathing.

"I think there's a way out, Murphy, Lemuel. This tunnel goes past the guard house exit, it doesn't just end there Murph, does it?" If my memory served, it went a hundred feet farther to a utility room. It had a manhole access.

"Yeah," he agreed. "Let's..."

He was interrupted by a distant harsh laughter that echoed faintly through the smoke. Now, my hands really began to itch.

An instant later, Lemuel cried out, "Hey, watch it!"

I turned the flashlight on his face. His expression was of shock and disgust. He was staring down. I swept the floor with my light.

"Ga–dammit!" Murphy roared. "What in hell are those things?" He started kicking with his feet.

"Cats!" I yelled back. I was doing my own kicking. Dozens of them, a river of the biggest, dirtiest cats I'd ever seen, had materialized around us –– yellow eyes bright with fear, small chisel pointed teeth bared, claws extended. Covered with wood ash and soot, they were almost unrecognizable.

"Get against the wall!" Lemuel seemed to be taking charge. "Let them get by. They're running for their lives."

We obeyed, and watched as the biggest cat –– a very familiar cat – stood for a moment on his hind feet and screamed a command. He gave me a quick glance before dropping to all fours and disappearing into the smoke. The rest of the pack followed him. Once out of their way, we were completely ignored. Harmless continued to repeat his command, and in a moment the last of the cats had gone into the smoke.

"They may know a way out. Maybe there's a manhole, an open manhole, up ahead," Lemuel said quickly. "We can follow them, even if we have to do it on our hands and knees." He started crawling after the cats. A second later Murphy and I joined him.

I don't know what was on the floor of that tunnel, but it was wet, slick, and smelled like it belonged in a toilet. I hoped it was mud. At least, close to the floor, the air was breathable, and in a few minutes, we passed the turn–off to the guardhouse, and left the worst of the smoke behind us. We stood and took deep breaths, and looked around with our flashlights.

"Where'd the damned cats go?" Murphy's voice was hoarse from the smoke.

They were not to be seen. At the end of the tunnel ahead of us, light was pouring in through an open manhole. Could they have climbed the vertical steel ladder and gotten out? Maybe. I didn't see how they could have done it that quickly.

That maniacal laughter came at us again. It was closer this time. A screeching followed the laughter. It was the sound of rusty iron against rusty iron. It was coming from ahead of us.

"It sounds like a manhole cover." Lemuel said. He started coughing. "C'mon, let's go while we can!" He grabbed my arm.

But even as we watched, the cover to the manhole was pushed shut. The closing clang had a deadly finality to it. When we finally reached it, Murphy climbed the ladder and tried pushing the cover open.

"Must be wedged shut," he said as he dropped to the floor. "Looks like we're stuck."

"One of you got a cell phone?" Lemuel asked.

"Won't cut through the walls," I answered. But I tried the phone anyway. So did Murphy, but not even the more powerful police models did any better than mine.

"Look at the smoke," Lemuel said.

We looked; it was drifting slowly back toward us. "Where's it all coming from?" he added.

"Not where is it coming from, but where is it going? That'll be our way out." I waved my hand around. "Where'd the cats go?"

The three of us searched the walls at the end of the tunnel and then went back as far as the smoke would let us. Nothing.

"How long before the smoke overtakes us?" Lemuel wondered out loud.

"Half an hour, maybe," I said. "We'd better find our way out before then."

Suddenly Murphy swore, "My damned light's going out!" The beam from his flashlight had turned pale orange. In a fit of frustration, he threw the dying Maglite so that it skittered along the floor and bounced off the wall at the end of the tunnel with a loud crack. He picked it up and threw it again. It struck near the corner, but this time it made a dull thud.

"That's it," I said. "Come on."

I felt around the wall where the flashlight had been thrown. "Turn your lights out," I said. In the following minutes of nearly complete darkness, our eyes adjusted. A faint, rectangular light formed an outline in the wall. I pushed on the center of the outline and a door swung outward almost effortlessly, then closed as soon as I removed my hand. Two or three cats could have opened it for all of them to pass through, and once it closed behind them there would have been no trace. Beyond that door was another tunnel, one so small that I wondered why it had even been built. Maybe they had guard dogs and the tunnels let them out and in. Even so, twenty or thirty feet away, the floor of the passageway seemed to rise up toward the ceiling. At that point, it would be too narrow for Murphy and me, if we could get that far. I turned to Lemuel, but he spoke first.

"Cats saved our lives," he said. "I'm going to go thank 'em." Without any further comment, he switched his light on and pointed it down the new tunnel. He was going to have a wet, nasty crawl, but there didn't seem to be any choice. "I suppose there isn't any doubt about the cats going this way," he muttered. "It's a giant rat hole."

"Take this, Lem," I said. "I don't know what's ahead, or even if this is a way out, but take this with you, just in case." I handed him my Beretta. He stuck it in his waistband, gave us a half–salute, and crawled away in the mud.

A minute later, he called back. "I'm stuck!" His voice carried the edge of panic, but he was still under control. "I can't move. One of you has got to pull me back."

Well, Murphy was the big man, and size did count, at least in that tunnel it counted; so the job was mine. The crawling was easy at the start but I was flat on my stomach long before I reached Lemuel. Whatever slimy foul-smelling stuff it was that was beneath me, it was like oil; and it helped me reach his feet. I gripped them both and inched my way back.

I didn't have to go far before he said, "Okay. Okay, Abel. I can make it now."

A minute later, we were back with Murphy.

"Too bad," Murphy said. His voice already sounded raspy from the smoke.

"Well, I'm not done yet," Lemuel said. "I could see the end of the tunnel past the dirt buildup. I just need to be a little bit thinner, and then I think I can make it."

He took off his jacket, shirt, and pants. "Have these ready for me when I get that manhole cover off. It's gonna be cold out there."

With the pistol in his hand, he began his crawl.

The last I could see of him was when he got down on his belly to pull himself through that narrow shallow section of the rat hole. Then, he disappeared around a turn.

All we could do was wait.

Chapter 23

And we waited. Five minutes passed. Murphy climbed the ladder and tried the manhole cover again. He looked down at me and shook his head. He tried his cell phone while he held it close to the cover. Nothing.

A gunshot startled us. It sounded far away. Murphy glared at me, then climbed the ladder once more and strained his muscles against the cover.

Two more gunshots, fired quickly and close together, echoed faintly through the tunnels.

The smoke was beginning to reach out and touch us. It burned our throats. Five, maybe ten minutes was about all we had left.

Then suddenly, above us, was the rattle of metal against metal. Two more gunshots rang out, and the cover began to move. Murphy pushed hard and it swung open. He climbed out; I was right behind. We dropped on the grass and sucked in the fresh clear January air.

Lemuel was pale and wheezing. He managed to get back into his clothes, and then collapsed on the ground. Through jagged breaths, he explained the gunshots. The first one had been to scare the cats out of his way when he had reached the small anteroom where the final door would open to the outside. A few of them had moved reluctantly, but most had just hissed and showed their teeth. The cats had been trapped. The door had been latched and the latchstring pushed to the outside where the cats couldn't reach it. A dozen cats had stood between him and that door, but they had arched their backs and bared their claws. Lemuel hadn't been sure he could make it through the pack alive, and he hadn't want to shoot any of them, not that doing so would have worked, anyway.

Then, Harmless had walked through the angry mob and stopped in front of Lemuel. He had eyed him for a minute, and then had turned and strolled across the room, a feline juggernaut pushing the other cats out of the way. Lemuel had followed. The latch had been secure but the hinge pins hadn't been. A shot into each rusted pin had blown them apart, and the door had fallen open. He had let the cats go first. Only Harmless had waited for Lemuel to stroke his fur in a sort of 'You're welcome' gesture, and then he had disappeared.

The tunnel had ended close to the river, inconspicuous under wide wooden stairs that went down to a boat landing. Lemuel had pulled himself out of what he still called a rat hole, and had found his way to our manhole. The last two shots had broken the padlock.

"Good job, Lem," Murphy said in unaccustomed praise.

"Yeah? Well, thanks, Lieutenant." Lemuel tried to rub some of the mud and filth off. He was obviously pleased by the compliment. "Right now, I'd like to know who tried to kill us —– and I need a shower"

"I'll give you a ride home —– there's a blanket in the trunk you can throw on the seat, so you don't smell up the upholstery. Maybe Houston can tell you who tried to kill us —– he usually knows, or Hobbes does and tells him. I sure don't."

I looked across the hospital grounds at the city street in the distance. It was early twilight, but I could see some kids riding their bikes. In half an hour, it would be too dark for them to be out on the streets.

Lemuel and Murphy followed my gaze.

"The bicycle," I said. "His bike is gone."

"Yeah," Lemuel said thoughtfully.

"So?" Murphy asked. "Someone took his bike, so what?"

I shook my head. "That's what he came back for. He straightened the rim enough to ride, and I know where he went. That's what I should have thought of before we went into the tunnel."

The light dawned for Murphy, too. "Dathan, you'll have to wait for your shower."

Lemuel Dathan nodded his head.

"Then, let's go!"

A few minutes later, we reached the cemetery. Rich was sitting on the ground near his dad's grave. He barely noticed us park the car and get out. His eyes were puffy when he looked up.

"I miss him," he said.

I nodded my head, "I understand. It'll be dark soon, though, and you'd better come home. You can ride with us. We'll put your bike in the trunk."

"Okay." He stood up and stretched, "We said goodbye a little while ago. I got school tomorrow, so I guess I should look over my homework." He seemed to see Lemuel for the first time. "What the heck have you been playing in, Lem? You smell like a hog farm."

"I'll tell you later," Lemuel answered. "I need to get cleaned up before supper."

"Yeah. I'm starved. What time is it?" He answered the question himself by looking at his wristwatch. "Six–fifteen. I've been here all afternoon? I bet nobody even missed me!"

Hobbes drummed his fingers on the desktop in the great room. It was eight–thirty p.m.; still Monday, and I'd just finished giving him my report on the trip into the tunnels.

"Who closed the manhole cover?"

"I didn't recognize the laugh, Chief. I only heard it twice. She was in the tunnel with us and locked the door, then she went out and around to the manhole, and locked the cover on it. It was a woman. At least, I think it was. It could have been anyone."

He grimaced slightly. "Not just anyone. Logically, it should be one of the four women already involved in this case; Katya, Linda, Kelly, or Agnes. If not one of them, then the whole city of Mercater is suspect. The question is, why would any of them want the three of you?"

I shrugged my shoulders. Ever since we'd found Rich, the question had been driving me crazy. I could see burning the guardhouse and its evidence of animal sacrifice, but three murders? "Maybe you could see who has an alibi for the time of the fire."

He shook his head slightly. "No, Abel. The moment the fire started is not the issue. Whoever was responsible for it could not have known you would go into the tunnels, and trapping you seems to have been a response to an unexpected opportunity.

"The puzzle is, who would know about the air circulation fans, and how to use them? Controlling the smoke, as she did, required special knowledge of the fans as well as the manhole location."

"But, it could have been the same person, Chief. She could have stayed to watch the fire, and then saw us drive up."

He leaned back in his wheelchair. "I recognize that possibility, Abel. What we lack are accurate backgrounds on all of the people living in the Butler house, and that makes it impossible to proceed. I have resisted deploying my forces in what is likely to be a fruitless search, but that in itself has been a mistake, and almost claimed three lives. It is time to correct that shortcoming. Will you summon Sally and Fred, and Charon if he is nearby? Tell them I want a meeting as soon as everyone is here. We have tomorrow to talk about. I want no repetition of today's deadly attack."

Fred was sitting in the kitchen staring at his oversized gas range, when I told him Hobbes wanted to talk to him.

"If he expects me to cook something tonight, he's gonna find another cook!"

I grinned at him as I poured a glass of milk from the fridge. "We won't be that lucky. He has another job for you."

"Yeah?"

"Yeah. You got a chance to use your brain for a change."

His whole attitude changed. "Digging up stuff for Hobbes? It's about time." He winked at me, "It'll give me something to do until I get my new electric stove."

"Hobbes wants Sally and Charon and me, too, when we're all together."

"Charon's in the boathouse; I can get him. Don't know what you'll do about Sal, though. She's on a date with the undertaker."

I almost choked on the milk. "A date? Did she tell you she was going on a date?"

"Not exactly, but that's what it was. She called right after the funeral and said they were going to the Abraham Lincoln National Cemetery while there was plenty of daylight, and then afterwards, they would go somewhere for supper. Some date, huh?"

"Some date. I don't think she'll mind a call when she finds out Hobbes wants to see her."

Fred tossed me the kitchen's cordless phone. "Speed dial number fourteen."

Sally said she was a long way from home, but she should be there by ten. Even so, it seemed to take longer than was necessary to tell Greg Frazier good night, and when she danced into the kitchen, she curtsied and said, "Ah, the nobility that some men can lay claim to!"

Hobbes' inscrutable face lost some of its inscrutability for about three seconds, but it didn't really reveal a lot to me. I couldn't tell whether he was pleased about Sally and Greg, or angry, disappointed, alarmed, or some other human emotion.

What he said was, "Is he your first boyfriend?"

She laughed, "No, you are. Then Charon, then Fred, and then Abel." She placed her hand on Hobbes' bald head, and tapped it gently, like it was a melon, and maybe not ripe. "That would make him number five, wouldn't it?"

Charon said, "Do ye think it wise, giving up four of us for one of him? Seems to me to be a poor trade, Sally."

"No," she said merrily. "It's no trade at all. I'm going to keep all five of you."

"Indeed," Hobbes said. "Now, perhaps you could put your many romances aside and sit with us for a while. We have some plans to make and some assignments to follow through on."

Sally sat down on one of the elevated stools, but then moved to a regular chair when Hobbes caught her eye.

"Thank you, Sally." He preferred that we all be at eye level when we were working.

He nodded to each of us, but spoke to us all. "We're going digging for anything that will help us. So far, I don't know what we'll be looking for. Maybe we'll dig up a lot of fool's gold and will have to count our time up to experience. But if we're lucky, we may find the entire gold mine."

He turned to his cook and said, "Fred, do you like to fish?"

Just like that, Hobbes changed metaphors from gold mining to fishing, which I thought kind of strange. When he got to me, what would I be doing; digging or fishing?

Fred answered dryly, "It's my life, boss. Right up there besides cooking with gas."

"Excellent. Then you won't mind going on a fishing expedition."

"Not unless I'm going after real fish. What am I going to be looking for?"

"I don't know. I wish I could be specific but frankly, I don't know exactly what kind of information is out there, if any at all. You'll be looking in Mercater when most of the principals in this case come from Watseka or Kankakee. However, people like to talk, and they like to talk about people who are unusual, and there is hardly a more unusual family than the one that lives next door. If there is anything of value to be found, you have a good chance of finding it."

"You want me to look at the riverfront bars, the VFW and places like that?"

"Yes, Fred. Any place where you would feel at home."

"Yeah. Give me some hints. Where should I start?"

"You'll be looking for anything relevant to the Butler and Ransom families and to witches, covens, and cats. My hope is that you will know it when you hear it. Abel will give you two hundred from petty cash, which may help to loosen the more promising tongues."

"I dunno. Two hundred don't seem like an awful lot for what you're expecting me to find out."

"How much then, Fred?"

"Four, five hundred. I'll bring back your change."

"Very well. Five it is. You understand that our client has limited resources and that my fee will be minimal. The expenses will be absorbed by Hobbes and Associates, or taken from certain designated accounts, such as the one earmarked for the new electric range." He gave Fred five seconds to absorb that, then added, "We may have to limit that purchase to one of the cheaper models."

After a moment of silence, Fred said, "Mebbe I could get by with just three."

Hobbes nodded and when Fred turned away, he looked in my direction and did something with his right eyelid that might have passed for a wink. One up on Fred, huh? Hobbes was rolling on the floor. You just couldn't tell it while he was sitting in his wheel chair.

"Sally," he said to the only woman who had ever been on his staff, "I would like for you to go to Kankakee in the morning, and then to Watseka. Stay overnight if you need to, but come back by Wednesday evening or earlier. I need background data on Linda and Luke, Lemuel, Kelly, Katya, and Katya's deceased husband, Frank. I also need to know if any of them seems to have an interest in devil worship, though that may be hard to find out. Also, Grandma Kelch is here because she is related to someone in that group. I should like to know who that person is and how they're related."

"I thought Linda was her granddaughter," I said.

"I seek verification."

Sally stood up, a sudden faraway look in her eyes. "Overnight? Why, Car'l, that could be a lot of fun!"

"Fun?" Hobbes said.

"Yes. Watseka is a very old town with some very old cemeteries. If we have time, we could visit one or two of them."

"We?" Hobbes sighed. "Will Mr. Frazier go with you in the morning or meet you there in the evening?"

"We'll meet for supper and then... Have you ever walked through an old cemetery on a clear night with only the moon and stars to guide you?" She put a hand on Fred's shoulder. "And someone to share the beauty with you? And always, always as the dark hours pass and the midnight chiming of some bell tower warns of the coming witching hour — always you wonder if some ghost or shade or dispossessed haunted soul will reach out and," she squeezed Fred's shoulder enthusiastically, "grab you!"

Fred jumped, then stood up and said, sheepishly, "Past my bedtime." He opened the door to the wide basement stairway that had been adapted to Hobbes' motorized lift, said, "See ya in the morning," and walked down the steps that Clyde Butler had built for Hobbes a few months ago, his boots going clomp, clomp on the bare wood.

Chapter 24

Clyde had planned on painting those steps over the holidays. Now, it would likely be a long time before that project was completed. The same could be said for a half-dozen or so other small jobs that were on a list somewhere. For some reason, the thought made me unreasonably angry. We missed Clyde already; now we would miss his handiwork. How many other people would feel that way? I didn't know, but I knew he had covered a lot of ground in his spare time. At any rate, it was Clyde that we missed, and his helpfulness was just a part of him.

"Abel?" Hobbes said. It took me a few seconds to realize that this was the second time my boss had called me.

"Yes, sir," I answered.

"Tomorrow morning, Abel, I want you to drive up to Starved Rock State Park and use tact and subtlety to investigate Jane Butler's death."

"Tact and subtlety, huh. I'll have to talk to the rangers who were working when she fell, examine the site, and so on. How subtle can I be?"

"That will be up to you, Abel. It's part of your talent as an investigator, and why I'm sending you and not Fred or Sally.

"And take the Lincoln. I may need the van."

I raised an eyebrow in question. Since he only insisted on keeping the van if there was someplace he wanted to go alone, would he tell me where? He ignored the eyebrow, as I expected.

Instead he said, "You can have some company if you wish."

I almost asked whom, thinking first of Lemuel, and then of Rich, either of whom would be an asset — at least they would be an extra pair of eyes — when I glanced across the table at the one person called in but not yet given a job.

Charon nodded. "Aye, Abel. If ye don't mind, I'll be going with you." So, a new country heard from.

I wanted to ask right up front what Charon was going to do at Starved Rock, but unless Charon or Hobbes volunteered the information, I'd have to wait for it to unveil itself. I'd learned years ago that Hobbes would tell me everything I needed to know to do my job, but that he relished springing surprises on the unsuspecting — so he sometimes kept secrets from me, and from anyone else, when it suited him.

It could be as irritating as hell, but unless I had a damned good reason to question what he was doing, I kept my mouth shut about that.

This was one of those times. The two conspirators waited for my reply. Even Sally smiled at me; she had had the same kind of frustrating instructions from Hobbes on occasion and knew how I felt.

I said simply, "Seven in the morning all right, Charon? We can stop at Flo's in Utica for breakfast; it might be better than those toaster things Fred's gonna fix."

"Toaster things," Hobbes said. His voice had a rare bleak quality to it. "Did he tell you that?"

"Look on the counter in back of you, Boss."

He didn't bother to look. "Will it snow tonight?"

"Not in the forecast," I said.

"Then I think I will get some fresh air and exercise in the morning."

"Gonna wheel yerself down to McDonalds, eh?" the ancient boatman said. "They got good biscuit sandwiches."

"I'll keep that in mind," Hobbes said dryly. "Goodnight, both of you."

Charon tipped his cap and went outside and down toward the boathouse where he had his own small apartment. Sally disappeared out the back door. Hobbes went to his room; I turned out the kitchen light and went upstairs.

For some reason, I went to the window by the stairs on the second floor and looked down at the front yard. I hadn't realized that Greg Frazier had waited for Sally, but there, in the driveway, was his eighty thousand dollar sports car; the two of them were leaning against it and talking. Well, that really wasn't my business, but I was starting to feel protective toward Sally. Greg had spent a lot of time here lately, I thought; but, well, the heck with it. As I said, it wasn't my business.

So I quit my spying and went on to my room. I took Neil Armstrong's picture off of the dartboard, and put up the new astronaut of the month. I didn't even recognize him, so it hardly seemed fair to throw darts at his picture. But flunking out of astronaut training hadn't seemed fair to me either. I needed the therapy. I grabbed a handful of darts, crossed the room and tossed them over my shoulder, one at a time, with my eyes shut. I turned the light out, went to the bathroom where I brushed my teeth, came back, got undressed in the dark, crawled into bed, and in two minutes, was sound asleep.

I didn't bother with the dartboard. What difference did it make if I had scored?

Sally had already left by the time I got out of bed at half-past-six, and neither Hobbes nor Fred appeared to be up when Charon and I left the house at seven. Fred had left a note saying he had changed his mind about going to bed right after our meeting. He had written that he might as well start right then seeing as how the hour hand was still in front of midnight, and that was the best time to talk to people in bars. Anyway, why waste a night? He probably didn't get to bed until two, so he wouldn't be likely to get up until nine or ten.

"Like riding in a hearse, ain't it, Abel?" Charon asked the question as we backed out of the driveway and headed west on River toward Main Street "Bet any other man my age wouldn't be riding up front if that's what this was, would he?"

I laughed to be polite, then asked, "And what would your age be, Old Timer?"

"Old as the hills," he said. "Older than dirt. Old as I feel. Old enough to know better..."

"But how old are you, really?" I turned north on Main and drove through town to Route Six, turned west and headed for Utica, which was right across the river from Starved Rock. Altogether, it was about half an hour's drive from Mercater.

He shrugged his shoulders. "Don't know for sure. Can't remember when I was born anymore. I guess it's like they always say — memory is the second thing to go."

I asked the obligatory, "What was the first?"

"I dunno. I forgot!" The old man laughed until tears ran down his face. It was going to be a long thirty minutes.

Over breakfast at Flo's, he admitted he didn't really know his age. "Been getting Social Security for thirty years, though. They admitted I was at least sixty-five back then."

"That would make you almost a hundred years old."

He stroked the long white beard that reached almost to his belt buckle and shook his head. "Beard's that old itself. I don't know how old the rest of me is." He chuckled, "I made that up about Social Security. Don't believe in getting something for nothing."

233

I caught our waitress' eye and indicated I wanted the check. She shook her head slightly and I said for Charon to look at her.

"Kind of pasty and nervous, ain't she, boy? Kind of like that biscuit and gravy you just ate." He said after a brief glance. "I'd say she's in trouble."

"Tried to eat, you mean, and yeah," I agreed. Two tough looking men were talking to her and casting hard looks our way. "I think she's in trouble and so are we. I don't like the way they're looking at us, and my damned pistol's in the car."

We were seated half way across the dining room — the only customers at the moment, if you discounted the two men at the register.

"Robbery?" Charon asked.

"Maybe," I said. My hands itched like I'd been in poison oak. I pushed my chair back and stood up. "Wait here, Charon."

My old friend stood up in front of me. "No, Abel. You wait. I'm bettin' they both got guns. They won't pay any attention to an old geezer like me, but they'd probably shoot you."

I started to protest, but something in his voice stopped me.

He stumbled his way across the room using the backs of chairs for support. One man, than the other turned to watch him. He walked with his head down, not seeing them, and only stopped when one of them said, "Where you going, old man?"

Charon looked up for the first time, and when he answered, his voice had a tremor that I hadn't heard before. "Sorry, young fellow, but I gotta use the restroom. My bladder ain't no damn good no more. If I don't get in there quick, I'm gonna piss all over myself." He started walking again.

The one who had been talking pulled out what looked like a thirty-eight Police Special and casually pointed it at Charon, who seemed unaware of it, but walked right up to the man. "Better stop, old timer." For emphasis he jammed it into Charon's stomach.

"Easy, Tom," the other man said. "He's not the one we want." He looked across the diner and grinned at me. He raised his voice slightly, "How ya doin', buddy?"

"Yeah, Vic, and we can't leave no witnesses, can we?"

"Well, I..." The man called Vic was suddenly staring at the pistol that Tom had held a second before. Tom was sliding down from the counter where his head had slammed into the cash register, bleeding, and already unconscious.

"Easy, boy," Charon said softly. "Raise your hands now and turn around. Okay. Now I want you to lay flat on the floor with your hands holdin' each other behind your head."

To the waitress, he said, "Miss, call the police."

From where I'd been standing, I was damned if I could see what he'd done. One second, Charon was about to be shot; the next, he had the gun. It was like watching a video that had a section of tape cut out and then spliced back together without the good parts.

About an hour later, Utica police had taken our statements and the two would-be robber/killers — one of them in an ambulance but both of them under guard — and had left.

It wasn't until then that the waitress, whose nametag said she was *Ellen Campbell*, tried to explain some of what had happened. It was an old story; she'd dated Tom, then broke off with him. He'd got mad and had come back to talk things out. She said she didn't think either Tom or Vic would have really hurt someone, and maybe Charon should have waited before he had attacked Tom. Why, he had given Tom a broken nose for sure, maybe a fractured skull.

"But, Ellen," I argued, "He had a loaded pistol shoved into Charon's stomach."

"No, no he didn't. The gun wasn't loaded. And besides, I think he was handing the gun to the old man, with the butt first."

"The gun was loaded," I said. I was beginning to wonder why I was having this conversation; the waitress was defending the two men who might have tried to kill us. "I checked the clip before the police got here."

"Oh," she said. "Ohhhh..." Like it was an epiphany. A sudden flash of brilliance. A revelation. A chance to save her boyfriend and get him back.

"Your gun! You brought the gun and put it in Tom's pocket because... because you wanted to get rid of it. But the police will find out the gun was yours because of your fingerprints on the clip."

She looked hard at Charon, "You were just being mean, weren't you? Shoving Tom into the counter like that. Were you trying to kill him? Why'd you do it? Why?"

The check was for eleven dollars and five cents. I put a ten, a single, and a nickel on the counter and said, "Let's go, Charon, before she has us arrested."

"Police cruelty!" she shouted at us as we hurried out the door. A saltshaker shattered against the thick glass of the door; a peppershaker followed close behind. I was going to tell her we were private detectives, not cops, but right then didn't seem to be the time to mention it.

On the way to the car, Charon said, "I don't think her old boyfriend will be going to jail."

"Yeah," I said. "She'll tell her own story so that the facts will be distorted, and the police will probably have to let them go. They could be out this afternoon."

"Too bad," Charon said thoughtfully. "That Tom's a dangerous feller. Vic ain't much better."

I pressed the button on the remote and unlocked the car, but I hesitated before opening the door. "Sounds like you already knew them, Charon?"

He shook his head. "Knew about them was all. I seen them once when they drove by the house Saturday morning, and once yesterday when I had breakfast at the New Tulsa. Millie, you know her — she owns the place — came to my table just to ask if they was friends of yours."

"Mine?"

"Yours, or Hobbes."

"I never saw them before."

"They been coming in for about a week, she said. Good tippers, but they didn't seem normal somehow. They looked like they were boiling underneath with some secret funny business. And they bragged about hitting some big old cat with their van. That's why she was asking about you, if you knew them."

"Then they didn't really ask about Mr. Hobbes?"

"No, but they told Millie they hit the cat in front of that big old house on River Street, the one with the wheelchair ramp. There's only one house like that."

"Yeah," I shrugged. "Cat was from the house next door. Maybe we can straighten that out when we get back home." We got in the car and I started the engine.

Tom and Vic had been asking about me in Mercater, and appeared here in Utica carrying guns. What the heck was going on?

"Did you see them hit the cat?"

"Nope. They must have driven by twice on Saturday."

"One more question, Charon. Where'd you learn to do that?"

"To take Tom's gun away? That's something I learned in the Big One. W-W-Two. Army Rangers."

World War 2. Sixty years ago. He'd be eighty or so now. I decided to let it drop.

"Well," I said, "I guess we're going to have to spend a few hours chasing their police records."

Chapter 25

I noticed an ancient, rusty, van parked in the handicapped parking area as we were pulling away. It didn't have a Handicapped placard hanging on the mirror or handicapped plates.

As we drove the car out of Flo's parking lot, Charon said, "Didn't tip her, did ya?"

I grinned and shook my head. "Not a penny."

"I'd' have given her ten percent." His eyes sparkled as he glanced over his shoulder — she was still watching us from the doorway. "Then, I'd have robbed her myself."

I had time to think as we drove across the river toward Starved Rock. What I came up with wasn't very comforting. I asked Charon what he thought I should do.

"For one thing, Abel, you better let Car'l know. Maybe there's something he can do."

Out here, far from civilization, my reliance on cellular reception faded dramatically, so I was relieved when we pulled into the parking lot at the Starved Rock lodge.

They had a direct dial system, so I was able to reverse the charges to Hobbes. I gave my report. He wasn't particularly pleased about anything except Charon's ability to disarm a gunman.

Ten minutes later, we left the lodge and drove around to the rangers' station, found a parking place, and went looking for a ranger. By the time I found one, Charon had disappeared into the twelve hundred acres of woodlands, waterfalls, and walking trails, doing, I supposed, whatever it was Hobbes had sent him to do.

I introduced myself as a private detective trying to expedite an insurance claim on behalf of the deceased woman's son, which was true enough.

The ranger, who said his name was Mullaney, tried to be helpful. "I remember the accident, but I wasn't working that day. I can show you where it happened all right. Everyone here knows about LaSalle Canyon at the waterfall. Beautiful place."

"I would like to see it, Ranger, but I would also like to talk to someone who was actually on the scene of the accident even before the body was moved."

"I think you want Jim Wilson, Ranger Wilson, that is." He spoke into his walkie-talkie.

After a few seconds, a voice answered, "Yo, Newt! What's cookin'?"

Mullaney explained the situation, and Wilson said to wait there. He'd pick me up in his jeep.

Fifteen minutes later, after Ranger Wilson insisted I call him Jim, we stood at the head of LaSalle's waterfall, which he properly called a natural beauty. We watched the water tumble over twenty foot high sandstone cliffs and into the lake below. "Caves down at the bottom are the result of millions of years of erosion," Jim said. "You can climb down, if you're careful. That's what Jane Butler was doing when she slipped and hit her head on the rocks. She fell into the water where it was deepest. The woman with her had called for help, but Mrs. Butler had gone right to the bottom; she drowned before they could get her out."

"The autopsy said she had a fractured skull," I said.

"I didn't know that," the ranger said. "Doesn't surprise me, though. I didn't see her close up, but from twenty feet away, it looked like the back of her head was flattened out."

"Where did she fall from?"

"The lady she was with, Linda something, said she was off the regular path."

"Ransom, Linda Ransom," I said. "Can you show me where?"

He moved about fifteen feet closer to the falls. "Right about here, she said."

I looked down the side of the cliff. "What do you suppose she was trying to do, Jim? There's no way down here."

"Probably just trying to see the waterfall better."

I had known Jane for years. I couldn't picture her slipping and hitting her head like that. She had been a cautious person. Too careful for this.

"She was lucky her husband was here," Jim said almost as an afterthought.

"Clyde Butler was here? No, he couldn't have been."

"Not him; the other woman's husband, Mr. Ransom."

As far as anyone in Mercater supposedly knew, Linda and Jane had come alone, and of course, Linda had been single at the time.

"Do you remember what he looked like?"

"Sure. I've got a good memory for faces. My camera's got an even better memory."

I was speechless. A camera? Pictures? This was almost too good to be true.

"Got an album in my desk. Come on, I'll show you."

We drove back to the offices. He had me sit on one of the ancient wooden chairs, while he dug out a plastic-covered album. He opened it and passed it to me. I stared at the pictures. Mr. and Mrs. Ransom. Sure. This might not be the gold mine Hobbes was looking for, but it sure wasn't the shaft. Hobbes was going to be proud.

The pictures were date-stamped. I picked out one that was slightly wide-angled, but their faces could still be identified, and one taken with a telephoto lens that resulted in a very detailed close-up. It was ironic that the man Jim took to be Linda's husband had thought he was protecting his eyes from the late sun by holding his left hand above them. What he did was prove that he was here when Jane fell to her death. I could clearly read the date as well as the time on the digital watch.

"Jim," I said, "I'd like to buy these two pictures if you'll sell them."

He shook his head. "Not for sale; they belong to the state. But if I loan them to you for, say, a couple of years, they might help explain how she managed to fall, right?"

"You got it."

"Look, I got six pictures here; some of them show the accident from different angles. There's even one that shows a dozen people who came to see what the hubbub was about before the police got here and run 'em off. You might as well take them all. The negatives are in my desk if I ever need copies."

"Jim," I said, "You're an angel in disguise."

"Just doin' my job," he said. "Look, I talked to Jane Butler before the, uh, accident, and she seemed like a nice lady. I hope you find out how she died. That's what you're here for, isn't it?"

"You got it, again," I said. I thanked him a couple more times.

I locked the pictures in the Lincoln's glove box, started the car, and went looking for Charon.

It was already lunchtime, so I parked in the Lodge's parking lot and decided to let him find me. A few minutes later, he opened the passenger door and slid in. He set a small cloth bag on the floor between his feet.

"Hungry?" I asked. I was, and we were parked next to one of the best dining rooms in the county.

It didn't surprise me when he answered, "Yup and nope."

"Yup and nope?"

"Yup, I'm hungry and nope, got no time. Hobbes be a-waiting for what you found out."

On the way back through Utica, I drove past Flo's. The diner was closed.

I was still hungry, so I stopped at a fast food drive-thru.

"I think I'll have me one of those Happy Meals," Charon said. "That won't slow us down none, and I'll save the toy for my grandson."

I glanced sideways at him, "Grandson?"

He kept a straight face. "Hell, I'm old enough, ain't I?"

Half an hour later, I pulled the Town Car up to the curb in front of Hobbes' house. I couldn't park in the driveway because it was already occupied. Two police cars and an ambulance had beaten me to it.

Hobbes sat in his wheelchair in back of his desk in the great room, staring at the painting of two children on a picnic. His face was cold and hard, as if it had been chiseled out of ice. He turned to face us as we walked across the room. His words were bitter and angry.

"I let them murder her right in front of me, Abel. Here, in my house. Four days after Clyde was murdered. I did not see it coming."

"Yes, sir. Who was she?" The EMTs had the body on a gurney. Her face was covered.

"Agnes Kelch," he said flatly. "Grandma Agnes Kelch."

"Houston!" The barely familiar voice of Bull Dickerson, Chief of Police in Mercater, put a quick stop to whatever Hobbes was going to say. "Come with me."

Hobbes nodded and said, "Later." He turned back to the painting. I watched his face return to its normal expression, which meant I couldn't read it. It also meant that he was going to do some heavy thinking.

Dickerson led me into the computer room. He took possession of the armchair that Hobbes sometimes used, moved it behind the desk, and sat down. He took a cigar out of his jacket pocket and lit it, inhaled a gallon or two of poison, and exhaled it as a dense black fog. It floated casually in my direction. Only then did he motion for me to take a chair — one that had wheels, but no arms. I sat down and pushed myself out of the range of the smoke.

"Alright, Houston, my boy. Talk to me." He leaned back in his chair and took another deep draw on his cigar and sent a passable smoke ring floating toward the ceiling.

I tried being polite; "Did you find the ashtray, Chief? Mr. Hobbes keeps one just for his old friends. Otis Slackmeyer used it about five years ago. Maybe you saw his obituary?" Polite? Maybe. Diplomatic? Maybe not. Tomorrow, this room would smell of stale cigars. I hated the smell of stale cigars.

"Smoke-free house, huh?" He looked at his cigar thoughtfully, then wet his thumb and forefinger with spit and pinched the end until the glow was gone. He flipped the dead cigar into the wastebasket.

"I can get by without it. Now, talk to me."

I put my hands out, palms up. "The rules say, you ask, I answer."

"If that's the way you want it. First question. Why does Hobbes say the old woman was murdered? The techs said it looked like a heart attack."

"Chief, I just got here, and I haven't seen the body, but I would say two people dying in the same house the same way might lead to suspicion of murder."

"Then how was it done? How would you do it?"

"I'd do it the way Hobbes told you it was done."

He held up his hand and stared at me thoughtfully. Then, he shook his head. "You know what he told us? Yeah, you'd know. Forget it.

"Question two. Hobbes called the coroner after he called the cops. Before we got here. Why? He said you could tell me better than him." He talked in short, abrupt sentences. Maybe that was his style of interrogation.

"If he's already talked to the coroner and told him what to look for in the autopsy, then, yeah, I know what he's looking for. It's not a true poison as such — except when someone drinks too much liquor — then the combination becomes deadly. We could all eat food with that poison in it without showing any ill effects. Most of us could even have one or two after-dinner drinks. A third might kill us."

"I read the autopsy report on Clyde Butler. There was nothing said about poison. Even the blood alcohol was pretty low. How do you and Hobbes explain that?"

"If you talked to Hobbes," I said, "then you already know."

"Question three. Why would they kill her? She's already eighty years old."

I answered that question and questions four to twenty-four the way I thought Hobbes would have, even though they seemed pointless or repetitive.

They ate up half an hour, but they kept me away from the crime scene. It took question twenty-five, "Where'd you go for breakfast?" for me to realize I had been suckered.

"That cigar was a good touch, Chief," I said as I stood up. "It distracted me for quite a while. I don't suppose you can tell me why you had to get me out of the way? Or was it Hobbes' idea?"

"Sit back down, Houston, or I'll have you tossed into the jug." He pushed himself out of Hobbes' favorite chair and walked around me to block the door.

"Huh-uh," I tried to make it sound like a snarl. "Move out of my way or I'll move you."

"You and what pack of girl scouts?"

A knock on the door saved either his butt or mine. Officer Carmody, one of the uniformed Mercater cops, called from beyond the door. "Hey, Chief. We need you out here."

"Be right there," Dickerson called back. To me, he said, "Forget it. I was through with you anyway." He opened the door and walked out, leaving it open for me.

I followed him into the hallway and stopped long enough to see the ambulance backing out into the street. One police car had already left.

The great room was empty except for Dickerson and Carmody, who had already begun gathering up their equipment, and for Hobbes who still sat looking at the same painting. As far as I could tell, he hadn't moved.

Chapter 26

After the police had departed and only Hobbes and I were left, he turned to me and said, "I'll listen to your report now, Abel."

I was ticked off, and of course he knew it; but, I had to tell him what I thought anyway.

"Had to be your idea, Car'l; Dickerson wouldn't have thought of it." In the past twenty years, I'd called him by his first name no more than a dozen times. Each time, because I couldn't think of anything worse to call him. "What is it that an ambulance crew and two cops can know, but I can't?" I stopped at the door on my way out. "When you get your report from Charon, you can keep that from me, too."

I went up to my room and sulked. Many years ago, when he had started keeping key elements of an investigation from me, he had explained it like this:

"Your face is remarkably ingenuous, Abel; so much so that you'd never be a good poker player or politician. You allow your emotions to show through unless you take great pains to hide them. A suspect spending time with you may deduce that we know no more than you know, and become overconfident, perhaps boastful. When he reaches that point, he dooms himself."

That was years ago. This was now.

The fact that he was probably right didn't make me feel any better.

"Bull," I said aloud. "You just want to be the hot shot private eye and get all the glory." I wished he could have heard me.

The truth was I was jealous.

I threw the darts over my shoulder again. Not a single one hit the target.

Ten minutes later, I came back down and gave him my report.

"A commendable job, Abel. Excellent pictures." He had studied them all, taking great pains to be sure he didn't miss anything. One of them, I couldn't see which, he studied for three minutes using a magnifying glass. He put them back in the envelope and placed them in a desk drawer. "Now, I have some more out-of-town business for you." He held up his hand before I could say anything. "This is not to get you out of the way; this time, I shall be going with you. Listen to this," he pressed a button on his answering machine.

Sally's voice. "Car'l," she had no trouble using his name. "If you can, you should come to the Kankakee Public Library tonight. There will be a speaker there whom you must see and listen to. I've already talked with him, and he is willing to meet with you after the seminar. He's supposed to be an expert on spirit possession. He has written a book about it. One of his cases is very interesting." She laughed delightedly. "Greg and I will be there, but if you can't, I'll see you at home in the morning. I've got a lot of things to talk to you about."

Hobbes said, "We should leave before six. Maybe by five. There are some good restaurants in Kankakee."

"Maybe the Homestead?" I suggested.

He nodded, and again turned his attention to the picture on the wall. The report was over. Hobbes barely commented on Charon's disarming the men at the restaurant, which was for me the highpoint of the New Year.

Fred came in as I was getting ready to leave. "Got a minute, Chief?" He sat down in the chair to the right, Hobbes' right, of the desk.

"Several minutes, if you need them."

Fred twisted the cap off of an imported beer, drank about half of it, and then wiped his mouth with the back of his hand. "Boss," he said a little reluctantly, "there ain't much out there. I talked to a hunnerd people, but nobody even hinted at something worth money. Ninety-eight of them said that there wasn't hardly any new folks in town that looked at all suspicious, so long as you left the Butler people out of it. And the Butlers just *looked* suspicious — they never done nothing." He tilted the beer and finished it off, then he continued slowly.

"The other two said some things I didn't want to hear."

"Like what, Fred?" Hobbes said.

"Part of it was about Sally and that undertaker. They was saying it weren't right for them to be dating, seeing as how they were dating in cemeteries."

Hobbes raised an eyebrow a quarter inch, a draconian effort for him. It showed how surprised he was. "They've pursued common interests for nearly a year; but dating? I'm not sure that Sally would agree to that, unless something changed last night."

"Nevertheless," Fred said woodenly, "that's what they're saying. And," he added, "one of them said she was too cute for an undertaker. If she wanted to be laid out, he said, he could take care of that — I damn near punched him. But, then the other one said, what's a mama's boy like him chasing around with her, anyway?"

Hobbes shook his head. "What was the other part that you didn't like?"

"Well," Fred opened a second beer and studied it for a few seconds, then placed it on the table without drinking any. "One of them said, 'That cripple's got it coming, wheelchair or not!' I said, 'What cripple?' but the other one gave him a look that shut him up, and I couldn't get any more out of them."

Hobbes put his hands to the ends of his moustache, then dropped them to the arms of his wheelchair. "Who were they?"

"That was at the *DIVE-INN* last night just before they closed. There were me and them and the barkeep, and that was all. When they left, I asked the barkeep who they were, but he didn't know; though he remembered one of them calling the other 'Tom.' They'd been in a few times, was all he could tell me.

"I'm sorry, Chief, but I didn't get home until almost four last night, and then I slept 'til noon. I went out soon's I got up and tried to find out some more, but there weren't nothing. So, I came back here." He picked up his beer and took a sip, then took a long drink, then said, "What the hell," and killed the bottle. He took out a roll of bills and handed them to me. "Didn't use any of it. Biggest waste of time I ever made."

"It was more useful than you think, Fred," Hobbes said. "Can you describe the two men?"

"Well, they was both about six feet tall, two hundred pounds, I guess. About Abel's age, thirty-five or so. One had thin black hair; the other was a blond. They both had a mean look about them. Come to think of it, when they left, there weren't neither one of them drunk."

Hobbes looked at me. I nodded, "Tom and Vic."

I briefly told Fred of our encounter at Flo's, and Hobbes promised to explain what happened to Grandma Kelch later.

I looked at my watch. It was already five o'clock; if we wanted supper before the seminar, we had to get going. It would take us forty-five minutes to get to Kankakee.

But, good food at the Homestead would have to wait. An hour wouldn't have been enough time to eat there, anyway.

Kelly Decker had rung the doorbell just as I was going out to bring the Town Car around front.

"Abel," she said, a hint of alarm in her voice, "Grandma Kelch, is she okay? Lemuel said an ambulance and police cars were here, and I haven't seen her for hours. I know she was coming to talk to Mr. Hobbes, but..."

"Come on," I said. "He'll tell you about it."

She stopped me with her hand on my arm. "An ambulance and police cars. She's dead, isn't she? Just like Clyde, in Hobbes' house."

"Yeah. She had a couple of drinks and passed out. Her heart stopped and they couldn't get it started. Look, Kelly, I wasn't here when she died; you need to talk to Hobbes."

She closed her eyes and kept hold of my arm. She tilted her head back and listened, "Hush, she's still here." She took a deep breath, and then whispered. "I've got to talk to her."

"Grandma Kelch is dead, Kelly."

"I know, but she wants to talk to me. To Hobbes."

"You want a séance, right now, with Hobbes!"

"Right now, while she's still here."

I shook my head. "Follow me."

Hobbes had backed his wheelchair away from his desk and was on the way out when Kelly stopped him.

"Please," she said. "Grandma wants to talk to us, to you."

Hobbes sent me a questioning glance.

I shrugged. "I told her she was dead, and that the ambulance had taken her to the morgue."

"Then, Kelly, you think her spirit is here. But there are only three of us; is that enough for a séance?"

"She's already here, Mr. Hobbes. I don't have to call her."

"Then we must go on with it."

"Yes, yes, we must hurry. Two chairs, Abel, and a small table."

It was the quickest séance I'd ever been a part of. I found a card table and set it and two chairs in front of Hobbes' wheelchair and then dimmed the lights as much as possible. Kelly and I sat across from each other; I took her left hand in my right, and Hobbes' right in my left. She took his left in her right, and we were ready.

She closed her eyes, and we waited a minute or two. Then, she began to speak in a soft voice, hardly more than a whisper.

"Grandma Kelch, we're here. Are you here?"

Kelly's voice changed; it became older, more forced. "Yes. Mr. Hobbes, do you know me?"

"Your voice is familiar," he answered.

"But do you *know* me? Do you believe in me?"

"I believe in anything that is real. Can you show yourself?"

The voice was silent for a minute, then it said, "My time grows short, so you must listen closely. The sickness comes from the roots of a rare tropical plant. The cure is in a compound made from the plant's leaves. Search Linda's room. You will find both. Also, tell Abel that she is back."

And with that cryptic announcement for me, the voice appeared to be finished. I felt her hand relax.

Kelly leaned back and let go of our hands. She shook her head enough to cause her hair to bounce a little, like she was trying to clear her thoughts. She looked at Hobbes first, then at me. It was me she asked, "Did Grandma Kelch tell you anything that I should know?"

"Yes," I said, "And it kills me to ask, but who was she talking about, when she said that she is back?"

"I'm only a conduit, Abel. I don't know what words are spoken through me."

Hobbes said, "It cannot be the one you are thinking of, Abel. Molly has been dead for a quarter of a century."

Kelly didn't seem concerned. "Spirits never die, Abel. Never, never, never."

"Is there some business concerning Grandma Kelch that is yet to be finished?" Hobbes asked.

"I think she wanted to be cremated," Kelly volunteered. "I don't know if she had any relatives that could say for sure, at least she never spoke about them. But then, she had only stayed with me for a few days."

"Did you know her before she came up here?"

"Oh, yes. I think everyone in south Kankakee knew her. She was one of the local characters."

"The burning question is, why did she come here for the holidays? She did not appear to belong here, yet she was staying with you. Are you and she related?"

"No," Kelly said. "She just called me a few days ago and said she was coming to visit. I said, sure, come on. She never gave me any reason."

Hobbes drummed his fingers on the arm of the wheelchair. It was a new habit he had acquired. It had a beat — I think it was *The Stars and Stripes Forever*.

Finally, he said. "Abel. It is after six p.m. If we are to be at the Kankakee Library by seven, we must be going. Miss Decker, thank you for your help. I shall probably call on you tomorrow. For now, I must bid you good evening."

"Then I'll say good night too, Mr. Hobbes. And good night, Abel." She waved her hand, and then let herself out the front door.

Half an hour later, when I first saw the van in the rear view mirror, we were a third of the way to Kankakee.

That old, ratty looking, white-mixed-with-rust van was badly in need of a drive through a car wash. It didn't have any rear side windows, just metal panels where glass ought to have been, so I assumed it was a cargo van.

What it didn't have was trouble keeping up with the Lincoln Town Car that I was driving. It never disappeared from my rear view mirror for very long, although I tested it twice to see if it could be following. Each time, I sped up until I was sure the driver couldn't see us and then slowed suddenly to make a turn off the main highway onto a secondary road; once on Highway 47 from Morris, and once on 113 from Coal City. Both times, only a few minutes had passed before the van showed up again in my rearview mirror.

Darkness had made us turn on our lights, so I had to watch the van by the shape and position of its headlights. By that time, I was sure it was the one that had hit Harmless Saturday morning, and as Lemuel had said, almost hit me; and it was the same one I'd seen parked at Flo's restaurant.

Chapter 27

Of course, I could have been wrong; maybe the van was just a look alike and had nothing to do with us. It could have been simply on its way to Kankakee, right? Yeah, sure. I nudged Hobbes with my elbow. He finished the paragraph he had been reading and marked the place with his finger, straightened the ends of his moustache with his other hand, and said, "Yes, Abel?"

I pointed over my shoulder. "They're following us?"

He twisted his head around to look out the back window. He saw mostly headlights. "Humph," my boss, Car'l Hobbes, said. "Do your hands itch?"

"They've begun to tingle."

"But not itch? As long as they're not itching, we don't have to worry." My itching hands had been our standard bit of contention for years. He had said it was either psychologically induced or coincidental. I had chosen not to debate the issue because it was our job to debunk cases of the paranormal or to prove that they were frauds or scams; saying that my hands itched whenever something bad was about to happen didn't seem to fit with our program.

The van disappeared when we reached Kankakee and turned east onto Court Street. We crossed the Kankakee River on the only small-town seven-lane bridge I had ever seen, and then drove halfway across town on Court to the courthouse. We turned right there and went two blocks south to the library. The van did not reappear in my mirror. I sighed in relief; it looked like the van hadn't followed us after all.

The library had its own parking lot half a block down and on the opposite side of its one-way street. It was a little far for Hobbes wheelchair, but there really wasn't any place closer that hadn't already been taken. So, I parked the car in the lot, got his wheelchair out of the trunk, and pushed him to the crosswalk. Then, because it was cooler than I had expected it would be, I went back to the car to get my jacket. A few cars went by us, but the growing darkness made it hard to notice any details.

Hobbes had started across before I got back, and it looked like he had plenty of time — the only vehicle approaching was half a block away. Then, I recognized the headlights.

I started running toward Hobbes. At the same time, the rear wheels on the van squealed in protest as the engine roared and the van lurched forward in sudden acceleration. Hobbes didn't see either one of us coming. His eyes and his concentration were focused on crossing the street without screwing up his wheelchair.

"Look out, Chief!" I yelled.

The van's intent was clear. Get him, or get him and me. There was no chance of Hobbes making it across the street on his own. The van's headlights shut off, as if the driver wanted us to see into the cab, to see who was coming after us. Then, they came back on and became twin spotlights focused directly on Hobbes and his wheelchair. He was its target, frozen like a wild animal caught in the bright lights of a car along some deserted country road. In seconds, he would be road kill.

But ironically, those same lights showed me how to get him out of there. They illuminated the curb and the sidewalk and the ramp that connected them. If I could get Hobbes to that ramp... I put on my wildest burst of speed, racing the van to get to Hobbes first. My feet barely touched the pavement until I slammed into the back of his wheelchair, forcing him to almost double up. I leaned on his back so that I could grab the steel rails on the wheels. I used my momentum to lift the wheelchair an inch or two off the pavement and take it flying forward six or eight feet, like a stock car clearing a ramp. I let go of the wheels an instant before they hit ground and gripped the wheelchair's armrests. Still running, but not as fast as I had been, I pushed Hobbes off the street and up the ramp. I let go of the wheel chair and watched it cross the sidewalk and come to rest against a building.

And then, I fell flat on the cement with my feet still in the street. The van raced towards me.

The driver wanted more than just my feet. He wanted me.

He swerved sharply at the last second and ran both of the driver's side wheels right over my stomach. At least six inches up and over my stomach. The sharp turn and the raised edge of the ramp where the van made impact were enough to tilt the van and cause it to run twenty feet on only the two right wheels. Nothing touched me.

The van righted itself and continued on down the street.

I stood up and checked myself for damage. I had escaped unscathed.

I looked around for witnesses. None of those were around, either. The incident had happened at a moment when the sidewalks were completely empty.

Hobbes turned his wheelchair around to face me. As usual, he didn't seem to be excited, but he did look puzzled for a moment. He put his hands on his knees and then shook his head. "Abel, are you alright?"

"A little winded is all, Chief. I'm sorry I had to rough you up. Did I do something to your legs?"

"I thought I felt some tingling in my muscles. The feeling's gone, but I'm alive and well. Thank you, Abel. It seems you have once again saved my life."

I waved his thanks off. "It was my turn, Chief. Are we going to call the cops?"

He shook his head. "Not yet. Not without witnesses."

My heartbeat was returning to normal. I didn't want to take any more chances with the traffic, so with eyes open, all eyes open, his and mine, I pushed him the rest of the way to the library.

We waited for the library's elevator. "That was the third time they've tried to kill me, Chief."

"Then, we must stop their clumsy attempts before pure chance gives them success. We shall find them and deal with them."

"Tomorrow," I said. "When we're back home."

"Tomorrow."

* * *

Under ordinary circumstances, if Barry Oldsmith could have chosen who would come to his seminar, Car'l Hobbes would not have made the list. Hobbes has earned a reputation of sorts as a vocal skeptic who has the annoying habit of taking apart a speaker's claim to anything supernatural, if not the speaker himself. For the moment though, Oldsmith's expression was one of pleasant neutrality as Hobbes wheeled his way into the main reading area of the library. The library didn't have any conference rooms, but other patron's weren't a problem; the library had closed for the evening, except for the seminar.

Oldsmith waited in silence as my boss backed into a free space by the wall and near the exit. Hobbes probably thought that his bald head and droopy moustache would be less conspicuous if he stayed pretty much behind everybody else. He was about as inconspicuous as prime rib at his dinner table would have been, if his pyrophobic chef had prepared it.

I pulled up a chair and sat down next to him.

A minute later, the librarian introduced the guest speaker as Dr. Barry Oldsmith, PhD, author of *Lost Souls of the Midwest* and eminent authority on reincarnation and spirit possession. The small group applauded politely as he stepped to the podium. He smiled briefly, not looking at Hobbes, and began.

"Of all the legends and folk tales of the supernatural, there are probably none more exasperating, more confusing, than those that concern Susan Kelch."

He had gone quickly to the reason Sally had called us out. Susan Kelch. He probably started that way because of whatever Sally had said to him. She wanted him to get the boss' attention right at the start.

Oldsmith absent-mindedly shuffled his thin sheaf of notes as he looked over the twenty or so people who had come to listen to him.

I followed his glance around the room. Retired teachers, retired doctors, retired preachers, and a few younger people, whom I supposed were trying to get a handle on life, made up the group. He let his eyes stop on me for a second and I felt slightly out of place — too young for the older group, and too old for the younger group.

He finally acknowledged Car'l Hobbes. He bowed at the waist, straightened up and said, "A pleasure to see you, sir," he said dryly. "Your reputation precedes you."

Several people looked back at the man in the wheelchair, then at each other and shrugged. Obviously, his reputation did not reach the entire room.

"Car'l Hobbes," Oldsmith explained to the group, "is a paranormal investigator without peer. You might call him the spokesman for the mundane. I look forward to his skepticism and his many thought-provoking questions, which I'm sure we'll hear before the evening is finished." He didn't sound as if he looked forward to anything Hobbes might have to say.

Hobbes didn't care to be singled out, but he returned the bow with a tilt of his head.

Oldsmith continued, "Does anyone here not know who Susan Kelch was?"

About ten hands went up, excluding Hobbes' and mine.

"Ah," he said. "Our expert investigator did not raise his hand. So, Mr. Hobbes, would you enlighten us?"

"All of these people have come to listen to you, Dr. Oldsmith," Hobbes said. "I would be a disappointment."

"Not in the least," Oldsmith said. "I presume you will have your say later, to my discomfort." He held up his book. "It's all in here; I have several copies available for those who wish to take one home." He placed the book on the podium and placed his notes on top of the book. Then, he put his elbows on the notes and his chin in his hands, as if he was gathering his thoughts.

He straightened up and put his hands in his pockets, and began his lecture.

"Susan Kelch was a real person, although the name I gave her in this book is Belinda Offwitch. I mention that now for the benefit of our friends from

Mercater, because they may know Susan Kelch. She was born in 1969 to real parents, but orphaned in 1983. For the next two years, she lived with her grandmother who, some said, quietly and constantly blamed her for her parents' death. In 1985, Susan attempted to drown herself, but failed. Her body continued to live, but her mind was gone." Oldsmith looked directly at Hobbes. "All of this is well documented in my book, referenced and cross-referenced, and taken from unimpeachable sources."

Hobbes nodded. "Most of whom are still alive?"

"Many of them, Mr. Hobbes. It's only been about two decades."

Not surprisingly, Hobbes didn't have much to say. He didn't want to risk antagonizing the man Sally had arranged for him to talk with after the meeting. At least not yet. Clyde Butler's murder and the attempt on his own life had him preoccupied, anyway.

Oldsmith continued, "According to the story, Susan had become an empty vessel. Her body was easily taken over by the spirit of a young woman — call her Linda — who had died in a terrible fire a few months before. Linda, wearing Susan's body, had been able to convince her family that she was really Linda come back from the dead."

Oldsmith's story was not unique in any major sense. There were many stories of a spirit losing its own body and possessing somebody else's, but this one seemed to have a lot of relevance to the Clyde Butler case.

Hobbes was quiet for the rest of the lecture, and without his questions, the meeting became something of a bore and I lost interest in Oldsmith. Five minutes later, I begun to doze off. I glanced at my boss to see if Oldsmith was putting him to sleep too, but Hobbes was wide awake and seemed to be enjoying himself. I watched him slide his hands down both sides of his moustache twice in thirty seconds. What made him so excited?

Frankly, I knew almost everything that he did and I didn't see any reason for joy. I had not even heard of Oldsmith before today, but Hobbes was still gleeful.

I leaned over and whispered in his ear, "What's so damned funny?"

"Study his face, Abel, and his mannerisms. You'll see for yourself."

So I did. Sixty seconds later I whispered, "Right on, Chief." I should have seen it earlier. Sally had known how much Hobbes would enjoy meeting Oldsmith. It set the Butler case one giant step forward. For the moment, I just wanted him to know that I knew, too.

Sally and Greg Frazier came in just before Oldsmith finished his lecture and waited back by the door until the main lights were turned on. Hobbes motioned for them to come over. His first question was, "How did you find him, Sally?"

"We went looking for his grave. We couldn't find it. We couldn't find any record of his death or official death certificate either, although the Ransoms had been living in Watseka at that time. They didn't seem to have any reason to bury him out of town, but he wasn't cremated, either." She smiled suddenly, and I could tell she wanted to dance. "Then, we talked to the local funeral directors to see if they remembered Frank Ransom from seventeen years ago. Greg," she took his hand as if she was used to it, "wanted to go partying 'cause he was sure no one would know anything that we didn't already know, but, I said, let's check one more place. Guess where we checked."

Hobbes studied her for a few seconds, and then said, "Would it be too much of a coincidence to say that the Frazier Brothers have a branch in Watseka?"

Sally jumped up and tried to lead an embarrassed Greg Frazier in an impromptu dance around the library. A minute later, she sat down. "Car'l, you are so smart! Yes. Greg's uncle was there, and he remembered the funeral. It had all been prearranged by Frank Ransom; everything but the body."

"And," said Hobbes, "I suppose he would have been cremated, so only ashes remained."

"There weren't any insurance claims so there wasn't any fraud. Frank wanted only one thing."

Hobbes nodded. "Exactly. What any sensible man would do, given his circumstances — to die or to disappear. Either choice would be preferred over living with that woman."

Chapter 28

Barry Oldsmith finished autographing a couple of his books, and walked over to our group, smiling. "Mr. Hobbes," he said.

Hobbes held out his hand, "Mr. Ransom, Frank Ransom, it's my pleasure."

"Please call me Barry Oldsmith. I am the only man left of the Watseka Oldsmiths. They have allowed me to use it as a *nom de guerre* for many years, and now I am the only living Oldsmith in the county, maybe even in the state, to carry that name. I should not care to have it associated with that other."

"Of course," Hobbes said.

"Your girl is a remarkable search engine. I still don't know how she found me, but I'll tell you, Mr. Hobbes, it was a delight to open up to her. It seems I had been waiting for years to finally talk to someone."

"Perhaps we could wait another half an hour," Hobbes began.

I interrupted, "Yeah, I don't know about Sally or Greg, but Hobbes and I haven't eaten since noon. By the way, I'm Abel Houston from the Piltdown Houstons."

"Piltdown?" Oldsmith asked.

"The lady we haven't yet spoken about said I was a Neanderthal."

"And you have evolved to what, Cro-Magnon?" He shook his head. "Katya called me many things worse than that.

"And this other young man," He held his hand out to Greg. "We have not been introduced. You are a friend of Sally's? When she first came to see me, she was alone."

Sally answered for Greg, "This is Greg Frazier, my associate in the cemetery business."

Greg said, "Mr. Oldsmith," and nodded his head, and then reluctantly shook the older man's hand.

Oldsmith looked thoughtfully at the younger man. "You are a part of the Frazier Brothers who run the funeral home of that name?"

"A hungry part," Greg said.

"Well, I think the Homestead is still open, and I'm hungry, too. So, let's go. You can follow me there. I have a little more to say." Ten minutes later we were at the Homestead. I hadn't seen the old van anywhere.

It was a long supper, partly because we took our time to savor the food, but mostly because Oldsmith did have a little more to say; quite a little more in fact, even though the serious talk didn't begin until the five of us shared a bottle of chilled champagne. Well, four of us shared it; Hobbes ordered an imported beer. An expensive imported beer, which he later told the waitress was almost as good as what he drank at home.

Oldsmith occasionally paused to study the ceiling, while he explained why he and Katya had gone their separate ways. "Marriage to Kate started out all right," he admitted, "until the miscarriages came. She had three in two years. They devastated her, and when the fourth pregnancy took hold, it kept her home and mostly in bed for seven months. Then, when the baby was born, Kate was terrified that something was going to happen if she left her alone for even a minute. She became obsessed with the idea. Her whole life became the baby. She smothered her with attention. Did everything for her. Almost never let her out of her sight. Poor Baby Linda. She never had a chance to be a baby with other babies, or a little girl with other little girls, either.

"A few months after she learned to talk, she quit calling Kate Mommy, and for no reason that I could see, started calling her Katya. Kate loved it. So, instead of teaching Linda to call her Mommy again, she insisted everyone else call her Katya."

When Hobbes asked about Lucas, Oldsmith said ruefully, "Who? Oh yeah, Lucas. Born when Linda was eight years old. Now, there was a sad boy. Katya resented him from the moment of conception, and resented me for being a part of it. She neglected him as a baby and as a child, and yet, he spent his life trying to please Mommy."

The waitress interrupted him, "We close in fifteen minutes. Can I get you anything else? Last chance."

Hobbes said, "Just the check, please."

Oldsmith said, "There's a lot more, but it's all in the book. Bluntly put, when Linda was twelve years old, spirits began talking through her, and continued until she was sixteen. They quit when some boy got her pregnant. Katya's world shattered. It seemed her little girl had a life of her own. Katya couldn't take it, so she sent Linda away until the baby was born, and then tried to get her back. Linda wouldn't come. Instead, she began having seizures, fits. They were so bad, the state took the baby and put Linda in the hospital, right here in Mercater. When she was twenty-four years old, her cottage caught fire and she died.

"It became impossible to live with Katya. And when I inherited some money, I put it all in a trust for her, cancelled my insurance policies so there wouldn't be any charges of fraud, and then arranged my 'death.'

"The rest is unimportant, and the night is late. I'll say this much, though, it has been a relief to tell my story to Sally and again to all of you."

Hobbes said, "There are many questions that I'd like to ask, especially about Linda's spirit possession. Can we talk again?"

Oldsmith shook his head. "Only if you are desperate. Some of the memories are painful."

"As a last resort, then." Hobbes held out his hand. "It has been a pleasure, sir."

It was past midnight when we parted company. Oldsmith said he was leaving early in the morning for another lecture in another city. Greg went looking for a pay phone to call home so that his family wouldn't worry, and ended up using the bar's phone because they didn't have a pay phone that was working. Like many people in Mercater where cellular service was so spotty, he didn't always think to carry his cell phone. It was a toll call to home, but the waitress said to forget it. Hobbes had left a pretty decent tip. Sally tried to get the bartender to dance with her, but he was too cautious, being a married man and all.

On the way home, Hobbes and I talked about the van and Tom and Vic, and our close encounters.

"Me three times and you once, chief," I said. "That could have been a matter of simple opportunity, since I am out and about more than you are."

"It isn't so much opportunity as it is motive, Abel. They are not professional or we'd both be dead by now, so they are amateurs. Who would hire amateurs?"

"Someone who wouldn't know how to find the pros."

"Does that make them less dangerous?"

"No sir, but only because they're persistent and only until we stop them." A pair of headlights appeared briefly in my rearview mirror then disappeared in one of the valleys the road led us through. A minute later they appeared again, then disappeared again. This time they were much closer.

Hobbes, who had been watching me watch the rear view mirror, asked, "Do you have a gun with you, Abel?"

"No, sir. I didn't think going to a library would be dangerous. In any case, the headlights behind us are not those of the van."

Three more sets of headlights appeared in the next few minutes, and I let them all pass us.

"Maybe they've given up," I said.

Hobbes didn't answer me at first, and when I glanced at him, he seemed to be deep in thought.

"Abel," he said suddenly. "Will your cell phone work out here?"

"Might. You can try."

"Do you know where Oldsmith is staying?"

"He said the Kankakee Crazy Eight."

"How quickly can you get us there?"

"Twelve, fourteen minutes."

"Do it. I'll work the phone."

I braked and made a hard U-turn without waiting for a cross road, or even a driveway to turn around in. It wouldn't have been a problem in Sally's Bronco, but the Town Car was longer, heavier, and had rear-wheel drive. The rear wheels spun the car around, cutting into the gravel shoulder that had been made soft by the unseasonably warm weather. Helplessly, I felt the car go into a skid and slide backwards into the ditch. The car had plenty of power, but no traction. I had successfully and completely grounded us.

"Damn, damn, damn!" I muttered my only defense.

Hobbes ignored our situation, and me as I got out and surveyed the damage. Nothing that a tow truck wouldn't handle.

He had better luck. The phone was in a working zone. I heard him ask for the Crazy Eight's number, and then dial it.

The volume on the phone was cranked up so that I could hear both sides of the conversation.

Hobbes said, "This is an urgent call. I need to talk to Barry Oldsmith. Will you ring his room for me, please?"

"Hey, Mister, it's one a.m. People like to get some sleep, you know."

"People also want to live through the night. Please connect me."

"Listen, two men have already been here and got his room number. I suppose they're going to kill him, huh?" He put a lot of sarcasm in those words.

"And you shall have to explain that to the police when he is found dead in your motel room. Now CONNECT ME!" The last two words came out in a roar.

"Okay, okay, keep your shirt on."

I heard the phone ring and Oldsmith's voice saying, ""Hello, just a minute, someone's at the door."

Again, Hobbes roared. "DON'T OPEN THE DOOR! DO YOU HEAR ME? DO NOT OPEN THAT DOOR!"

After a moment of silence, Oldsmith picked up the phone again. "Hobbes, is that you? Two of your men just called from the office, and they're at my door right now."

"They are not my men, Mr. Oldsmith. They are assassins. If you open the door to them, they will kill you. You must hang up the phone right now and call the police. Do you understand?"

"Yes," the man answered in a badly shaken voice. "I will. I will." He hung up the phone.

"If they don't break the door down," Hobbes said, "we may have been in time."

"Okay, then. Right now, we need to get out of here. Do you want to call a tow truck, or do you want me to?"

His answer came in a different form as a white Ford Bronco flashed by us, and then suddenly stopped. Hobbes said, "Forget the tow truck, Abel. An angel of the highway has arrived."

The driver backed up and stopped on the shoulder near the Town Car. Sally got out, and seeing we were both okay, laughed at our distress. Greg followed her, but he seemed to be more concerned about the time than alarmed about our being in an accident. He glanced several times at his wristwatch, making sure Sally saw him.

"This won't take long, Greg," she assured him.

He reluctantly agreed. "You know Uncle Herman. He worries himself into a frenzy if I'm late."

"You can use Car'l's phone to call him," she said.

"Well, I guess we'll only be a few minutes."

Uncle Herman, he'd said. I'd known Herman Frazier was his adopted uncle, but not much else about his family. Well, I thought, big deal. As long as Sally knew. My mind rambled on — Sally was an angel of the highway, right? So what should we call Greg? He was an undertaker, so maybe we could call him an angel of death? The thought seemed unkind, so I kept it to myself. Greg Frazier didn't seem to have that sort of a sense of humor, anyway.

How many girls had a winch on the front of their cars, I wondered, or felt comfortable using one? I could think of two or three possibilities, but only one certainty; our own Sally Hudson. She set out two warning flares, backed her Bronco to about thirty feet in front of the Town Car, unwound enough cable to make the hookup, told me to put the tranny in neutral, and engaged the winch. Sixty seconds later, the car was out of the ditch. The whole operation up to that point had taken less than ten minutes.

Rewinding the winch and saying she'd see us at home took another five, and then she and Greg were gone.

Sally hadn't asked how we'd ended in the ditch, and Hobbes didn't offer an explanation. Neither the lack of a question, nor the lack of an explanation surprised me. For good or for bad, that was the way things were often done in Hobbes' house when we were working on a case.

Before we put the Town Car in motion, Hobbes made one more call to the Crazy Eight. When he identified himself, the night clerk exclaimed, "Man, you really got things going around here! As soon as you got off the phone, I decided those two guys didn't look right and I called the cops. It was, like, so cool. Like they were right here. Man, they caught one guy trying to kick the door down, and the other guy breaking the window. They actually had a shootout! Like they were Wyatt Earp and the Clancy brothers at the OK Corral. Like they shot it out with the police. They had to take both of them away in ambulances!"

"Dead or alive?" Hobbes asked.

"They didn't look too much alive, for sure."

"Thank you, my friend," Hobbes said. "Now, could you connect me to Mr. Oldsmith's room?"

Barry Oldsmith was on an emotional high. "You saved my life, Hobbes. They came with automatic weapons. I'd have been a dead man now if I'd opened that door."

"Do you know who they were, or who sent them?

"All I know is one of them said you sent them with a package you were supposed to have given me at the library. Then, the cops showed up and used a bullhorn to tell them to surrender. A lot of gunfire exploded around me, so I jumped behind the bed. The police are here now. I've been trying to explain that I don't know why those two were trying to kill me."

"Their names are Tom and Vic," Hobbes said. "And I do not yet know why they were after you. We will return to Kankakee if the police will allow me to talk to them."

'You could talk to them, but I don't think they'd talk back. And you'd have to go to the morgue to do it."

"Well, then," Hobbes sounded defeated. "No justice would be served by my return to Kankakee tonight, but perhaps you would like for me to keep you apprised of the progress in the case. Your right to live has been challenged, and it may be challenged again."

"Then, you want my phone number?'"

Hobbes shrugged. "If it's convenient."

Oldsmith recited the number, and added, "Call me, Mr. Hobbes. I shall be glad to discuss things of merit with you."

"Things of merit?"

"Yeah," Oldsmith said. "That means anything that's of interest to you."

"Then, expect to hear from me." Hobbes sighed, and then added, "The police will wonder how I knew to warn you, and they will wish to talk with me. Ask one of them to come to the phone."

Fifteen minutes later, Hobbes finally convinced the Kankakee policeman that he had told them all he knew, and that if they would send an officer to his house in Mercater sometime tomorrow, he would make a statement. Perhaps Chief Dickerson could take care of that for them, and they wouldn't have to send someone. Finally I started the car and began the drive home.

"It's already tomorrow, and things don't look a lot better so far," I grumbled at Hobbes. I had the feeling that something big was going to happen. Bigger than Grandma Kelch's murder.

Stephen Stillwell

My hands began to itch, again.

Chapter 29

I slept late the next morning, Tuesday morning, but I woke up wondering how much we had really accomplished the day before as far as solving Clyde's murder went. We didn't have any evidence of foul play where he or Jane was concerned; and as far as I knew, Grandma Kelch had died a natural death.

Details about Vic and Tom were sketchy at best, but I still had to go into Kankakee to identify them, and to explain why I thought they had been trying to kill Hobbes and me. The police weren't satisfied with my explanation, but then neither was I.

*****

Rich had ridden his bike to the cemetery very early in the morning and spent a couple of hours leaning against a tombstone near Clyde's grave. He had taken some pictures he'd laminated in plastic and mounted them on a small easel that was attached to a metal rod. He had driven the rod deep into the ground where the headstone would eventually be planted. The pictures were three-by-fives; one was of Clyde, Jane, and Rich in a family portrait that seemed serious but was somehow alive with feelings for each other. A second picture was a candid shot of father and son playing one-on-one with a basketball on the asphalt in front of their garage. The third was Clyde alone, a much younger man in a tuxedo, his face glowing, his right hand pointing to the ring on his left hand.

In the course of that evening, Rich had told his plans for the next day, Wednesday. He had said he would ride the bus to school in the morning, even though he could have stayed home a couple more days. He said his grieving was done, and Dad would have wanted him to get on with his life. He'd stop at the cemetery after school for his final goodbye and then walk home. Those were his plans.

Wednesday morning, we had no reason to think he hadn't spent the night at home; Linda Butler, though she had rapped on his door to get him up for school and hadn't been answered, assumed he'd spent the night on Hobbes' couch. He wouldn't have been missed until that evening, if it hadn't been for Lemuel.

And if it hadn't been for Lemuel, the Hobbes' household would probably all have died that Wednesday morning.

That morning had come, and with it a phone call from Lemuel. I had said "Hello" and heard the handset on the other end clatter against the floor. For a few seconds, I had wondered how good an oversized dart my phone would make if I threw it at the Astronaut of the month.

Frankly, I was getting tired of Lemuel Dathan's early morning calamities. They played havoc with my peace-of-mind, especially on mornings like this when I was trying to catch up on a little sleep.

"Abel," he said with a curious calmness to his voice. "Is Richard somewhere in your house?"

I didn't have a ready answer for him because special alarms began going off in my head. The smell of sulfur dioxide was heavy in the air. SO2. Rotten eggs. An additive in city gas to warn people about a gas leak. Gas. I could smell it upstairs in my bedroom with the door closed. A bad leak. For the moment, Rich took second place. I said, "Call the fire department, Lem. This house is full of gas. I've got to get everyone out."

"Gas? Yeah, sure. Right now!"

I took a deep breath and opened the door and ran down the hallway yelling, "Sally, Sally! Gas leak! Get up and get out! Sally, do you hear me?"

"Yes, Abel. Yes, I hear you."

I held what was left of my breath as I took the stairs three at a time to the main floor, ran through the kitchen, and opened the door to the basement stairs. I yelled down to Fred, "Gas leak, get out!"

The rushing hiss of gas was coming from behind the stove, but I didn't bother looking for the leak. I grabbed a wrench from the tool box near the back door and ran to the gas shutoff valve that fed the outside meter. It took only seconds to shut it off.

I hadn't worried about Hobbes to that point. He always slept with at least one window open and the door closed. He probably hadn't even smelled the gas, though I was making enough of a racket to awaken everybody in the house. Nevertheless, I yelled at him through his window. He answered, and I told him what was happening.

Hobbes was calm, of course. He merely said, "The wind is from the west, Abel. If both front and back doors are open, the gas will be dispersed through the back door, and there should be no further threat of a gas explosion."

"Yeah, but are you coming out, Chief?"

"The danger seems to have passed. I shall wait here."

The front door was locked and my keys were upstairs, so I had to hold my breath again as I ran through the house. In a minute or two, I had the front door, patio doors, and all the windows I could quickly access flung opened.

Sally and Fred met me in front of the house. Sally was still in her pajamas, but Fred had pulled on a pair of overalls. They had both checked on Hobbes; he had said for them to wait out front for me.

A minute and a half later, the first fire truck arrived. The fire chief showed up a minute later. Two firemen went in wearing gas masks, and opened all the windows and doors they could find that I hadn't already opened, and then set up an exhaust fan to pull out the rest of the gas. It took more than an hour to satisfy them that the house was clear.

The chief said I'd handled the emergency well, and then proceeded to chew me out for going back into the house to open the front door, and then he chewed Hobbes out for staying in the house. Before he left, he showed us where one end of the flexible copper tubing behind the gas range had somehow come unscrewed and dropped down, venting unrestricted natural gas into the kitchen.

"My guess," said the fire chief just before he left, "is that the installer did not, I repeat, did not forgot to tighten the fitting. And I don't think it just unscrewed itself and dropped off. If you'd waited another hour, just turning a light on or off could have given a big enough spark to blow this house up. I call that attempted murder and I've informed Chief Dickerson. He'll be out later this morning."

After he left, Fred said, "I knew that damned gas range was trying to kill us." He stood outside near Hobbes' window as he said it.

Hobbes' answer was, "Get dressed and meet me in the kitchen."

Back in my room, I remembered the phone call that had awakened me. What had Lemuel said? "Is Richard somewhere in your house?"

My throat suddenly felt dry. I called him back and he said, "Did Richard spend the night there?"

I had a vision of the boy lying somewhere overcome by gas. The firemen hadn't been looking for any bodies because we'd assured them everyone was out.

"I don't think so, but we'll look. Are you sure he isn't home? In the workshop or garage, maybe?"

"Huh-uh, Rich and I were supposed to meet on our steps at six o'clock and go to McDonald's for breakfast before he went to school. I came down a few minutes early and waited until ten minutes after but he never showed up. I looked through the house, but the only thing I found was that his bed hadn't been slept in. I woke up Linda and Luke, and they said he'd probably spent the night at your house. Did he, Abel?"

"No, Lem, I'm sure he didn't, but we'll look around and then I'll call you back." It took forty seconds to change from pajamas to street clothes and exit my room to the upstairs hallway. I rapped loudly on Sally's door at the end of the hall. She answered, "What is it?"

"Crisis," I answered. "We need you downstairs."

I went on to check the guest room and the room that used to be Fred's until he had set up housekeeping in the basement. Rich wasn't in any of those places, alive or dead, nor was he in the bathroom. I hadn't expected him to be.

Downstairs, I checked the kitchen, dining room, great room, computer room, bathroom, and then pounded on Hobbes' door. He opened it immediately, already in his wheelchair.

"What else has happened, Abel?"

"Rich has disappeared. I'm going to check the basement."

Fred was still in his basement room, but he had the door open and was watching one of the early morning talk shows. "Hey, Abel, you gotta see this! They got a guy on here who's married the same woman seven times. Now, they're getting their first divorce and she's asking for seven-eighths of everything he's got."

"Rich has disappeared, Fred. We've searched the house except for the basement. He's not here, is he?

He clicked his remote to shut off the TV. "Nope. Did you check the boathouse or the garage?"

"The garage? No. C'mon." I checked the garage's attic while Fred looked inside the Town Car and the van, and then unlocked the door to the finished but almost unused workshop that took up a third or more of the garage. The shop had been there when Hobbes had bought the house, but with a neighborhood handyman like Clyde Butler willing to do good work at a reasonable price, the incentive to do our own work had been almost nonexistent. With him gone, would that change? I didn't know.

The garage had been built with a tall, roomy attic. Years before Hobbes bought the property, it had been made into an insulated, paneled, decent one-bedroom apartment with a small kitchen and a large living room. No one had ever lived there as far as I knew, but we called it the Mother-in-Law's Escape.

It was empty. So, said Fred, was the rest of the garage.

Charon was just coming back from his morning patrol of the river when we knocked on the door. He called to us from the riverbank, "Go in, it's open."

We waited for him, anyway. When he was close enough that we could talk without yelling, I said, "Rich is missing. He wouldn't be in here, would he?"

Charon opened the door and we followed him inside. "Ain't seen the boy since yesterday, and there ain't no place in here for him to hide."

"We're grasping at straws, Charon," I said. "He could be anywhere."

"Butler house clean? Who looked at it?"

"Lemuel called us half an hour ago. He said Rich wasn't there. Anyway, Hobbes is going to want us pretty quick.

"I'll be a-waitin', my boy."

"Nothing?" Hobbes asked Fred and me as we came into the kitchen. He had set the coffeemaker to work and pulled his wheelchair up to the table. Sally was stirring up some pancake batter while the griddle was heating, and had some bacon cooking in the microwave and a bowl of scrambled eggs waiting to be stirred into a frying pan. Fred took a deep breath and let it out slowly. It was supposed to be his kitchen, but with Rich missing, the situation was changed. We needed a good breakfast. So, Fred kept silent and let Sally do the cooking. No one said anything more about the gas leak.

"Nothing," I repeated.

"I had intended to discuss the gas leak, and who was responsible for it, but that will wait. Instead, I would like to have Mr. Dathan join us for breakfast, or at least for coffee."

"Right," I said, and reached for the phone.

It was nearly nine o'clock when we all took a place at the table. Breakfast was good, although Lemuel took only coffee, but I couldn't say just how good. I was too busy studying him. I thought he might at least knock over a salt shaker, but he didn't.

Hobbes asked him if he had any suggestions.

"Yes sir. Call Rich's friends. Call the police. Check his father's gravesite. I feel we have until midnight, no longer."

"I shall leave it to the police to talk to his friends, most of whom none of us would know. I will send Abel to the cemetery, although I think he will not have spent the night there."

Dathan clasped his hands together, put them behind his head and tilted his chair back. That seemed a pretty reckless thing for him to do, and I started to say something along that line when the chair tipped over. Dathan rolled out and came lightly back to his feet. He picked up the chair and sat back down. "Excuse me," he said. "It's hard not to do that."

Hobbes said pointedly, "Hard not to be clumsy? Is your clumsiness deliberate?"

He shook his head. "Not deliberate. More of a subconscious thing. Believe it or not, I was a gymnast in high school. Until I started bumping into things."

"You were a gymnast?" Hobbes repeated.

"Yeah, and a pretty good one. I was small and quick and competed one year in the state semi-finals. Then, suddenly my coordination went south, and I had to give it up. I had an inner ear problem, and the cure took a year. By that time I had become interested in genealogy and decided I had to find out what kind of people my ancestors were. I'm adopted, but I do know that some of them were actually from around here."

"So, you just moved to Mercater?"

"It was almost that simple, Mr. Hobbes. Mercater High School needed a history teacher and when I applied for the job, they hired me. At about the same time, Clyde was looking for renters. We met, liked each other, and I moved in."

Chapter 30

Lemuel seemed ready to say more, but then he shook his head. "It's Rich we're here to talk about, Mr. Hobbes."

"You are right, of course, Lemuel, but I still need to know how you fit into this mystery."

"I don't, really. I rented the apartment from Clyde, and started teaching at the high school. I didn't know anything was going on until a few days before New Year's."

"I see," Hobbes said. He didn't sound either surprised or disappointed; nor did he sound convinced. "Remember the van that hit the cat on New Year's Day?"

"Harmless? Of course. The cat that came back from the dead."

"The van was driven by two men, Vic and Tom. Did you know them?"

Lemuel suddenly sounded evasive. "I've seen them around now and then."

"They made three attempts at murder," He looked up at the clock, "during the last eighteen hours and maybe one as early as last Saturday."

"Who... how?"

"The 'who' are Abel, Barry Oldsmith, possibly Charon, and me. The 'how' was to run Abel and me down with that old white van, or to shoot Abel and Charon during a phony robbery, or else to shoot Oldsmith in his motel room."

Lemuel seemed surprised. "They are residents at MerSH. I've seen them when I went looking for backgrounds, for genealogies."

"How long have they lived there?"

"I don't know. I've heard twenty years or so. Why not ask them?"

"They wouldn't answer."

Dathan didn't ask why they wouldn't answer. Instead he grew thoughtful. "I was thinking, Kelly might know them. She was a patient there a long time ago. She almost got killed in a fire. She had to have a lot of plastic surgery to get her looks back."

Hobbes suddenly held up his hand for silence. He closed his eyes and gripped the wheel rails and rocked the wheelchair slowly back and forth.

Three or four minutes passed by. Sally refilled our coffees, and we waited. Hobbes was in the midst of a revelation. I sipped my coffee and tried to figure out what it was. I thought I should be able to reach some sort of conclusion; hopefully, the same as he had. As usual, I was wrong.

When he stopped rocking his wheelchair and opened his eyes, it was to say, "Fred, will you bring the car around. Abel, I'm going to the Administration building at MerSH where I hope to be given access to some records. While I am gone, I would like for you to prepare the great room for a meeting. The guest list and the time, I shall give to you when I return."

"Should I still check the cemetery?"

"He is unlikely to be there, but it is worth a look. Also, you should call Bull Dickerson and talk to him about the gas leak and about Richard's disappearance. Ask him to check Richard's school. There is the slightest chance that he spent the night somewhere else and is at school this morning. Finally, tell him we shall have a meeting this afternoon, and invite him to come. Tell him the meeting will be at five o'clock and that I will name the person or persons who killed Clyde Butler.

"After he agrees to that, tell him we may need his help convincing one or two people that they should be here."

"Sally, go to the county clerk's office in Watseka and get copies of the birth certificates of Luke and Linda Ransom and of Susan Kelch, and see if the doctors who delivered them or treated them as children are still practicing, and if they are, talk to them. Get any impressions they are willing to give you. Ask if Luke and Susan could have pulled off the deception as they so claimed? Ask if they have fooled other people."

The rest of the morning passed, and early afternoon came. Hobbes had returned from his visit to the Administration building. He wasn't happy. He had the look of a storm brewing inside, with thunder and lightning ready to strike out.

Sally called at 1:30, and Hobbes had me listen in.

"Nobody knows anything," she said, "except that Frank and Katya Ransom adopted Susan after Linda died, and then changed Susan's name to Linda. Frank died about a year later, they said, and then the Ransoms pretty much dropped out of sight. They didn't have many friends. Even Luke, who was a good looking boy, never seemed to have any girlfriends."

"Luke and Linda weren't boyfriend and girlfriend?" I asked.

"No, Abel. I think they took the brother and sister act seriously.

"Sally," Hobbes said suddenly, "I think you may come home. You have helped me immensely. I shall have a meeting with all of the people involved in this case at five o'clock, and I would like you to be there."

"Can I bring Greg?"

"You may bring anyone you wish, Sally."

To me, he said, "I have waited as long as I dare. We must act quickly."

"Then you have a plan, Chief?"

"No. I have a forlorn hope."

That was around a quarter to three. The weather had started to change, becoming more like March. What should have been snow and arctic winds that belonged with January were blasts of cold damp air with dark clouds that came rolling in from the west. The fog wasn't going to be around this time, like on New Year's Eve. Just rain — maybe a lot of it.

The weather didn't seem too important, though, and by half past four o'clock, I had the office set up as Hobbes had requested.

The office was really the great room, of course. Hobbes' desk dominated the west end; all of the chairs and both sofas had been turned to face it. By five o'clock, everyone on the list was present. A few had come in willingly enough; guile and threats and police coercion had contrived to bring in the rest of them. None of the latter group looked pleased to be there.

Linda Butler sat alone on the gray sofa that we'd placed a few feet from the front of the desk and just a little left of center. The blue sofa, we put next to the gray, but a little right of center, and Katya Ransom and her son Luke sat there as directed. Kelly Decker had been instructed to sit next to Linda, but had refused, as had Lemuel Dathan. Both of them sat in straight-back chairs in the second row.

Rich had developed a custom of standing in front of the distant cold fireplace. He wasn't there.

Forrest Green and Lieutenant Murphy sat in upholstered chairs, but on opposite sides of the room.

Bull Dickerson was in plain clothes, having been lured in by the Boss' promise to expose a murderer. I had seated him near the south wall next to Green.

My chair, as was usual when we called together everyone who was a significant part of whatever case we were working on, was five feet in back of Hobbes' desk, but near the north wall. It was one of the few times I would wear my shoulder holster with the .32 caliber Beretta in easy reach.

For atmosphere, I had made sure the patio doors were closed, but I had kept the drapes open. The coming storm had darkened the sky and had somewhat set the stage for Hobbes.

A loud meow from the other side of the patio doors brought Katya quickly to those doors. She slid one open, and called to the cat, "Harmless, my baby, come; come to me." The cat took several steps backward, then turned, and walked away. Katya called again, "Harmless! Harmless!" But the cat crawled under some bushes, stretched out on his belly, and watched Katya. His expression seemed to be one of detachment.

Slightly bewildered, Katya returned to her seat.

At exactly five o'clock, Hobbes wheeled in and parked his wheelchair behind the desk.

He glared at the people in front of him.

"Today," he said without preamble, "I shall explain how Clyde Butler was murdered, who did it, and why."

"Well, it wasn't me!" Katya said sharply.

Hobbes fixed his gaze on her. "Indeed?"

He looked the small group over, but he spoke to Linda, "There is room for Richard to sit next to you when he comes in."

Linda put her face in her hands. Katya Ransom started to say something, but Hobbes held up his hand and shook his head. "Without a doubt, he has good reasons for being late. In the meantime, I have questions for others among you.

"Mrs. Ransom, I shall start with you. Your husband Frank died in 1985. Tell us about him."

She stiffened her back and tightened her lips as if nothing could make her talk. She tried to stare Hobbes down, but his inscrutability was a little more than she could handle.

She leaned forward on the sofa as if to stand, but stopped when Hobbes said softly, "Mrs. Ransom, would you prefer someone else to tell your story? I don't think so. You are not the kind of woman who would enjoy listening to a biased version of your life. Now, let me make this clear: once you move from that sofa, you will not be allowed to make further comment, nor will you be allowed to leave the room."

"So that's the way it is," she said.

Hobbes nodded.

"About Frank?" she snorted. "You want to know about Frank? What about him? He died of a heart attack. What else is there to say?"

"But he didn't die penniless, did he?"

Katya was slow to answer. "You already know, so why ask me?"

"Because you want to tell us. Because you felt cheated."

"Yes. I did feel cheated. We could have lived a good life; Frank and Linda and I. He had inherited some money, but you'd have sworn he was a bum from the way he hoarded it."

"A large sum of money, wasn't it, Mrs. Ransom. Almost half–a-million dollars. What became of it?"

"Before Frank died, he put all of his money into some program managed by a banker and a lawyer that was supposed to take care of me for the rest of my life. Hah! The whiny little bastard."

"The money was not enough?" Hoobbes asked. "Was there no life insurance?"

"Oh, I suppose the money would have been enough for me, but it wasn't enough for the three of us. But then, he cancelled the life insurance right after he got that inheritance."

"And when you pass on, what will your children get?"

"Nothing. After my final expenses, the rest goes to some charity or other." Her voice was almost gleeful.

"Then," he murmured, "There was enough to keep you alive."

"That idiot should have left the whole thing to me."

"He excluded both Linda and Luke. Were they not loved by their father?"

"Hah!"

"Nevertheless, children are not usually excluded from a father's will, barring a strong and persistent animus."

"Right!" She looked slyly at her son and daughter. "They didn't even know about the will until after he died."

"A moment ago, you said 'Frank and Linda and I' could have had a good life. You didn't mention Luke. Why?"

"Didn't I? Well, he was always sucking up to me, trying to weasel in on Linda's birthright. Still, I didn't mean to leave him out. Luke was always there."

"He was there when Linda died, wasn't he?"

"Yes, he..." She clamped her mouth shut for thirty seconds, then spoke through tightly clenched teeth. "What do you mean, when Linda died? She's right here."

"You know what I mean, Mrs. Ransom. The real Linda died in a fire when she was twenty-four years old. You knew that."

She looked toward the ceiling −− her face became blank, unreadable.

She spoke softly, "My little girl never died. She just left me for a while."

"But you still had Luke, didn't you?"

"Luke?" She seemed to be looking into the distant past. "Yes, Luke was there. He was the first to see..." her voice dropped off.

"See what?"

"Why, Linda of course. He saw her in... in..."

"Susan Kelch?" Hobbes prompted. "Mrs. Kelch's granddaughter?"

"Mother!" Luke interrupted. "Don't answer any more questions. He's making you look like a fool." To Hobbes, he said, "She is not competent, hasn't been for years. She can't tell the difference between truth and make–believe."

Katya ignored her son. "My daughter, Linda, was taken from me because they thought she was insane. For four years, they wouldn't let me see her. Then, her body died in that terrible fire. I prayed to God above to bring her back to me, but He wouldn't do it. I prayed again and again, but He went to His enemy and offered him my soul for Linda's return. The Master said to wait. To worship him and wait. I learned how to call up the coven; to sacrifice animals. Then one night, we tied a living human being to the altar. The Master appeared, silent, tall, cloaked, and hooded in red. He took up the ceremonial knife and offered it to me, but I couldn't take it. I couldn't see his face, but I knew he was angry at me. I ran out crying! It took years for him to forgive me."

"Stop it, Mommy, dear. No one here can understand what you're talking about," Linda Butler had left her sofa and was standing in back of Katya. She tentatively put her hands on the older woman's shoulders and squeezed gently.

Katya shook the hands off. "No? If I hadn't refused to do his bidding that night, you would have come back in your own body." She quit talking, as if she were suddenly aware that she'd already said too much.

"Mrs. Butler," Hobbes said to Linda after a moment's silence. "Please return to your seat. We have much to discuss, and you will soon find your turn has come too quickly."

"For the moment, Mrs. Ransom, I have only three more questions: One, are you sure neither Linda nor Luke knew the contents of the will? Two, do you know who fathered Linda's baby? And Three, do you know, and haven't you known since the beginning, that the Linda Butler we have here is a fake; that she is, and always has been, Susan Kelch?

"I would add a fourth question: Do you know deep in your heart that the daughter whose death you blamed on yourself is truly dead?"

Chapter 31

Katya stared at Hobbes for a long minute, then glanced sideways at the very pale Linda Butler, then back to Hobbes.

Through gritted teeth, she hissed, "I will tell you nothing more than this; I'm glad that my ancient sister made you into a cripple. I wish she had killed you!"

Hobbes looked at her speculatively. "Molly Beecher was your sister?"

"I've said all I care to say," she said flatly.

"No doubt. I'm sure Mad Molly Beecher would have been your sister in the coven, had you met. Such spiritual relationships, real or imagined, can be more enduring than physical ones.

"But I have little interest in your relationship to the women who preceded you." His voice became sharp and derisive; the corners of his mouth turned down in a sneer. "In Molly's time, her coven was a deadly force to be reckoned with; in comparison, your little coven of play witches has been more entertaining than frightening. It has none of the strengths it had when Molly had been its leader. It is weak, meaningless, useless –– a circle of neutered cats and dogs and cowardly weasels and rats. But then, its leader is little more than that, isn't she? No! Less than that. Even her cat, her link to the underworld, rejects her."

She gripped the arm of the blue sofa; her face made a sharp contrast in red. Her free hand shook in anger as she rose from the sofa, walked to his desk, and leaned forward. Her voice trembled, "You miserable crippled bastard. You think we're nothing? If you want to see how nothing we are, then go to 403! See what happens to the blood of innocents! Ask them who called the boy out..." Her voice faded away, as if she was surprised at the words that came out of her mouth.

Hobbes' voice returned to normal. "Thank you, Mrs. Ransom. Abel, take Lieutenant Murphy with you. Do what you must."

"You got it, Chief. Keep them here, but wait for us to get back –– I don't want to miss anything."

I didn't hear his answer; Murphy and I were out the door, down the sidewalk and into his overpowered Mercury in ten seconds.

"403," he said as the tires squealed and the car fishtailed. "Where is that?"

"Lincoln south to Grand, turn right to Jackson, and follow it around. I'll show you."

It was two miles of city driving. At the end of three minutes, Murphy parked the car on the street in front of 403.

"There'll be a side door to the basement," I said. "I don't have a key."

"Yeah," Murphy answered. "Neither do I." He opened the trunk and took out a short pry bar and two flashlights.

"Batteries are probably dead," I said when he offered me one of the flashlights. We hadn't bothered with them after getting out of the tunnel.

"Yeah?" He looked at me curiously, flicked the switch, said, "Damn," and tossed the light back into the trunk.

We found the stairwell and descended the four steps. "Door's locked, Murph."

"Don't matter." The door opened inward, so he didn't need the pry bar. He gripped the doorknob with one hand and pushed against the door with his shoulder. The heavy metal resisted for a minute, then the hundred-and-twenty-year old striker plate gave way with a sharp snap and the door swung open. I followed him into the basement.

The building above us was probably two hundred feet long by fifty feet wide. The basement was the same size. Its layout would be similar to others I'd been in, with a central corridor down two–thirds of its length that gave door-less access to a dozen or so large rooms. Midway down would be the broad walkway to the other three dormitories in the cluster. The far end of the main corridor would open into a dining room big enough to feed a hundred or so people. It should have been empty, unused for its entire existence.

We had entered the boiler room. Had the boiler been working and fired up, it would have provided heat for all four dormitories in the cluster, but all useable parts were gone, salvaged to keep other boilers working. We passed through it into the corridor. The early winter's night darkened the basement, so we had to wait for our night vision to become effective. It was just as well we didn't have flashlights —— they would have given us away.

Some kind of light should have been visible, if people really were there. We walked down the corridor, checking every room. Nothing. We walked back and stopped at the walkway to the cluster's hub.

"She said 403, didn't she?" Murphy asked, just loud enough for me to hear.

"Must be in the tunnel access."

"Can you find it?"

"In my sleep. They're all the same; twenty feet ahead, exit left."

The door to the tunnel was locked. It opened toward us so Murphy's shoulder wouldn't be of help this time.

"Pry bar," he said.

I handed it to him. He had to feel around in the darkness to find a gap big enough to wedge in the bar, but the ancient door and frame no longer fit together tightly. In a few seconds, the metal squealed and yielded with a loud crack as the door swung open. We stepped inside and pulled it shut behind us.

The tunnel was barely lit by a smoking torch in a bracket at the far end of the hallway, a hundred feet distant. It kept us in shadows as we came closer. We could hear faint voices singing.

"Let's go!" I said.

We ran quietly, but as fast as we dared. I didn't know what the singing meant, but it sounded like it was building to a climax. We stopped at the doorway and peered inside. I heard Murphy suck in his breath. I drew out my gun —— I'd seen this before.

Nine people. Three groups of three. Three trinals. There should have been four. Dog, Weasel, and Rat were here. Three sets of costumed worshippers. The Cat was missing. Dog, Weasel, and Rat were waiting. Gathered around a flat altar stone that was prepared for a sacrifice. Waiting for the Cat —— waiting for their leaders.

Richard Butler was strapped to the altar.

Murphy pulled out his gun and stepped through the door. "All right, everyone. Stand back. Your game's over. Up against the wall. Now!" I was right behind him, my Beretta held straight out.

Nine pairs of eyes turned toward us in surprise. No one moved.

"I said against the wall!"

The eyes looked to the doorway behind us. I heard angry hissing and knew where the Cat was.

"Hit the floor, Murphy!" I yelled, and dropped, twisting around, trying to avoid the poisoned darts. I fired my gun at the ceiling, and Murphy fired his, neither of us hitting anyone.

When the smoke cleared, we were alone with the boy. All the trinals had run.

"Too many back doors," I said to Murphy. "We'd never catch them."

I walked to the altar, knelt down and untied Rich. He sat up slowly, groggy from the drugs they'd used on him.

"What took you so long?" he mumbled.

I looked at Murphy; he seemed a little unsteady on his feet. "Did a dart get you?"

"Just a scratch –– barely broke the skin." He leaned against the wall for support. "How bad is that stuff?"

"Bad enough, but if you haven't fallen by now, you should be okay."

"Then, let's get out of here."

"In a minute. You bring that pry bar with you?"

He pointed to the doorway.

I helped Rich up and leaned him against Murphy. Then I found the pry bar and walked back to the altar. Two thin sheets of polished marble lay on cement blocks before me, strapped together, side by side to form the altar top. Those sheets had been the mysterious content of the wooden crates I had seen at the Butler's house. Even in the weak light of the torches, the red of the marble was made brown by streaks of dried blood. I had no way of knowing if it was the same altar top that I had been strapped to twenty years ago, but... I knew it was, if that makes sense.

Its time had come.

I raised the bar over my head and brought it down violently on the first sheet of marble. It screamed and shattered into a hundred pieces. At least it seemed to scream. So did the second sheet when its turn came.

I picked up two small pieces of the broken marble and shoved them into my pocket.

With Rich leaning on one of my shoulders and Murphy on the other, we left the tunnel and building 403, got into Murphy's car with me driving, and headed toward Hobbes' house.

I looked at my watch. We'd been gone less than forty–five minutes.

The rain had started. By the time I had parked in Hobbes' driveway, it had become a downpour; the strong wind whipped heavy droplets into our faces.

Forty-five minutes can be a long time in Hobbes' house, especially when we're nearing the end of an investigation. Today, time seemed to have stopped. Hobbes was still in his wheelchair behind his desk. Katya still sat in the same place with Luke next to her; Linda hadn't moved, as far as I could tell — she still had her head buried in her hands; Kelly and Lemuel sat in back of her, and Forrest Green had opened up his laptop and was apparently working. Sally had gone to the kitchen with Fred and Charon where they could listen in through the secret mike, but Greg had taken a straight-back chair by the bookcases.

All eyes turned to me as I entered and crossed the room. I shrugged off my wet coat, letting everyone see the Beretta in its holster. I placed the two pieces of marble on Hobbes' desk, stained sides up, but let only him see them.

He didn't touch either piece, but simply looked at them for several seconds. He spoke in a voice too low for anyone else to hear, "All of the stains are old?"

I nodded.

"Excellent. I am greatly relieved. Is he with you?"

"In the computer room with Murphy. Murphy took a small hit so he's a little groggy, but he'll be all right."

"Will you ask the lieutenant to come in?"

"Alone?"

"For the moment. I would like to establish a police presence."

It took me a few more minutes to help a pale and sweating Murphy stumble into the great room and find his chair. He glanced briefly at Forrest Green, who seemed about to say something, but didn't, Then, he glared at the three people on the two sofas.

Hobbes watched their expressions; Linda seemed puzzled by Murphy's actions, Luke rubbed his chin, and Katya turned her head away.

"Lieutenant Murphy," Hobbes said, "shall we call a doctor?"

Murphy shook his head. "Ten minutes, I'll be okay. They were waiting for someone, not us. I want to know if it was the old woman."

Luke spoke up, "You've kept us here far too long, Hobbes. You were going to tell us how Clyde died. Let's get on with it."

Hobbes drummed his fingers on the desktop. "He was murdered. Stress from seeing what he thought was the ghost of his first wife while under a hypnotic drug, an already-weakened heart, a poison administered within the hour before midnight on New Year's Eve and triggered by the shock of strong liquor — combined, they were too much for him."

"What poison?" Luke interrupted. "Wasn't there an autopsy that showed his death was a completely natural heart attack?" He took his sister's hand, "I'm sorry, Linda, but we need to clear this up."

"That's right; the autopsy showed nothing."

"I don't get it. How do you know he was poisoned if you couldn't find any poison?"

Hobbes grimaced. "By deduction. Let me explain. Clyde's sudden death was the third in a series that all occurred during a little over four years. In each case, the coroner didn't know what to look for, and foul play hadn't been suspected, anyway. It wasn't until I saw photographs of the exotic plants being grown in Clyde's cistern that I knew poisoning was a possibility. One of those plants could yield a deadly substance that would kill quickly, yet in a few hours, convert to simple sugars without leaving a trace of the original poison. Clyde hadn't been examined until at least twelve hours had passed."

"No poison, no murder. Right?" Luke sounded annoyingly smug. It wasn't until that moment that I began to think I knew what was going on. I looked at the other faces; Linda, Katya, Kelly, and Lemuel — even Greg Frazier. None of them had that same look. They all seemed to be confused, maybe guilty of something. Luke alone, looked respectable, above such things as murder.

"Proof of poison came in a different package, Mr. Ransom. Early this afternoon, Grandma Agnes Kelch came to talk with me. She had had a late breakfast at the Butler's, she said, and now she needed something to brace herself with —— to build up her courage. 'There are things that need saying,' she told me. She wanted a double anything, as long as it was one hundred proof or better. I poured two or three ounces of scotch into a highball glass and gave it to her. She drank all of it.

"'It's about my granddaughter,' she said, then she grabbed her chest and collapsed onto the floor. I called for help; Fred came and gave her CPR; a few minutes later, paramedics arrived and did their best, but she died in this house.

"As the ambulance was leaving, I called the coroner and advised him of the nature of the poison he would find and how to find it. I told him he had to work quickly and why. He said he was on his way."

Suddenly, Hobbes slapped both hands on his desk, and glared at everyone. "Clyde Butler and Agnes Kelch died in this room, and I was powerless to help either one. I could not have known of Clyde's danger, but I knew enough about the threat to Mrs. Kelch that

I could have warned her. I do not consider myself blameless where she is concerned."

He held up a thin red binder. "The coroner obliged me with a preliminary report on the death of Mrs. Kelch. It proves that she was murdered. It names both the poison and the plant it was derived from. That plant was one of those growing in the cistern-turned-hothouse in the Butler's basement. If you doubt me," he held up a manila envelope, "I have pictures of the plants. They were taken the day after Clyde's death."

Chapter 32

He paused for a moment. Only one person who lived in the Butler house seemed especially surprised about the revelation. That was Linda — and she didn't look guilty, only surprised. She glanced quickly at Luke, but he had already put on his poker face. If anything, he looked slightly relieved.

Linda's voice trembled slightly when she spoke. "Clyde made that hothouse," she said slowly. "Everyone knew about it. Clyde grew tomatoes for me, and some herbs. He let Mother grow some things in there, too. He said anybody, even the renters, could use it. I don't know what was grown there."

"Liar," Katya said flatly. "You had the only key."

"But I never locked it."

"It was always locked when I went down there."

"Clyde would have given anyone a key."

Another moment of silence passed, and then Luke spoke.

"So Linda grew some strange plants," he said. "That doesn't mean she killed anyone. So did Kelly. Ask her what she used hers for."

Linda turned slowly to gaze at Luke. He met her eyes and nodded reassuringly.

To Hobbes he said, "How could anyone have managed to poison Kelch? You really couldn't know, could you? She died before she could say anything."

Hobbes checked his moustache for shape; the droopy tips were perfectly aligned. He raised the corners of his mouth slightly. "First, Mr. Ransom, I have accused no individual by name, not even Linda. Second, Mrs. Kelch had eaten breakfast in the Butler's kitchen where anyone could have slipped something into her cereal or juice. It was common knowledge that she started most days with a strong drink or two, so the chances were good that the poison would work. And, third, she did tell me something very revealing."

"Then, you didn't tell us all she said."

"Yes, yes I did. She said only four words just before she died, but they were revealing. She said, 'It's about my granddaughter.' In retrospect, I found it most odd that she would talk about her grandchild. None of her relatives, as far as I knew, had ever had any dealings with the Butlers or the Ransoms." He let his hands touch the pieces of marble.

"Hah!" Katya Ransom voice crackled.

"Quiet, Mother," Luke ordered. He had risen up slightly, trying to see what I'd placed on the desk.

Hobbes placed a sheet of paper over the marble pieces. "My associate Sally Wilson and her friend, Greg Frazier, spent Monday afternoon in Kankakee and much of Tuesday and today in Watseka, Illinois. She is talented in the realm of research and seldom fails to produce. She outdid herself this time. The five of you, Linda, Luke, Katya, Kelly, and Lemuel, all supposedly

315

came from Kankakee —— that was the most any of you would tell us about your background. That was as true as far as it went, say, for the past five years. Prior to that, though, your lives were far different from what you led people to believe."

Luke interrupted him, "Our lives were quiet and respectable, Mr. Hobbes, and weren't anybody's business but our own. Be careful what you say. We are willing to sue to protect our reputation."

"Whom do you speak for, Mr. Ransom? Everyone, or just yourself?"

Luke looked at each of the other four briefly, then turned back to Hobbes. "For my sister and my mother. I don't know about Kelly and Lemuel."

"You should have learned about them before today."

Luke's smile was thin as he said, "Then, tell us now."

"In her research at Watseka —— the court house, the library and the newspaper archives, especially —— Sally put together a Ransom family history. I shall summarize:

"Katya and Frank Ransom were married in 1959; four years later, after three miscarriages and a difficult pregnancy, Linda was born. That was in 1963. For the next eight years, the mother smothered the daughter with unceasing care and devotion —— leaving nothing to chance, making all the decisions —— perhaps to the point of taking away the child's identity.

"In 1971, you were born, Luke. Your mother resented you because you took time away from Linda, and as devoted as she was to Linda, she was indifferent to you. Even so, you did everything possible to win your mother's love and attention, but you weren't successful, were you? You were the perfect son, but that wasn't enough, was it?'

Luke only glared at him.

"When your sister was twelve years old, something very remarkable happened. She began talking to spirits. She would go into a trance and unknown spirits would speak through her. She would talk of things that happened when she wasn't around. She was said to have been very convincing. This continued until she was sixteen, when she met Clyde Butler and began dating him. At the same time, contact with the spirit world ceased. Katya became jealous and angry and tried to break up their romance."

He suddenly raised his voice, "Mrs. Ransom, is this accurate so far?"

"Everything you say is a lie," she said matter-of-factly. "You made it all up. I suppose next you'll say he got her pregnant."

Hobbes nodded his head. "Of course, because that is what happened. Then, what did you do, Mrs. Ransom?"

She sneered at him. "Nothing, because nothing had happened,"

"Linda knows. So does Luke. So does Kelly."

"Kelly?" Luke said, startled. He twisted around to look at her. "How could she know anything about our personal lives?"

"She is at liberty to speak or remain silent, insofar as my investigation is concerned."

Kelly shook her head. "Not now."

"Then I shall continue with my brief history.

"You, Mrs. Ransom, in an attempt to regain control over Linda, who was then seventeen, sent her to a private home in Galena where she was to stay until her baby was born. Even so, everything might have worked out, but the spirits returned. She was possessed and they talked through her daily. It was more than the people in Galena were able to deal with, so they sent her to a hospital for the insane." Hobbes smiled slightly. "Mercater State Hospital. Odd, isn't it, how things come together? She had the baby and took care of it for three years, until it was put into a foster home. She stayed in MerSH until 1977, sharing a cottage apartment there until an early morning fire killed her and severely burned her roommate."

Hobbes fixed his eyes on Luke, and spoke gently, "For the first time in your life, you might have become someone in your mother's life — the son she had barely acknowledged while your sister lived."

"That's enough, Hobbes. I'm warning you." The pitch of Luke's voice went up an octave.

"It didn't work though; your mother still ignored you. Susan had nearly drowned and lay in a coma, and there were only you and your memories of Linda. You were alone, terribly alone. And then, Susan woke up."

Hobbes turned to Katya. "It must have been difficult, Mrs. Ransom. On one hand, you wanted your daughter back, but on the other hand, you did not want a son, regardless of what he did for you."

"Just a minute, Hobbes," Luke's voice was still high-pitched and strident.

Hobbes raised his hand. "Sue me later if you must. Right now, I am busy."

He continued, "As I said, Susan woke up. Luke and Susan had been talking about just such a fantasy for two years, and suddenly, an opportunity presented itself to make the fantasy real. . She had only to pretend to be Linda and everything would be all right."

"You're crazy, Hobbes," Luke's voice had returned to normal.

"The pretense has worked for almost twenty years."

"You are an idiot, Hobbes. She could not have fooled me," Katya Ransom said.

In the brief silence, Hobbes looked at Kelly and raised an eyebrow.

"I could use a dozen aspirins," Murphy said.

"Be right up. They're in the computer room." It was a chance to check on Rich. He'd been by himself for quite a while, considering what he'd just gone through.

He was sitting at the computer playing solitaire.

"Who's winning?" I asked.

He smiled. It made him look like his old self. "Sounds like Hobbes is," he said. "When does he want me to come out?"

"Shouldn't be too long, Rich. He needs the timing to be just right."

"Does he always have to talk so much, Abel? Why doesn't he just say how they killed Dad and let the cops arrest them?"

"He probably doesn't have any proof."

"So, what's his plan?"

"He'll keep talking until he wears them down. Keep listening; he'll let you know when it's time to show yourself."

I grabbed a couple of extra–strength aspirin, went to the kitchen for a glass of water, saluted Fred, Sally, and Charon, who were listening to Hobbes dissect the Ransoms from their kitchen chairs, and returned to the office. Murphy said thanks for the aspirin, swallowed both, and followed with a chaser of Mercater city water. He spat some of the water back into the glass, and glared at me. "What the hell?"

"Tastes good, huh? The water company hasn't learned to get sulfur out of the water supply yet." I took his glass and set it on the hall table, then took my seat five feet behind Hobbes' desk, near the north wall, same as before.

Hobbes was still waiting on Kelly, but finally she shook her head just enough to indicate 'No.'

He nodded and finished a can of beer. He dropped the empty into the wastebasket, then addressed the entire group. "I have said that I would explain how Clyde Butler was murdered. I shall also reveal why and by whom. The guilty will provide part of the proof, perhaps unintentionally. There are two things I shall discuss: motive, and opportunity.

"The motive. At first glance, it would appear to be money; certainly a lot of money was involved. We shall discuss this in a few moments.

"Opportunity? That is more difficult. Several times, the guilty would almost have to have been in two places at once.

"Mixed in with those two elements are a few more tangible items. For example," he pulled out a small plastic bag and emptied it on his desk. "A hand rolled cigarette butt given by Lucas to his mother. A red herring. It was nothing more than a hand rolled cigarette.

"Clyde's glasses. They had bothered him, gave him headaches. Why? Clyde had worn glasses for many years without problems. What was different about this pair? Abel, look at them. Tell me what you see." He handed them to me; I had to stretch to get them without standing up.

I held them up to the light and looked through each lens. Except for one being cracked, I couldn't see anything wrong. "They look all right to me, Chief." I handed them back.

"Clyde Butler and Katya Ransom both saw the image of Jane Butler clearly; Kelly and Abel saw a blurred picture. The explanation lies in the glasses that both Clyde and Katya wore and both hated. I sent this pair to an optician for examination." Hobbes paused and studied the three people on the two sofas. Linda looked a little scared, Katya's mouth had dropped open, and Luke was staring at Hobbes as if in disbelief. The boss continued, "He said the lenses were polarized, but one had vertical polarization, the other had horizontal. Such lenses are used for viewing three-dimensional motion pictures. They were used in this case, without Clyde's or Katya's knowledge, to give depth and life to the projection of Jane's ghost."

"She was real!" Katya insisted. But there was a crack in her voice.

He shook his head. "A hypnotic gas hidden within the smell of lilacs and introduced by way of the heating ducts in the basement would help make the ghost real to those who breathed the gas, Mrs. Ransom. Under the spell of that gas, Clyde was easily made to believe he was going to die. When it was no longer needed, a small fan in the basement expelled the gas under the front porch, a place considered by Harmless the Cat to be its own lair. The gas made him temporarily insane, and that is probably why he survived being hit by a vehicle and buried alive.

"My cat? Harmless?" Katya turned slowly to look at Linda, then turned back to gaze at Luke.

The air in the house had taken on a heavy, stuffy, oppressive atmosphere. My claustrophobia acted up at times like that, so I tried opening a patio door a few inches. A rush of rain-filled wind pushed itself by me and cleared the air somewhat. During the three seconds I had the door open, power-driven raindrops misted the whole south end of the great room. The view from the house down to the river disappeared completely behind that cascade.

I called for Forrest Green to come look at the storm.

Hobbes continued, "And then, I have pictures taken by a park ranger on the day Jane fell to her death. They show a grief-stricken Linda being comforted by a man the ranger took to be her husband. The man was not her husband, merely her brother Lucas who had never told anyone that he had been at the top of the cliff when Jane had fallen to her death.

Chapter 33

Before I even realized he was on his feet, Luke had taken three steps forward and grabbed the edge of Hobbes' desk and shoved it aside. "You sonofabitch, Hobbes," he was almost crying as he dropped to his knees, his hands reaching out, opening and closing in uncontrolled spasms. He knelt there as if he was frozen in place. And then, I had my arms around him before he could do anything, like strangle the boss.

"Take him back to his seat, Abel," Hobbes said, and when I had put Luke back down, added, "There will be no further outburst, will there, Mr. Ransom?"

Luke had begun to shake. "We didn't have anything to do with her falling. We were... looking at something else."

"The pictures only prove you were there," Hobbes said, as he slid his desk back in place. "Nothing else. We may say more about them later, if doing so helps clear up Clyde's murder."

"He did have a heart attack." Luke insisted, his voice frigid. "It's still a natural death."

"How many 'natural' deaths have you been a part of, Mr. Ransom?"

Luke seemed to have regained control of himself. He glanced at his watch and said, "Linda, I think it's time for us to leave." He stood up and after a moment,

Linda sighed deeply, then pushed herself up from the sofa.

"Mother?" he said to Katya, "we're leaving."

"Harmless was almost killed," she whispered. "Buried alive. Why?"

"Mother!" Luke insisted. He put his hand on her arm to help her up.

"I'm staying until I know what happened to my cat," she said. "Remove your hand."

Surprised, he stepped back. "This cannot end well, Mother. It may cost you your daughter."

"Then so be it. I have put my children in enough danger."

"Children? They're dumb animals, Mother. Cats."

"They are more my children than you ever were, Luke."

"More than I was, Mother?" Linda dropped back onto the sofa and tried to meet Katya's eyes. Tears ran down her face.

'Oh, Linda," Katya's voice was suddenly soft. "Why couldn't you have stayed the way you were? Why did you have to leave me for him?"

"Leave you for whom?" Hobbes' voice was sharp, commanding.

"For Clyde, you idiot. I thought you knew everything!"

"I know that Linda was born in 1953 and in 1969 dated Clyde for six months, then they quit seeing each other, and four years later, she died in a fire. She is said to have returned in 1977, not as the twenty-four year old the calendar would indicate, but as a healthy seventeen-year old girl."

"No. You still don't know everything, do you?"

"That's true. I don't. But it was a blessing, wasn't it? Getting your daughter back, I mean. An answer to prayer, but not quite what you had expected. We'd like to hear the true story about what happened; would you tell us?"

I don't know how he did it, changing his way of speaking from commanding to pleading in a matter of seconds, and establishing an almost hypnotic control over his victim. But I'd seen him do it many times over the years.

Katya looked at the ceiling, as if she would see the complete answer there, then dropped her gaze to Hobbes. "Linda's soul took over the body of Susan Kelch after Susan tried to drown herself, and Luke rescued her. He brought her home and told us Linda was back. She didn't know anything about Susan any more, but she knew everything about me and Frank, and about Luke, and herself when she had been alive before. A month later, we adopted her."

"You adopted a seventeen–year old girl and she moved in with you and your husband and her new seventeen–year old brother. Didn't it seem somehow too convenient?"

"They were good kids," she said. "They both went to college."

"Yes," Hobbes agreed, and then added, "And after graduation, they both moved out and found good-paying jobs."

The sarcasm wasn't wasted on her. Her reply was dry and quick. "Yes, they moved out and got good-paying jobs."

She held up her hand before anyone else could speak. She took her time with the real answer, and even Luke had quit trying to keep her quiet. "Yes," she said. Then, she snorted, "No, they lived at home. Loafers; educated cretins. Frank had a little money, and they stayed as long as he was generous to them."

Hobbes nodded, "Then in 1984, Frank inherited some money; a considerable sum of money. It must have seemed like a fortune to you and Linda and Lucas"

"Hah. It turned him into a miser!"

"A dead miser? Shortly afterwards, he died of a heart attack, at least according to the records at one funeral home; but not before he put most of his money into an annuity for you. Linda and Luke wouldn't get any cash other than what they could get from you, and if you died, they wouldn't even have that access.

"As I have said before, the money kept you alive. Were the three of you surprised by the will's content?"

Luke answered for her. "Of course, we were, Hobbes. I don't like your inference. You are dangerously close to accusing Linda of faking her way into the family, so she could get her hands on Dad's money, and then killing him for it."

"It gets worse, friend Luke. Consider the death of James Larsen in 1997. A recent widower, he had remarried; just a few months later, he had a sudden fatal heart attack. His new young wife was found to be his sole beneficiary. Two years later, Oscar Field, also a widower, in his turn left a small fortune to a new young wife as he, too, succumbed to a heart attack. Last week, Clyde Butler continued the pattern, except that in his case, half of the estate was to go to his wife and half to his son, as long as they both lived.

"Larsen, Field, and now Butler. Each of those men was in his turn, married to the same woman. Each died within the year." He paused and waited for a response.

Luke acted as if he was too stunned for words.

Linda would not meet Hobbes's eyes.

"Do you have anything to say, Mrs. Butler?"

She stared at the floor.

"You grieve the death of Agnes Kelch, do you not?" Hobbes was sympathetic; at least his tone of voice was.

She nodded. "I guess I'm still her granddaughter. I tried to keep track of her."

"You'll miss her more, even, than any of your husbands?"

"I don't know."

"What about Katya Ransom when her time comes; will you grieve for her?"

"She is the woman, Mr. Hobbes, who allowed me to come back from the dead. I don't thank her for that, and I doubt if I'll miss her."

A lot of eyes turned toward Katya. Her expression was one of mild surprise. After a moment she smiled. "My cats will grieve for me."

Hobbes turned his attention to Katya. "No doubt, Mrs. Ransom. Will you have the stuffed and mounted animals cremated with you?"

"They go to the coven."

"Ah, yes. The coven. How did you become a part of the Mercater coven of witches?"

"Its master called me one night and said I was needed."

"He called you how, in a dream?"

"On the telephone, you idiot!"

Hobbes allowed a trace of a smile to cross his face. "They never really sacrificed anything but stray dogs and cats, did they? Richard might have become the first human?"

"I would not have allowed it, if I was there."

"Just so," Hobbes said, and turned back to Linda.

"Are we agreed that you are the granddaughter Grandma Kelch spoke of?"

Linda hesitated for a moment, and then glanced at Luke, who turned his head away. She finally said, "Yes, I am."

"Then, who are you now, Linda or Susan?"

Again, she waited for Luke to say something, but it was clear he was letting her dig her own grave. "Linda. I've been Linda since I was a child."

"Then how can Agnes Kelch's death really mean anything to you? She has not been your grandmother since the soul of Linda possessed that body."

Linda was startled; again she looked to Luke for help, and again he ignored her. "Help me, Luke," she pleaded.

Luke turned back to Linda, and met her eyes. "Three men, Linda. Three men. He's going to say you killed them. Did you? Why?"

I had never seen a more innocent look on a man's face. I was disgusted. I glanced at Hobbes to see if he felt the same way. He was tapping a finger on his desk. Impatiently. What was he impatient about? Wasn't this the time when he would name the killer and get a confession?

She had no answer.

"Please come to my desk, Mrs. Butler. I would like you to see something."

She reluctantly got off the sofa, and walked to where he indicated.

Hobbes slid a sheet of paper off of the pieces of marble that I had brought to him. He gave her a moment to look at them, and then asked, "Do you know where these came from?"

She shook her head.

330

Hobbes continued to tap his finger. He was tapping the sheet of paper that had covered the broken marble. It had writing on it. Large print. She read it and gave no response. I looked over her shoulder.

It said, "Mrs. Butler, bear with me. You are a victim. I shall help. I will soon name the killer. Until then, be defiant but say no more than you must."

The note could have been meant for me. I was a victim of Hobbes' deception. I didn't know what was going on, and I was defiant. Quiet, but defiant.

She gave Hobbes a scornful look and then returned to her seat.

I gave Hobbes a scornful look and then returned to my seat.

He flipped the paper over, covering the chips once again.

She fixed her eyes on Luke, but it was Hobbes who talked to him.

"Here's the scenario, Luke," he said. "It was pretend, from the attempted drowning to the present, always calling herself Linda, always acting. At first, she just wanted to be near you. Then, she liked the new life and what money could buy. But the money ran out, and she couldn't live forever on Katya's annuity. She married for money and killed for the inheritance; when the money ran out she repeated herself, and then did it again with Clyde. Is that right, Linda?"

She continued looking at Luke.

"Clyde's will had one problem, didn't it, Linda? The estate was to be split between you and Rich, and Clyde's estate wasn't that big –– maybe four hundred thousand. So you had to get rid of Rich."

"No. I didn't want that."

"But you helped kidnap him anyway. Where is he now?"

She shrugged, defeated. "You wouldn't believe anything I say."

"Mrs. Butler, would you like to talk to your grandmother?"

She answered with a flat, "Grandma is dead."

"Ah, but we have an intermediary with us. A medium who can patch us through to her. Kelly Decker. Please come forward, Kelly."

Now, what the heck? I thought. Hobbes calling someone who was a part of a murder investigation by her first name? He even sounded like he believed in her. Something strange was going on. I tried to see where he was leading us, but gave that up quickly. I didn't want to miss anything. I shot a quick glance at Hobbes and he looked up at me. We caught each other's eye, and he nodded. The first name usage had been to get my attention. This was it, he was telling me. Be ready.

"Miss Decker," he said to the group, "is able to communicate with certain spirits without the benefit of the lighting and atmosphere of a traditional séance. Half a dozen people around a card table are all she needs. That's right, isn't it, Miss Decker?"

"Yes," she said shortly.

"Kelly," he said in his softest, most gentle voice, "for honor's sake, and so that I may bring this meeting to a fitting close, would you at this moment, and in front of all these people, summon Agnes Kelch?"

She cleared her throat, and then looked at my innocent face. Finally she nodded.

"Abel," he said, "There is a card table and four chairs in the hall. Please bring them in and set them up in place of my desk. Your chair and my wheelchair will complete the six."

For the next two minutes, the only sounds in the great room were the ones I made, except for the occasional rolling thunder that shook the old house and threatened to knock the windows out. The flashes of lighting became a distraction; I could have taken a few seconds to close the heavy curtains over the patio doors, but for some reason, I chose not to. The rain stopped abruptly, but the water on the concrete patio continued to evaporate into a gray mist — the second fog I'd seen in a week.

Shortly, I couldn't see anything out there but blackness. Nothing but the reflection of light from a cat's eyes. Harmless was still out there, watching. He meowed a question at me. I nodded my head; he shook some of the water off of his fur, entered, and walked to the east end of the room. He settled down on a thick throw rug. If the boss wanted atmosphere, he was getting it now.

Chapter 34

All the eyes in the room, except for Hobbes' and mine, were on the table and the chairs. Hobbes had set the stage, and his audience was hooked. Once the table was in place, he said, "Miss Decker, I'm sure, will allow me to choose who will sit with us." He didn't really give her a chance to object, but seemed to assume his choosing would be all right. "Kelly will be at the foot of the table with her back to the rest of you, Abel on Miss Decker's right, Linda Butler on my right, Lucas between Linda and Miss Decker. For the sixth person I wanted someone relatively unknown to the rest of us, so I am asking Greg Frazier to sit between Abel and me. You don't mind, do you Greg?"

The young mortician sat there, apparently too surprised by the request to respond. Sally had entered the room while I had been moving the chairs and had sat down next to Greg.

"Greg, please come join us. Sally will assist you."

"No," he said, as Sally stood and then pulled him to his feet. "I don't like, I mean I don't believe..." but to his obvious reluctance, he allowed Sally to lead him to the last seat at the card table, between Hobbes and me.

She kissed him lightly on the forehead. "You'll be the hit of the show, Greggy." She danced her way back to her chair.

Hobbes had called him 'Greg.' We had two first namers at the table.

"Kelly," he said, "You know Greg, don't you?"

"We met at the funeral home," she said. Greg nodded in agreement.

"Excellent," Hobbes' smile was so bright, it was alarming. I could see the cutting edges of his teeth. "Kelly, the table is yours."

For a few seconds, I thought she was going to change her mind, and then I saw where Hobbes was headed. I didn't see how he was going to get there. It depended on what Grandma Kelch's spirit had to say. Or maybe how she said it. Kelly must have read that on my face –– my trusting, open, nothing-held-back face.

Anyway, she smiled, and said, "Let's hold hands."

I took a firm grip on Greg's hand; I saw Hobbes grasp the other.

Kelly allowed a minute to pass, and then, "Grandma Kelch, are you here?" A lightning flash lit up the room. Barely a second later, thunder threatened the old house again. That was too close — besides, it was January. We weren't supposed to have thunderstorms in January.

She closed her eyes and let her breathing become slow and shallow. A soft, deep voice that sounded like Agnes Kelch spoke. "I am here. I must leave soon. When the person who killed me is named, I will go home."

Katya Ransom snorted.

Chapter 35

"Who killed you?" Hobbes asked.

"You know who," the voice said.

"Was it Lucas?"

"No."

"Was it Linda?"

"It is as you say."

"I need proof. How can I find proof?"

"You will find it in her room, in her closet, under things. Now, I must go."

"Please," Hobbes said, "Grandma Kelch. You are Agnes Kelch, aren't you?"

"Of course I am." The voice sounded irritated.

Hobbes said, "I have a few brief questions. May I ask them?"

"Do it quickly."

"First, will you tell everyone what happened to the real Linda Ransom? I know who she is, and she isn't dead, but is in fact here in this room at this moment!"

"What? What?" The voice suddenly sounded like Kelly's.

Hobbes continued. "I need confirmation. You can give it to me. She stays in the background, watching, manipulating... murdering." He paused. The room became silent with apprehension.

He went on gently, "Second, isn't Greg Frazier her son? Third, isn't...."

"I am done," the voice said.

Kelly snapped her eyes open. "What's going on? What's happening?"

I felt Greg's hand moving toward the inside of his jacket, but I tightened my hold. His other hand was held in Hobbes' vice-like grip. He probably wasn't armed, but why take chances?

"The idiots have found you out," Katya Ransom laughed out loud.

Kelly stared at Hobbes. Her stare turned to a glare. She had been suddenly betrayed. He knew that Linda Ransom was still alive and that Greg was her son? Her lips tightened; apparently she would say no more.

"No, you are not done," Hobbes said. "I can prove Grandma Kelch was not the one talking through you."

Her silence didn't last; she relaxed and said softly, "How can you do that? You'd have to bring her back from the dead, and even Car'l Hobbes has his limits."

"I won't attempt to exceed that boundary, Miss Decker. It is not necessary to bring her back from the dead. Look behind you."

Kelly turned and stared. Grandma Kelch came walking in through the hallway door. Her smile was nearly wide enough to break her face.

"Hello, my dear," she said to Kelly. "As Sam Clemens said, 'The report of my death was exaggerated.'"

"It was Mark Twain said that, Dummy!" Katya Ransom said, almost involuntarily.

"Mark Twain was Clemens' pen name, my dear Katya," Grandma Kelch said loud enough for everyone to hear. Then, she lowered her voice, "You shouldn't call other people 'Dummy.' The name fits you too well. Besides, there are those here who use names other than the ones given at birth; names like Linda, and Susan, and Kelly."

Kelly shot a quick glance at me, but I was almost as surprised as she was. It explained the time Dickerson kept me away from the ambulance while the EMTs got Grandma Kelch out of there, or appeared to. She probably had never left this house.

In the meantime I had thought she was dead, and it showed on my face. That was what had given Kelly the willingness to go ahead with her phony communication with the other world.

Now, she was speechless.

Hobbes wasn't. He had plenty to say.

"I will answer those questions I just asked you myself:

"First: the real Kelly Decker perished in that fire, not Linda Ransom. The surgeon that had performed the restorative plastic surgery on your face was nearly finished when he realized that he had been working with photos of the wrong woman. That surgeon, who

338

now lives in South Venice, Florida, talked to me on the telephone this morning. He said you were pleased with the new look.

"So, since Linda Ransom never died, your spirit could never have possessed Susan Kelch or anyone else.

"That farce is over; the hoax is ended.

"Second: Greg Frazier is the adopted son of Herman Frazier, whom he calls Uncle Herman, and the real son of Clyde Butler and Linda Butler. You... do I keep calling you Kelly, or change to calling you Linda?"

"My name is Kelly."

"Indeed. Well, Sally has retrieved copies of your son's adoption papers, and has talked to Herman Frazier. Mr. Frazier is pleased with his adopted son, although he doesn't know how Greg is able to buy an eighty thousand dollar sports car. But, then, he knows little about Greg's activities.

"Third: Greg probably didn't know that Clyde Butler was his father. For him, I think it was a matter of money where all three murders were concerned. For you, Miss Decker, money had nothing to do with your motivation. It was revenge. Revenge for all the things that Clyde had done, or that you had imagined he did; for getting you pregnant, for leaving you alone to raise his baby. For having a happy marriage while you were nearly killed in a fire. The fires of revenge burned against others as well; against your brother, your mother, and mostly against the woman who took your place. The list of wrongs is long, but you know what I mean, don't you, Miss Decker?" He leaned forward, his eyes intent and penetrating. "Don't you, Miss Decker?"

"You can't," she swallowed hard, "You can't prove a thing."

"Wait, wait, wait!" Greg Frazier said suddenly. "He was my father, my real father?" Greg's hands tightened their grips. "Clyde Butler was my father and you killed him?"

Kelly stared across the table at her son. "What difference does that make, now? I have what I wanted. Yes." She smiled grimly. "Yes. I've got my revenge. Everything he loved. His wife, Jane. Clyde himself. His son, Richard. Even you, the son he never knew, will have to live knowing that you helped kill your father. All are dead, destroyed, or about to die anyway."

Kelly finally stood up and walked to the side of Hobbes' desk, and turned to face everyone. She looked at Linda first. It was a look of satisfaction, of smugness. A brief glance at Luke showed a measure of disappointment, and little else. She held back the big guns for Katya. It was a victory salute, a look of immense pleasure — a gloating, self-satisfied smile that reached unfamiliar territory around the eyes and the corners of her mouth.

"There is no need for me to continue the charade, is there?" she said it softly, almost to herself.

"Don't you know who I am? Come, on! Weren't you listening? Hobbes just told you!" She said suddenly, raising her voice. She tantalized them by changing from one half-familiar posture to another.

Those three faces, Linda's, Luke's, and Katya's, seemed puzzled, and then bewildered.

"Luke," she said after a long minute passed, "Don't you know your sister? And Katya Ransom. Mother, dear. You must surely know your own daughter. And Linda Butler, you of all people should know me; after all, I am really you!"

Luke and Linda stared at her. Katya alone had something to say. One word. "Liar!"

"Genetic matching would prove it, if we wanted to go that far," Kelly said. "The fire that you thought killed me only disfigured me. It killed my friend whose name had been Kelly Decker. It is her body that lies under the headstone that says Linda Ransom.

"I say I was only disfigured, but it was bad enough that I required plastic surgery. I convinced the surgeon that I would be better off with a face that wasn't mine, and I came out looking like this."

She bowed mockingly at the silent three, and then whispered, "One of you killed Clyde Butler and tried to kill Grandma Kelch. Which one was it? Mr. Hobbes is going to tell us, and won't we be surprised!" She laughed and walked to the patio doors and pulled the curtains back. She studied the darkness outside for a moment. The darkness of the fog. The thunder and lightning. Even as she watched, a flash of lightning and a sharp crack of thunder happened almost simultaneously; the bole of an old walnut tree in Hobbes back yard exploded. The tree toppled partway to the ground, stopped only by the strength of the power lines.

Kelly turned away from the window, and with a nod of her head, relinquished the floor to Hobbes.

Of those three faces, Luke was stunned; Linda seemed relieved; Katya rubbed at her eyes. They all looked at Hobbes.

He shook his head. "I have explained the motive; now I must go into means and opportunity.

"Who had the opportunity to administer hypnotic gas and poison as well? To replace two pairs of glasses and set up the projector? Who had been here long enough to become a part of the coven and persuade it to actually get ready for a human sacrifice? The ritual sacrifice of cats had been going on for a long time before Katya had arrived, and she would not have been a part of such a crude slaughter. Who would have been familiar enough with Mercater State Hospital to know of the coven, or to know the two residents who had attempted to kill Mr. Houston and me? It had to be someone who had lived there for many years, and then maintained contact with those residents, and others who could build up a coven. There is really only one person in this room who fits those questions. It was not, of course, Katya Ransom, or Luke Ransom, or the one we've been calling Linda Butler.

"There are some other details that point to the same person. For example, who sent me some fax that were, at best misleading, and sent them from the machine in my office? Traces of her perfume told me who she was. It could only have been," he paused for effect, "Kelly Decker — or as we know her now; Linda Ransom." His smile was tight and his tone harsh as he said, "And now, what do we call you, Kelly or Linda? Kelly, I think, to avoid confusion."

Kelly just stood silent and still, her smile gone.

Hobbes continued: "She did not, however, have the means to direct the one we've been calling Linda to three widowed husbands in five years, and to introduce them to her. Nor, could she keep track of our investigation well enough to know where to send two killers to find us.

"Another person was needed to take advantage of those opportunities."

Hobbes paused for a few seconds, but no one seemed ready to say anything.

He continued. "Again, that could only be one person; Greg Frazier. Who better to find lonely men whose wives have just died than a funeral director? Who else could become a trusted friend to our Sally and keep abreast of our plans? Who would be quick to call Vic and Tom to kill the newly found Frank Ransom in another act of vengeance on behalf of Kelly — this one against the father who deserted her? One more fairly small point; who would have a masculine enough voice to call Katya to a meeting of the coven?

"I had another question to ask during the séance, but didn't get the opportunity to voice it. I'll ask it now. How did you get Linda Butler to turn over the moneys she had inherited from her first two husbands to Greg Frazier?"

But Kelly Decker had had enough. "Figure it out yourself." She turned again to the patio door, only to stare at a reflection in the glass. She spun around and stood face to face with Richard Butler.

"You're dead," she said.

"No, I'm not," he said.

"And I have these," Hobbes said. He held up the two pieces of broken marble.

Kelly recognized them immediately. She gasped and shuddered. "You fools," she said. "You risk the fury of Satan. You cannot get away from his wrath!"

Lieutenant Murphy had walked up behind Greg and placed his big hands on his shoulders. Hobbes and I both let go of Greg's hands not realizing that Murphy was still a little slow from the poison. Greg kicked the chair back, dodged Murphy and scrambled to Kelly's side. He slipped the pistol from his pocket into Kelly's hand.

"Mother," he said.

"Oh, shut up," she said. "You're not my son. You're just a dupe. Someone I used." She shoved him away and watched him fall hopelessly into Murphy's arms. She waved the pistol with one hand and slid the door open with the other. "I'll be leaving as soon as I take care of one more detail."

She pointed the pistol at Rich. "Goodbye, Clyde's son."

She started to squeeze the trigger.

From behind her, an almost human scream, a caterwaul, startled her, caused her to whip the gun around. She aimed high; the bullet created a small hole in the safety glass. An instant later, the glass fractured into a thousand dull pieces. The cat came in low with the howling wind and rain, but made a giant leap against Kelly's chest. He was big enough and fast enough to knock her to the floor.

She lost the gun when she fell.

For a long second, no one else moved; not me, not Murphy or Dickerson. No one. Just Kelly. She started crawling — only Harmless stood between her and the gun, his back arched, claws extended, hissing. He glared at me as if to say, "Do something. I'm only a cat!"

So I yelled, "Get the gun!"

Forrest Green beat us all. He darted forward and swooped it off the floor, just ahead of Kelly's grasp. He tossed it to Lieutenant Murphy. Murphy made the catch and saluted him.

As if the weather was a part of the melodrama, the wind died down and the rain stopped.

"Harmless, my baby Harmless." Katya held out her arms, but the cat ignored her. "Harmless, come here." It was a command, but the cat turned his back.

Harmless walked over to Rich and rubbed against his leg.

The boy smiled sheepishly. "I've been giving him kitty treats," he said.

Epilogue

Later that evening, Kelly and Greg were taken away in handcuffs, and Linda — who we were starting to call Susan — and Lucas were warned not to leave town. Susan and Lucas took rooms at the Crazy Eight, but Katya simply disappeared. Harmless was sticking with Rich.

Hobbes called a meeting for the rest of us.

Present were Murphy, Green, Dathan, Richard Butler, and the Hobbes' household — Sally, Fred, Charon, and me.

"Perhaps," Hobbes began, "We can clear up some loose ends. At least the important ones."

He turned and smiled at Sally. "I must apologize to you. I was not aware of the danger you were in until after you had pulled my car from the ditch."

She laughed and danced her way over to Hobbes and kissed him on the forehead. "I knew he was a phony the first time I saw his car. Eighty thousand dollars for a funeral director's car? You have to be kidding."

To the fireman, the boss said, "Fred, you shall have your new electric range."

Fred shook his head. "Nah, this one will be okay, now, no more than I cook. The danger's been taken out."

Rich raised his hand, as if he was in school.

Hobbes nodded.

Rich said, "I was just wondering why you didn't think Linda or Lucas had pushed my mom over that cliff."

Hobbes handed him the pictures the ranger had given me. "Look at the group picture," he said.

Rich studied it, and then said, "Oh. She was there, in the background. Kelly."

"She will be charged with your mother's murder, as well as several others."

Rich handed the pictures back to Hobbes. "I thought for a while that Greg was my brother, I mean my half-brother. I'm glad he wasn't. I wouldn't want a killer for a brother."

"Nor would I. Now, I understand you have expelled three people from your house?"

The boy nodded his head, "Yeah, Lucas, Linda, and Katya. If they had never come here, Dad would still be alive. I told Linda, or Susan, whatever you want to call her, that her marriage to my dad was made under false pretenses, and she had nothing here. I used Lt. Murphy as my bouncer."

"Excellent," Hobbes said. "But you should keep in mind that your dad and Susan were legally married, and she may yet be entitled to half the estate."

Rich smiled slyly, "I already called Dad's lawyer and told him what happened. He said he would see to it that all of Dad's accounts were frozen until the courts could straighten things out. To be honest, I don't care if she does get half the money, but she can't have half of the house. That's mine."

"You're not yet eighteen, Richard; you know you won't be allowed to live alone."

"I know," he said.

"Ideally, you would have a blood relative that you like and trust who could move in with you. Do you know of such a person?"

"No, I don't," Rich stared hard at Hobbes, and then added, "Do you?"

"I know that you have a half-brother," Hobbes said. "I can arrange an introduction if you like. I think the two of you would get along quite well."

"Please do that. Someone you recommend has got to be a lot better than the people I've been living with. Who is he? What's his name? What does he do?"

Hobbes used his thumbs and index fingers to align both sides of his moustache, then let the corners of his mouth go up a sixteenth — no an eighth of an inch into a broad smile. "Actually, Richard, you and he have already met. He had been trying to chase his father down through genealogical searches. It was that which brought him to Mercater. Unfortunately, he had not been able to establish anything before your father's death."

Rich looked at Hobbes, then at Lemuel Dathan. "Oh, man," he said.

Hobbes held up his hand: "Don't let knowing who his mother was affect any decision you make. He is nothing like her."

"I won't!"

"Then, Richard Butler, let me introduce your brother, Lemuel Dathan."

The brothers met in the middle of the floor and gripped each other's hands. "Let's go outside where we can talk." Rich said. He tripped over a footstool on the way out. They both began laughing.

Sally joined in, then Fred, then Charon, and then I witnessed something I never would have expected: the corners of Hobbes mouth rose another sixteenth of an inch. For him, that was absolutely rolling on the floor. I shook my head and chuckled politely.

I didn't speak until Rich and Dathan had left the room. Then I caught the boss' eye.

I said: "I have a couple of questions, Chief."

"All right, Abel. Fire away"

"Number one, why did Luke and Linda mess around with those boxes?"

"Because of Katya, and her mysterious phone calls that no doubt came from Frazier. Kelly had somehow found the marble slabs, or been led to them, and decided to put them back into service. Luke and Linda's job was just to move them."

"Question two: what about that stuff that Charon brought back from Starved Rock?"

"That was just pure ginseng," Charon answered for himself. "I get it natural. That's what keeps me young."

Epilogue 2

Hobbes leaned back in his wheelchair and admired the new painting that hung where the Children's Picnic had been. An old woman in a rocking chair on the porch of an ancient house had taken their place. In small letters at the bottom of the picture was the disclaimer, "This ain't me no longer Car'l, I'm free now and I'm going places. Grandma Kelch."

"It was her self-portrait, no doubt. She was a sad and lonely woman then. But not anymore. Right, Chief?"

"Neither sad nor lonely." Hobbes pushed an envelope toward me. "This came in the morning's mail."

A photograph of her and a much younger man dropped out. It took a minute for me to recognize him.

"Barry Oldsmith?" A.k.a. Frank Ransom. I raised my eyebrow to Hobbes.

"Read the letter."

"'Wish I was twenty years younger. When are you going to send me a bill?' It's signed, 'Grandma Kelch.'"

I handed them back to Hobbes. "Cute couple. Are you going to bill her? It's been three months."

He drummed his fingers on the desktop. "I called it a trade; her portrait for my services. She still wants to pay me. I told her any money would be too much."

"You solved three murders, exposed a fraud and nearly got killed twice. What does that deserve, a free ticket to a performance of CATS at the high school?"

He wheeled around to the patio door, slid one side open and eased the wheelchair across the threshold and onto the flagstones. He waved his hand across the back yard. "A tree is gone, struck down by lightning. Elmer's Woodworkers removed the carcass and paid me seven hundred and twenty dollars for the good walnut lumber that had remained undamaged, but I miss that tree."

"Send her a bill for seven hundred and twenty dollars. We will plant two new trees, but we will have no more parties."

The doorbell rang. We'd both heard the Mercedes drive up.

"Do you have a question to ask her?" he said.

"I don't know, sir. I really don't know."

I went to answer the door anyway.

Come to think of it, Nero Wolfe's Archie Goodwin never married Lily Rowan, and they lived happily ever after, at least until the series ended.

So why should I be in a rush?

I opened the door with a cheerful heart.

Marilyn put her arms around my neck, pulled me down and kissed me. Then she kissed me again, and standing there in the doorway, with her mostly on the outside and me mostly on the inside, I said, "Will you marry me?"

She said, "And be your wife? Huh-uh. I've got a six-month date in the Outback with a tribe of Aborigines. If you want to, you can ask me again when I come back."

Then she smiled at me and said, "But I do have this weekend free."

And, you know something? A weekend now and then is enough.

Really.

About The Author

Diagnosed with Parkinson's disease in 1994, Steve Stillwell retired from his work as a master electrician the following year. This allowed him to pursue his lifelong dream of becoming a writer. He returned to college and took several creative writing classes. Since then, he has written three novels and more than one hundred poems and short stories.

Steve and his wife live in Bourbonnais, Illinois.

www.ingramcontent.com/pod-product-compliance
Lightning Source LLC
Chambersburg PA
CBHW051326250626
47155CB00007B/2466